Leaves Before
the Storm

Leaves Before the Storm

ANGELA ARNEY

ROBERT HALE · LONDON

ISBN 978-0-7198-1178-4

Robert Hale Limited
Clerkenwell House
Clerkenwell Green
London EC1R 0HT

www.halebooks.com

2 4 6 8 10 9 7 5 3 1

Typeset in 10½/14¼ Sabon
Printed by Berforts Information Press Ltd.

CHAPTER ONE

Easter 1939

'You're not marrying Henry for his money are you?' Arthur wheeled himself into the bedroom and looked at his sister who was brushing her hair. 'I couldn't bear to think of you selling yourself.'

Megan leaned over and grabbed at Arthur's hand. 'I'm marrying him for me. I want to be Mrs Henry Lockwood and then perhaps one day I shall be Lady Lockwood of Folly House if Henry is made President of the Royal College of Physicians.'

Arthur sighed. 'Well, I hope you get what you want, and there are no nasty surprises along the way.'

Megan laughed. 'Stop worrying.' Leaping from the bed she spun Arthur's wheelchair around and pushed him towards the door. 'Now go! Lady Lavinia is coming to help me get dressed, and you've got to get yourself ready to escort me down the aisle.'

Once Arthur had gone Megan sat back down on the bed. The wedding dress hung in the wardrobe, a mass of cream silk and seed pearls. She worried. What really happened between a man and a woman in bed? She had only the haziest of notions, picked up from romantic novels and school gossip. In novels the heroines always sank blissfully into their lover's arms at the end of the book, and at school the only book that gave any information on sex concentrated entirely on rabbits.

Megan had tried, but found equating Henry to a rabbit was too difficult so had given up. Now, on her wedding day she was counting on Henry knowing about such things and teaching her. After all he was ten years older than she was, and a doctor. He ought to know.

Besides, she had other things to worry about. The wedding. Would everything go smoothly?

Crossing her fingers she prayed that her father, the Reverend Marcus Elliott, wouldn't drink too much. He was inclined to over-imbibe, especially when he was depressed, and these days old age and being a widower seemed to depress him. Sometimes when he took Sunday service he was definitely the worse for drink, but his parishioners loved him and forgave him when his sermons became long, maudlin and muddled. Although after last week's sermon Lady Lavinia had taken him aside and given him a stern lecture on the perils of the demon drink.

Suitably chastened, Marcus Elliott had promised not to overindulge and Lady Lavinia departed, hoping that her reprimand would at least keep him sober for the forthcoming wedding of his daughter Megan, and her nephew Henry.

Today both Megan and Arthur wanted him in a cheerful frame of mind. All the bottles had been hidden, and Arthur had temporarily nobbled the wireless. Every day the news was about the deepening crisis in Europe and the possibility of war with Hitler's Germany. Marcus had served in the trenches in the 1914–1918 world war and was distraught at the thought of another war. Today Arthur tried to make sure he didn't hear anything.

Lady Lavinia arrived at the rectory, a vision in lavender silk, carrying her hat in an enormous hatbox. Amy, the young maid at the rectory, showed her upstairs. 'I can't risk damaging the ostrich feathers,' Lady Lavinia said, putting the hatbox down carefully. 'I've had them imported especially from South Africa, and I do want them to look their best in church.'

'I'm sure they will look lovely,' said Megan, who had seen the feathers. They were large and a violent purple colour. On most people they would look ghastly but Megan was sure that Lavinia would carry them off with her usual aplomb.

Amy bobbed a curtsy at Lady Lavinia and Megan. 'Can I go now to Folly House, miss? I've got to help in the kitchen.'

'Yes, off you go,' said Lavinia, answering for Megan. She turned back and lifted down the wedding dress. 'Right,' she said briskly, 'let's start buttoning you up. There must be a hundred pearl buttons here at the very least.'

Megan slipped her arms into the tight leg-o'-mutton sleeves, and turned around. 'Thank you,' she said.

'It's no bother, my child,' said Lavinia with a curiously tender note in her voice. 'Nothing is any bother for a bride on her wedding day. Everything should be perfect.' She sighed. 'I do hope that you and Henry will have a long and happy marriage, and that it won't be spoiled by the war.'

'I refuse to think about war,' said Megan stubbornly. 'I refuse to let hateful politicians spoil everything. Germany and the rest of Europe are far away. Nothing that happens there can affect what happens here in the New Forest, and anyway, there may not be a war.' She turned to face Lavinia who was regarding her with a grave expression. 'Well, it can't affect us can it? Not here. There won't be fighting here.'

She didn't want to think about it because she had waited for this day for years. She had made up her mind to marry Henry years before he had even noticed her, Henry had inherited Folly House and it had always been Megan's overriding ambition to be the mistress of Folly House, therefore she had to marry Henry. Not Gerald, his younger brother, who attracted her, but who would never have the house.

After Henry had inherited the house Gerald, his younger brother, also got his inheritance, a large sum of money. He was ambitious, and immediately left university and moved up to the Midlands, near Sheffield, bought a factory and a steelworks and now had even more money.

'He's making guns,' said Lavinia in a disapproving tone of voice.

Gerald still visited Folly House and pursued Megan whenever he came. She was glad he was no longer around all the time, as despite the fact that she was sure she loved Henry, she still felt an undeniable attraction to Gerald and knew he felt the same about her. He kissed her whenever he got a chance, and his kisses were quite different from those of Henry. Henry's were warm and comfortable whereas Gerald's were rough and demanding and his hands wrought havoc with her body. So she'd made certain that she was never alone with him on his last few visits, as the feelings he aroused in her were quite alarming and she wasn't sure whether she was scared of Gerald or herself.

Even thinking about him frightened her and today, of all days, she didn't want to think of him. Although she couldn't avoid him as he was to be best man at the wedding. But at the end of the day she would be married and would move from the vicarage to Folly House to join Henry. In preparation Lavinia had moved out into the dower house at the main gate, where Gerald was staying temporarily. Soon Megan would truly be mistress of Folly House.

It was planned that Gerald would return to Sheffield the following day, then it would just be herself and Henry at Folly House. They were not having a honeymoon, just a few days in Devon as Henry was heavily involved in the Civil Defence Committee for London; as a surgeon he had been co-opted to organize plans for mass casualties in the event of bombing. But Megan would not be entirely alone in the house when Henry was in London. Tilly the housemaid would attend to her needs and would sleep in the attic room on the far side of the house near the stables. And in the older, semi-detached part of the house, which had originally been the nurse's cottage, lived George Jones, the gardener and handyman, Bertha Jones his wife who was the cook and housekeeper, and Dottie Jones their daughter. Dottie was sixpence in the shilling, as they said in the village, but at sixteen years old was expected to earn her keep although she didn't get paid. She just got board and lodging with her parents. Their accommodation was rather basic, but the Jones family were more than happy with their lot.

'Well, my dear, I certainly hope nothing happens.' Lavinia carefully adjusted the veil with its long train. 'As you say, we are a long way from Europe, but in the last war we were all touched by it. Even me,' she added softly.

Megan was startled. She'd been lost in her reverie and had almost forgotten that Lavinia was there. The war! Of course Lavinia had been affected. Sir Richard had been blown up and apparently that was the reason they'd never had children. 'He wasn't a proper man any more,' Bertha had told Megan. Now she felt guilty. She'd forgotten that other people's dreams had been dashed to smithereens.

But she had waited for this day for so long. Before Henry had even noticed her, when he and Gerald came as orphaned boys to live at Folly House with their widowed Aunt Lavinia, after their mother and father both died in a car accident in Italy. As the eldest boy, Henry inherited Folly House, and as it had always been Megan's over-riding ambition to be mistress of Folly House, she therefore had to marry Henry. Not Gerald, his younger brother, who attracted her, but would never have the house.

'Yes, I'm sorry,' she said, and meant it.

Lavinia sighed. 'Water under the bridge, my dear. I pray nothing happens to you and Henry.' She stepped back. 'There, that's you finished. Just be careful coming down stairs. I've asked Jim the stable lad to help you into the carriage, you mustn't let your dress get near the wheels, and I do hope Thunder is on his best behaviour.' Thunder was the big dun-coloured shire horse who was pulling the bridal carriage, a converted dray, to the church. She hesitated, then leaned forward and planted a lavender-perfumed kiss on Megan's cheek. 'I think you'll make a very good Lockwood.'

'Thank you.' Megan smiled shyly. It seemed a lifetime ago since Henry had proposed. Of course, he hadn't known that he was merely setting in motion the plans Megan had made years before. He thought it was all his own idea.

In 1938, when Megan was nineteen years old, and Henry, now a qualified surgeon, working mainly in London, Lavinia thought that he should marry so that Folly House could have a mistress. She was anxious that Folly House should stay within the family, and thought that Megan, Henry's second cousin would be an ideal candidate. Marcus was also anxious to get Megan off his hands; he couldn't afford to have her presented at Court, and anyway Megan had let it be known in no uncertain manner that she was not interested in being introduced to Society. She loved the country, riding ponies, swimming in the sea, and appeared to have no ambition. Marcus and Lavinia thought she lacked a purpose in life, little knowing that her one purpose was to marry Henry.

They were slightly surprised when she fell in with their plans and even more surprised when Henry also was quite amenable when they suggested Megan. He liked his dark-haired cousin. She was beautiful, and appeared easy-going, which suited Henry. He didn't want a troublesome wife, just someone who would be content to live in Folly House while he worked in London and shared a house with Adam Myers, a friend since school days.

Adam was an actor of some repute, and lived a hedonistic lifestyle. Henry was happy to dip in and out of Adam's world of parties, alcohol and women, without actually belonging to it, but was surprised when Adam objected to his marrying, especially Megan, whom he considered a country bumpkin.

'Women always spoil things,' said Adam. 'We're happy as we are. Footloose and fancy free. You can have your pick of any woman in London. You don't need a permanent woman in the picture.'

'You're an actor. It's different for me. I'm a doctor and I need a wife for Folly House. I've got to be more respectable.'

'Respectable! What a dull word,' Adam grumbled. 'But I suppose if you're determined I'll have to put up with her.'

'I am determined,' said Henry, surprised at Adam's vehemence. 'But you'll only have to put up with her when you come down to Folly House. Here in London everything will be more or less the same. You can still have your string of women, but after my marriage I'll remain celibate, in London anyway.'

'Oh my God!' Adam exclaimed. 'I don't know whether I'll be able to bear it. I'll be living with a saint.'

But Henry knew he would bear it. Friends since prep school, they were too close to let anything come between them, not even a wife.

And in 1938, as Henry slipped the diamond and emerald engagement ring on her finger and gave her a chaste kiss, Megan decided that she *would* fall in love with him. Wives should love their husbands. They did in romantic novels. Henry was tall, blond, good-looking, charming and rich, and master of Folly House. What was there not to love? Life stretched out before her just as she'd always wanted. Her dream was complete.

CHAPTER TWO

Easter 1939 – The Wedding

Megan insisted that all the permanent staff from the house and gardens should be invited to the wedding. This included the Jones family, even though Bertha was doing most of the cooking for the wedding breakfast at Folly House. Temporary staff were hired in from the village to help Bertha, and no one refused the request to help. The villagers were only too glad to have the chance of peeping inside Folly House at the village wedding of the year.

On the morning of the wedding the lane to the squat flint stone Norman church of St Nicholas on the edge of East End, was busy. The day dawned misty with heavy dew, the promise of a fine day to come. The hedgerows sparkled, laced with diamond-draped cobwebs glittering in the sun as it pierced through the mist. Translucent green leaves were a reminder that the year was exploding with fresh life, and newborn lambs in the fields skittered with the sheer excitement of being alive while their mothers stolidly munched at the fresh grass and hedge sparrows competed noisily in the hedgerows.

The rumble of steel-rimmed wooden wheels and the clip-clop of old Ned's hoofs along the flinty lane heralded the arrival of the Jones family on their way towards the church.

'Look at the way they've tied up them pony and traps,' grumbled Bertha, feeling bad-tempered and flustered because of the rush to get ready. 'The way them are all jammed up on them banks will ruin the blackberries for the autumn. There'll be none worth picking after this.'

George was more patient than his wife. 'They've got to be parked up there, dear. In a minute the big dray with the bride in it will be coming along, and it's going to have a terrible squeeze to get past.'

'Do you think Megan will be late?' asked Dottie.

'Don't be so familiar,' said Bertha sharply. 'You must call her Mrs Lockwood after today.'

'But she said I could call her—'

'Never mind what she said. I'm telling you. You mind your place. You're a servant girl, for what use you are. And don't you dare sing the hymns too loud when we're in church.' Bertha turned to her husband. 'We should never have brought her. She'll make an exhibition of us.'

'She was invited,' replied George, the stubborn note creeping into his voice as it always did when Dottie was mentioned. 'She has a right to come. And if she do sing the hymns too loud, well, at least she sings them in tune, which is more than can be said for some folk.' He glanced pointedly at Bertha, whose vocal talents were renowned for being far from musical.

Bertha sniffed bad-temperedly. 'Well, she's got to mind her place. She'd get the sack anywhere else. If it weren't for us she'd have no job at all.'

'If it weren't for us,' said George quietly, 'she wouldn't be here at all.'

Bertha didn't reply, merely rammed Dottie's straw hat down straighter on her head, but George knew she felt guilty.

When they arrived at the back of the church the sun was becoming higher in the sky and it was beginning to be hot. Pigeons crooned softly, 'croo, croo,' from the inky darkness of the ancient yews bowing low over the leaning tombstones. Old Ned was tethered to a ring outside the gate, well away from the poisonous yews and clumps of ragwort. A nosebag was put on his head and he was left munching happily. George offered his arm to his bad-tempered wife and, with Dottie following, the family walked back to the main door of the church.

'You're wrong about her getting the sack,' George said, continuing their previous conversation. 'Lady Lavinia has never complained about her, and neither will the new Mrs Lockwood. They're both very fond of Dottie.'

'*They* haven't got her for a daughter,' was Bertha's bitter reply.

George sighed. He knew only too well how disappointed Bertha had been when Dottie was born. They'd waited so many years for a child, their joy turning to sorrow when a small sickly baby was born and diagnosed as a mongol child. He knew too, although Bertha had never voiced her thoughts, that she hoped the feeble baby would die young, as most such children did. But Dottie did not. She survived against all odds, and was now growing into womanhood. Only her mind remained that of an innocent child. George was more philosophical than Bertha. 'There's normal and normal,' he always said. 'It takes all sorts to make the world, and I love her. She's made in God's image the same as you and me, and we've got to thank God for what we've got.'

But Bertha could never find it in her heart to thank God. In fact she doubted there was a god. As far as she was concerned Dottie was a burden and a shame.

In church Henry was in his place in front of the altar with his best man, Gerald. Lady Lavinia was there in the Lockwood pew, resplendent in lavender silk, her large hat covered in deep-purple ostrich feathers.

Dottie, entranced by the sight of the waving feathers, breathed loudly. 'Cor! Don't she look lovely.'

'Be quiet,' snapped Bertha. 'The whole village is here, they don't want to hear you.'

Nervous at the sight of the crowded church, Dottie slipped her hand into her father's. 'There's such a lot of people,' she whispered.

'That's because it's Mr Henry's and Miss Megan's wedding, my love,' said George tenderly, adjusting the ribbon on her hat so that it hung straight down her back. 'Now be a good girl and try not to annoy your ma. Don't sing the hymns too loud, will you.'

'I'll sing very, very softly,' promised Dottie.

Megan entered the church on Arthur's arm. He was walking with his crutches and only Megan knew how much pain this caused him, but he insisted. 'I'm not going to take my sister up the aisle in a wheel-chair,' he said.

As they paused in the doorway for Arthur to get his breath back, the first thunderous chords of *The Arrival of the Queen of Sheba* echoed through the church and Megan felt a thrill of triumph sweep through her. She'd done it. She was about to become Mrs Henry Lockwood, mistress of Folly House. The entire village was there dressed in their Sunday best, the men's suits too tight and shiny at the seams, the women's hats overflowing with flowers, ribbons and feathers.

They turned with one accord to look at her. Megan knew she looked beautiful. The simple oyster-satin dress cut on the cross clung to every curve of her slender body, a million seed pearls glimmered in the light from the windows, and the creamy white veil covering her face gave an air of mystery.

Henry too turned towards her. He was the most handsome man in the church. His fair hair gleamed in the light sliding through the narrow slit of the chancel window as he smiled at her. She was aware of other people smiling, but it was only Henry whom Megan had eyes for. He was the man she was marrying.

When they reached the altar steps her father moved forward, solemn and dignified in his surplice and cassock. He always seemed taller in stature in church, and possessed a florid handsomeness, which made ageing almost a compliment. His dark hair streaked with silver added to the air of distinction, and when he began the service the timbre of his baritone voice rang through the church with august resonance.

The wedding breakfast was a small affair; neither the Lockwoods or the Elliotts came from large families, therefore it was decided to use the gold drawing room and the rose dining room, opening the connecting wooden doors between the two rooms. The windows looked out onto the lawn, which stretched down to the shore with the distant view of the Isle of Wight. By the time the guests arrived back from church it was exceptionally warm and the guests spilled out through the wide French windows into the garden with their champagne and canapés. The casual help from the village, mostly cousins of Tilly as well as Tilly herself, were kept busy. Meanwhile a perspiring Bertha and her niece Milly, plus Amy from the rectory, the only people she would trust in the kitchen, made sure the dining area was laid out perfectly and all the food prepared. Bertha wouldn't let anyone carve any of the meats; in her opinion no one could carve properly except herself, and therefore no one was allowed to touch the assembled joints of beef, ham and pork.

The meats were assembled on the enormous rosewood sideboard and Bertha was just finishing paring the crackling from the pork when Henry came in to see how things were going.

'Give me five minutes,' said Bertha to Henry's enquiry. 'And I'll get Tilly to sound the gong for the guests to come in.'

Henry, always irritated by anything less than perfect efficiency when it came to organization, found himself wishing he'd listened to Gerald's advice and hired a professional company from London to do the catering. Now, he said without thinking, 'Oh dear, perhaps this is all too much for you, Bertha.'

'Too much for me!' Bertha raised a beetroot-red face and glowered at him. 'I'm *enjoying* it.'

'Oh, I'll wait for the gong then.' Henry backed out, accepting defeat. 'But you will give the guests five minutes to be seated won't you?'

'Of course.' Bertha sounded even more affronted. 'I knows what to do, Master Henry.'

Henry paused in the doorway. 'Bertha, you can't go on calling me Master Henry now I'm a married man and master of the house. You must call me Mr Lockwood, Mr Henry or Sir.'

Bertha fixed him with a steely eye. 'Yes, *sir*,' she said.

Henry rejoined the rest of the guests, wondering how it was that the word *sir* hadn't sounded polite at all.

Gerald joined him, puffing rather ostentatiously on a large cigar. 'When is lunch going to be served?'

Henry pulled a face. 'When Bertha decides it's ready,' he said.

Gerald snorted. 'The trouble with the Jones family is they're treated almost like friends. I keep my servants' noses to the grind-stone, and they are certainly not my friends.'

'And they don't stay with you for long. I've heard they never stay for more than a few months,' replied Henry.

Gerald flung himself down bad-temperedly on a garden seat. 'So what? Plenty more where they came from. All willing to work for a few shillings. I shall make good use of them now; they won't be around once the war starts. Cannon fodder, all of them.'

'Let us hope that we can avoid war,' said Henry. 'The politicians are trying hard enough to avoid it.'

Gerald laughed and stubbed out his cigar. 'As far as I am concerned war is a money-maker. The more fear and chaos there is in Europe and the rest of the world, the more armaments I can sell. Business is good.'

Henry stared at his brother, impotent anger boiling up inside him. 'In my view the political situation in Europe is a tragedy. People are suffering. The Nazi regime is disgusting.'

'Depends on your point of view.' Gerald was unrepentant. 'Personally I admire their talent for organization. We could do with a bit of that here in England. The government is bloody useless. Besides money is power and I intend to accumulate both.'

Henry didn't reply, he just walked away across the lawn towards the shore. Adam left the other guests and joined him, and they walked to the water's edge side by side.

'The lawn looks beautiful,' said Adam, lighting a cigarette.

'It's been especially mowed by George Jones to within an inch of its life,' replied Henry with a wry smile. He'd seen George the day before going up and down with the mower, practically measuring the lengths of the blades of grass.

Now it looked like green velvet, stretching in neat stripes down to the tamarisk bushes, their pink fronds fluttering in the gentle breeze. The stone walls of the folly glinted in the afternoon sun. Such a peaceful scene, thought Henry, so far removed from the upheaval across the channel, where people were piling their belongings on to carts, prams and bicycles, anything with wheels, and moving themselves and their families to what they hoped were safer places. Poor devils, he thought. Henry was a pacifist at heart, and couldn't imagine himself going to war.

'Such a peaceful scene,' said Adam, echoing his thoughts.

'Yes, England is safe for the moment,' said Henry slowly. 'All because of that reassuring strip of water separating us from the anarchy of other lands. But maybe not for long.'

Adam walked slowly to the water's edge and threw his cigarette stub into the sea. 'There's something I have to tell you,' he said quietly. 'I've been accepted into the Royal Air Force as a pilot. I begin my training next week in Essex.'

Astounded, Henry joined him at the water's edge. 'But what about your new play in London? It's only just started. What about your career? Everything?'

'Everything is different now,' said Adam, lighting another cigarette and inhaling slowly. 'You are married, so there's nothing to hold me in London apart from the theatre. There will definitely be a war soon, we all know that, and I want to defend my country against the Nazis. I shall come back to the theatre when the war is over.'

'But you don't have to do anything as drastic as joining the Air Force. You could do something else. Join the Civil Defence, like me.'

Adam laughed. 'Don't be ridiculous,' he told Henry. 'I haven't got organizational or medical skills like you. I'd be useless. But flying, that's a different matter. I'm damned sure I can give the Nazis something to worry about.' He leaned against the barnacles on an ancient breakwater, got out another cigarette, then threw the packet to Henry.

Henry felt shocked. Suddenly the war seemed ominously close. To disguise his unease he lit a cigarette, then said, 'I'll miss you. I won't have anyone to talk to.'

'You'll have Megan.' Adam carefully blew a smoke ring and looked at Henry through the wavering, fragile circle of blue as it disappeared.

'I can't talk about anything serious to her. Nor Lavinia. They both are only interested in the house and village. Neither is interested in life outside East End and Stibbington, and neither is willing to acknowledge that war is imminent.' He drew on his cigarette. 'I supposed it's because they are women.'

'Maybe,' agreed Adam. 'But it's the way things are. We have to accept it. That's why I'm joining the Air Force.'

'I'll miss you.'

Adam laughed. 'Just wait until you see me in my blue uniform. I'll be so handsome you'll be green with envy, because all the women will be throwing themselves at my feet.'

Henry grinned. 'No change there then,' he said.

They stood smoking in silence, then Adam said. 'It's not surprising no one thinks about impending war down here. It's so different from London.'

Henry nodded. 'Yes, Megan hated what she saw in London when she came up for the fitting of her wedding dress. She couldn't believe it was necessary to dig trenches in the London parks, or that huge barrage balloons should be flown everywhere. She said it looked as if the sky was full of elephants.'

'But they're having Anderson shelters in the gardens here,' Adam reminded him. 'You've got two in the kitchen garden if I'm not mistaken, and everyone has got their gas masks.'

'George Jones is using the shelters as an extension to his potting shed,' Henry said wryly, throwing his lighted cigarette butt into the sea. 'And the gas masks are gathering dust in the hall.'

Their conversation was interrupted by Gerald, who offered Henry a cigar, but he waved it away. 'Best quality there is,' said Gerald, snipping the end off and lighting it. 'I import them from Havana.' He drew on it expertly. 'Funny,' he said regarding Henry through a pall of cigar smoke. 'I never thought of you as the marrying type. And then to marry little Megan from the vicarage: that's a turn up for the books. Although I must say she's turned out to be a stunner and not so little any more.'

'Everyone has to settle down at some time or another,' said Henry. 'Besides, I want a son. Someone to inherit the house.' He didn't add *otherwise you will get it,* but he knew Gerald was thinking that too.

Gerald inhaled deeply on his cigar. 'Ha! Not exactly a love match, then?'

'Of course I love her,' said Henry quickly. 'Anyway what exactly do you mean by a love match?

'Dunno,' sniffed Gerald. 'Overrated term, if you ask me. But I suppose it means overwhelming passion, can't live without the woman in question. Can't say I've ever felt it myself. Overwhelming passion, yes. But once I've bedded a woman I lose interest. By the way, have you and Megan. . . ?

'No,' said Henry quickly. 'Megan is not that sort of girl. I'm marrying a virgin.'

Gerald gave a lecherous laugh. 'Tonight should be fun then.'

They were interrupted by the gong sounding loudly as Tilly came out of the French windows. It was time to go in for the wedding breakfast.

A rosepink sunset heralded the end of the day. Tilly and the girls flitted around the departing guests, gathering together empty champagne glasses, while Megan and Henry circulated, saying goodbye and thanking everyone for their gifts. Then they went into the kitchen to thank Bertha and all her staff.

The staff stood in a row, Bertha at their head. They were all red in the face but beaming with pleasure. 'It's been a long hot day for you,' said Henry. 'My wife,' he turned to Megan who blushed, it was the first time he'd called her that, 'and I, thank you from the bottom of our hearts for making our day absolutely perfect.'

'And we have a little thank you to give you,' said Megan. Henry passed her some envelopes and she distributed them. One for each girl and Bertha.

Dottie tore hers open immediately. She held up a pound note in one hand and a shilling piece in the other. 'A guinea,' she said gasped. 'I've never been paid so much before.'

Everyone else had the same except Bertha who when she opened hers discovered that she had three guineas. Her face went an even darker shade of puce. 'What can I say,' she stuttered.

'Nothing,' said Henry firmly. 'You deserve it. All the guests agreed that the food was worthy of the Ritz in London. You should be very proud.'

Megan felt proud too. Henry was generous to a fault. He was a marvellous husband. She knew she was going to be very happy at Folly House. They linked arms and left the kitchen to a round of applause.

19

As they walked back through the gold room and out on to the darkening lawn which was now empty of guests, Adam appeared. Henry dropped Megan's arm immediately and moved across to Adam. 'I'm taking the Daimler and dropping Adam off at Stibbington station now,' he said to Megan over his shoulder. 'He's got to get back to London tonight.'

Megan stared at him. Surely he couldn't leave her now, not on their wedding night? Couldn't someone else take Adam to the station? Then common sense kicked in. Of course, Adam was joining the Air Force, it was only natural that Henry wanted to say goodbye to his friend. Stifling her disappointment she smiled meekly as Henry kissed her. 'Of course,' she said, holding out her hand to Adam. 'Goodbye and good luck.'

Adam took her hand and, bending low, kissed it. 'Goodbye and good luck to you,' he said, and as he raised his eyes Megan shivered at the bleakness she saw there. His grey eyes were cold, like stones. Adam didn't like her. Well, did it matter? She tried to tell herself that it did not, but was not convinced.

'Won't be long, darling,' said Henry.

Lavinia was the last to leave. She unbuttoned Megan upstairs in the bedroom she was to share with Henry. 'Tilly's much too busy washing up,' she said, 'and I don't want any of them dropping my precious china.' She looked at her watch. 'Do you want me to stay, dear?' she asked.

Megan shook her head.

Lavinia looked at her watch again and tutted. 'Adam must be on the train by now. It really is too bad of Henry to leave you alone tonight, of all nights.'

'I think he's upset that Adam is joining the Air Force,' said Megan.

Lavinia sighed. 'It's the coming war,' she said, 'disrupting our lives before it's even begun.'

'Don't stay,' said Megan quickly. 'I'm all right.' So Lavinia left.

Megan was alone, wishing she could join the servants down in the kitchen. She could hear the clink of glasses and laughter. To fill in the time she took a rose-scented bath before slipping into a cool white satin nightdress with a matching gauzy negligee. The woman who looked back at her from the mirror was tall and slender, with a cloud of dark hair surrounding a pale, anxious face.

Thinking she heard the sound of a car on the gravel she went downstairs to greet Henry. But no one was there. Restless and even more nervous now, she lit a cigarette and stepped out of the French windows into the garden. Dew on the lawn soaked through her satin slippers, but Megan didn't notice. Without thinking she drifted towards the folly, where a sea mist was swirling over the gently lapping waves on the shore. It eddied around the walls and tower of the folly, clinging in shifting shapes and forms, and closing around her like a mysterious blanket.

Leaning against the rough stone wall of the folly Megan drew on her cigarette, watching the red pinprick of light at the end of her cigarette glow in the darkness. A thin sliver of a crescent moon gave a cold light.

She felt alone and unwanted. What had happened to her dream? A hot tear trickled down her cold cheek; she wiped it away with the back of her hand and sniffed.

'Here, take this.' A hand materialized out of the darkness and proffered a large, white, man's handkerchief.

The next moment she felt the warm bulk of a man's body pressed close beside her. 'Gerald,' she gasped. 'What are you doing here?'

'I might ask you the same question.'

'I'm waiting for Henry.' As she stuttered her reply she turned towards him. The next moment she was in his arms. They were warm and comforting and involuntarily Megan relaxed in his embrace.

'What a fool Henry is.' Gerald's voice was rough.

The next moment his mouth found hers. *I'm married. I'm married to Henry. To Henry.* The words echoed through her head but they didn't stop her responding to Gerald's urgent, demanding mouth.

Everything was forgotten. Nothing mattered but the overwhelming feeling surging through her, obliterating everything else. Kisses became more urgent. Suddenly she was lying naked on Gerald's jacket. She heard herself groaning as she clasped her hands behind his neck, pulling his face down to hers, pulling his whole body

21

down, down, down, deeper and deeper. They were moving together in an ecstatic frenzy. Crying out, she wanted it to go on forever, but it was over too soon, leaving them both breathing hard, and lying tightly locked together. Then Gerald's mouth closed over hers once more, this time in a long, luxurious, lingering kiss that left a delicious feeling in the pit of her stomach. At last, content, they lay in each other's arms.

'You should have married me,' said Gerald at last. 'I told you I'd be rich, but you didn't wait.'

His words brought Megan back to reality. To reality and the enormity of what had just happened. *I've betrayed Henry. I've made love with his brother.* Panic-stricken, she grabbed her nightclothes. 'I shouldn't have, I shouldn't have,' she muttered feverishly.

Gerald sat up and lit a cigarette. 'No, you shouldn't,' he agreed, then laughed softly. 'But by God, it was worth it. I can't wait until the next time.'

'There won't be a next time. I don't know what came over me.' She started to leave, but Gerald was too quick for her.

He grabbed her shoulders and turned her to face him. 'I'll tell you what came over you,' he said. 'It was lust, Megan. Pure simple lust. You and I were made in the same mould. We know what we want and we know how to get it.'

He let her go and Megan ran back to the house, praying that no one had seen her and that Henry hadn't returned.

When Henry arrived ten minutes later Megan was ready for him. Fresh and fragrant in a demure cotton nightgown.

'Darling,' said Henry holding out his arms. 'I'm sorry I'm late. But I'm here now.'

'Yes, darling,' Megan replied, fixing a smile on her face, praying that the weight of her monumental guilt did not show. *You are here now, but you are too late,* she thought, letting herself be enfolded in his embrace. But as she raised her face to his she could only remember Gerald and feel his rough urgent mouth on hers. So different from the smooth, cool kiss of Henry.

CHAPTER THREE

August 1939

Gerald returned to Sheffield the next day, much to Megan's relief. She would forget him, she told herself firmly. But every time Henry made love to her she found she was comparing his slow, gentle love-making with Gerald's fiery passion. Not that they made love very often; Henry was away in London, and never seemed to have time to come back to Folly House. Megan suggested that she should visit him in London, but there was always a reason why this was not possible. Henry's war work was taking up more and more of his time. 'I'll come down to the New Forest,' he promised. But his visit somehow never materialized.

One day while looking at her diary, trying to find a date when Henry could visit, she realized that they had been married four whole months, and she hadn't had a period in all that time. Surely it was not possible to be pregnant so soon? Besides, she felt very well. No morning sickness. But what were the other symptoms? She didn't know, and she didn't know Lady Lavinia well enough to broach such a delicate subject. There was no alternative but to visit Dr Crosier, the village GP.

He confirmed her suspicions. She was pregnant. 'Four months gone, if I'm not mistaken,' said Dr Crozier in his broad Irish accent. 'You must have conceived on your honeymoon. Well done, lass.'

Well done! Megan didn't think so, and Dr Crozier mistook her worried expression for fear of the coming confinement. 'Don't worry lass,' he said. 'You're a good strong country girl. You'll have your baby as easy as shelling peas.'

But Megan's worry was that it might be Gerald's child, not Henry's. How could she tell? How could anyone tell?

Of course Henry was delighted, as was Lavinia. Everyone in the household thought it was good news too, only Megan worried about it. Unable to sleep at night she often sat by the bedroom window gazing out into the garden towards the folly where she and Gerald had made love on her wedding night. Whose child was it? Guilty thoughts scurried round and round in her mind. To make matters worse she had nothing to do to take her mind off her worries. Everyone wrapped her in a cocoon; she was not allowed to ride the pony or her bicycle; they seemed to expect her to sit around and look decorative.

Before her marriage Megan had thought she would run Folly House, and had made plans. But this was off limits too. Bertha insisted that she and only she should oversee the purchase of all provisions, as well as deciding the weekly menus.

'I've always done it, Miss Megan,' she said firmly, puffing up her not inconsiderable bosom. 'I'm well known with all the purveyors of produce in these parts. They'll not get inferior food past me for Folly House.'

'But I thought I ought to be getting my hand in, get some experience as the new Mrs Lockwood.'

'Lady Lavinia never wanted to get her hand in,' replied Bertha woodenly. 'She was content to let me do it.'

And that was where the conversation ended.

Lavinia was no help. 'It's best not to upset Bertha, dear,' she said. 'Don't interfere.'

'But I thought that was my responsibility,' Megan objected.

However, Lavinia was firm. 'She's always done it and I don't see the need for change. That's another thing you need to learn now you're in charge. It's essential not to upset the staff.'

Megan fumed silently. The trouble was she wasn't in charge. Henry didn't care who did what as long as the house was in order and his meals on time when he came back from London, which was not often. So Megan had nothing to do, and often no one to talk to. Being Mrs Lockwood was not how she had imagined it.

Lavinia changed the subject. 'I'd like you to meet Violet Trehearne,' she said.

'Why?' asked Megan mutinously. She'd seen her once or twice at concerts she'd attended with Arthur, but had never formally met her. Neither did she want to. Violet was small, plain and timid, and apparently filled her time doing good works for the poor. Not Megan's type at all.

'Because,' said Lavinia, 'she and Gerald are to be married.'

'Gerald? Married?' Conflicting emotions suddenly raged in her. Megan didn't know whether to be pleased or sorry. Vanity demanded that Gerald should still be attracted to her, although she had every intention off rebuffing his advances; but there was also disappointment that he'd found someone else, and was marrying. 'I shouldn't have thought Violet Trehearne was Gerald's type,' she said.

Lavinia had smiled wryly. 'She's not, my dear. But she's recently come into a fortune. She's inherited Brinkley Hall in Wiltshire, a mere thirty miles from here, and more money than she'll ever know what to do with. That makes her Gerald's type, as I dare say he has plans for her money.'

So Megan spent several very boring afternoons with Violet, not choosing wedding gowns, which she would have been quite happy to do, but talking about Violet's various charities.

'What does Gerald think about your charity work?' she couldn't resist asking.

'He's not interested.' Violet was quite honest. 'He says I can do as I like once we're married. He's going to be too busy making more money.'

'Oh!' Megan was surprised at the bluntness of Violet's answer. 'Don't you mind?'

Violet looked at Megan, who noticed for the first time how steely grey were her eyes. 'I know he's marrying me for my money, not my looks,' she said quietly. 'The deal is I get a husband and respectability. A married woman has much more freedom and opportunities than a single one. I get that, and Gerald gets Brinkley Hall plus some of my money. The only other thing I have to do is provide an heir. Something you seem to have managed spectacularly well.'

Megan felt her face flushing. What would Violet say if she knew the baby might be Gerald's? But she didn't know. No one did.

The marriage between Gerald and Violet was a discreet affair held in the small family chapel in the grounds of Brinkley Hall. Only a dozen people attended: some aunts, uncles and cousins of Violet, plus Lavinia, Henry and Megan from the Lockwood family. The wedding breakfast served in the ballroom of Brinkley Hall was absolutely sumptuous. Oysters, champagne, caviar, beef Wellington, suckling pig, stuffed mushrooms, glazed vegetables and mountains of fruit with flowers flown in from southern Italy, as well as ice-cream made to a special recipe for the occasion, containing champagne.

'Gerald likes to impress,' said Violet wryly to Henry when he remarked on the quantity and quality of the food.

Megan was very impressed. So this is what money can buy, she thought, remembering the simple fare for the wedding breakfast at Folly House. For a moment she envied Violet, but only for a moment. Gerald drank too much, was rude to Violet and flirted with one of her younger cousins. Violet said nothing, but Megan knew she was hurt from the expression on her face.

Later, before the couple left for their honeymoon, Gerald managed to waylay Megan on her way to collect her wrap. Before she could escape he drew her from the corridor into the library and shut the door. Holding her in a tight embrace he kissed her roughly, his tongue exploring her mouth as if he would devour her. Against her better judgement Megan found her treacherous body responding.

He drew back a little, and whispered against her cheek, 'Well? Whose child is it that you're carrying? Mine or Henry's?'

'Henry's of course,' Megan whispered back.

Gerald held her tighter. 'Lavinia told me it is a honeymoon baby. That means . . .'

'It means I conceived on our honeymoon,' interrupted Megan, vainly trying to struggle free from his embrace. 'It is Henry's baby, and you should keep away from me. I'm married and I'm pregnant and—'

Gerald gave a low laugh, and dropping his hand down caressed her rounded stomach. 'It doesn't make any difference. I still want you,' he said. 'Don't tell me you don't feel the same, because I wouldn't believe you.' Cupping both her breasts with his hands, he bent his head and kissed her again.

Megan closed her eyes and kissed him back. Why couldn't Henry make her feel like this? Then the very thought of Henry galvanized her into action, and she tore herself free, pushed Gerald away, wrenched open the library door and stumbled down the corridor to the room where the ladies' cloaks and wraps were laid out. Collapsing on the couch just inside the door, she whispered to the maid, 'I feel a little faint. Do you think you could get my husband to come and escort me to our car?'

It was a lie, but the maid bobbed a brief curtsey and went to get Henry. Anything, thought Megan, to make certain she couldn't bump into Gerald again when she was alone.

When leaving on Henry's arm, with a concerned Lavina in attendance, Megan caught a brief glimpse of Gerald and Violet. He was laughing, and Violet was looking rather lost and miserable. Megan felt sorry for her. At least she knew Henry loved her, even if he wasn't a very good lover.

'They are going to bloody Italy for their honeymoon,' said Henry savagely. 'He's got some armament deal going with Mussolini's lot. It's a business trip, not a honeymoon.'

'Poor Violet,' said Lavinia. 'But she has her charity work to keep her mind occupied.'

Megan said nothing. She remembered Violet's steel-grey eyes. Yes, Violet had a purpose in life, whereas she didn't. I need something to do, she thought. I need something to stop me from thinking about Gerald. He threatens my happiness, mine and Henry's. I've made one mistake, but there's no need for me to make another. Like Violet, I must find something to do.

The week after Gerald and Violet's wedding Henry told Megan he was engaging an estate manager.

Something clicked. This was her opportunity. She could do it, and she had to make Henry see that she could. 'I can do it,' she said.

'No,' said Henry firmly. 'I need someone I can trust. I'm needed more and more in London now, I haven't time to do the accounts and all the other things that are needed here.'

Megan pressed home her point. 'All the more reason to let me take over running the estate. I could do it. I'm competent, and anyway, if you get a man in he'll be called up to go into the army before you know it. Everyone will be called up soon, that's what the papers say.'

Henry looked at Megan in surprise. 'I didn't think you bothered with the news.'

So she had surprised him. This was her opportunity. 'Well, I do read and listen. I know what's going on, and I know how it's going to affect us. We've got to make the estate and the home farm much more productive. Every bit of spare land will need to be turned to the plough, because England has to be self-sufficient. Nazi Germany has plenty of U-boats, which will sink our merchant shipping; we won't be able to import food.'

Henry looked even more surprised. 'I didn't think you took any of this seriously. I'm glad you do, but you'll have your work cut out looking after our son.' He was determined that the baby was a boy.

Megan grasped his hands. 'I'm not a silly little girl any more, I'm a married woman, and what's more I'm a country woman. I know a lot about farming, and what I don't know Silas Moon and George Jones can teach me. I'm good at maths and can do accounts. I'll make Folly House and the home farm the best-run business in the whole of the New Forest.'

'But the baby . . .' began Henry.

'Will be looked after by me, Lavinia, Bertha and Dottie. In fact, I suspect I'll have to fight to get my hands on it. They are all waiting with bated breath for me to give birth.'

Henry suddenly laughed. 'That's true,' he agreed. 'All right, I'll give you a year to show me what you can do. You'd better come into the office now and I'll show you the accounts, which I've had set up ready by my accountant in London. From now on they will have to be done down here as I can't keep carting files of paperwork back and forth from London.'

So Megan officially became the manager of Folly House Estate and the home farm. There was united opposition from Lavinia, George Jones and Silas Moon, as well as Bertha, who as usual had the last word.

'It don't seem right,' she told her friends in the Women's Institute. 'She should be sitting at home knitting and being quiet. Everyone knows a woman's mind is not normal when she's pregnant.'

But these pearls of wisdom went unheeded by Megan, who set to work with an enthusiasm that amazed everyone. Her first task was a confrontation with Albert Noakes. As well as being the air-raid warden he'd been appointed a government inspector for the East End area to designate land that needed to be put into arable production. Soon inhabitants of East End were wishing there would be an air raid to keep him occupied, anything to stop him officiously demanding that rose beds and lawns be dug up and planted with vegetables. He arrived one rainy morning at Folly House full of zeal, officiously demanding to see the farm manager.

'Do you mean the manager, Mrs Lockwood?' asked Bertha, equally officiously.

'I mean the man in charge,' said Albert.

'There isn't a man in charge. It's Mrs Lockwood.' Albert opened and closed his mouth as Bertha continued. 'I'll see if she can spare a moment. Wait there.' She shut the kitchen door in Albert's face, leaving him outside in the rain, and went to find Megan. She was in the office deciding how many pounds of runner beans they could spare for sale in the newly opened farm shop. Bertha was to salt down as many as possible for Folly House for the coming winter, the rest were for sale.

'Albert Noakes is here,' Bertha told Megan. 'I'm thinking he'll be wanting us to dig up the lawns. He's made everyone else dig up theirs.'

'I'll see him in five minutes,' said Megan. She'd already decided where the new vegetable plots should be and had no intention of destroying the lovely expanse of lawn, which stretched from the house to the sea. This would be her first battle as the new estate manager and she was determined to win it. And win it she did. Albert Noakes retreated with the compromise that the scrubby area with a few wild rhododendrons in it would be grubbed up and put to the plough. Oats would be planted there, and all the fallow beds in the kitchen garden would grow leeks and swedes for the coming winter.

Albert happily put all this on his maps and left, not realizing that he'd fallen in exactly with Megan's plans.

Megan was happier being occupied, but wished that Henry would sometimes visit Folly House, not dash off to Biggin Hill where Adam was stationed, whenever he had a spare moment.

Lavinia defended Henry. 'I think it's because he feels guilty,' she said. 'He feels he should be in uniform too, and doing something for his country.'

'Why should he feel guilty? We're not at war yet.' Megan couldn't help feeling jealous of Adam, who always seemed to demand Henry's attention.

'We soon will be,' replied Lavinia sombrely. 'And then Adam will be a fighter pilot, a dangerous job.'

Megan didn't reply. What could she say without appearing selfish and petty?

Megan decided to fill in one afternoon by driving to Stibbington to the bookshop. She'd buy a book, then have some afternoon tea in one of the hotels before returning home. Driving across the cobbled yard on the way out she caught sight of Dottie walking along, clutching a piece of paper in one hand and a shopping basket in the other; her gas mask slung across her back. 'Where are you going, Dottie?' she called.

'Stibbington,' said Dottie. 'I knows the way,' she added proudly. 'Mum says I can walk there on my own. I'm going to Clarence Stores. Mum wants some more Kilner jars for the runner beans. I've got it written down.' She waved the piece of paper.

'Well, hop in,' said Megan. 'No point in walking all that way when I'm going into Stibbington as well. You might as well come with me.'

Dottie didn't need a second invitation. Throwing her gasmask box onto the back seat first, she clambered in and settled herself down with the basket on her lap. Megan tried to ignore the gasmask. It wasn't necessary to carry them yet, although Dottie always did. To Megan it was yet another reminder of war. War, always war, she thought crossly. Even here on a peaceful sunny day it poked dark unwelcome fingers into the tranquil life of rural England. It was impossible to escape it. The reminders were everywhere.

Dottie sat up straight beside Megan in the front of the car. She was beaming from ear to ear and Megan felt a flash of tenderness at the girl's obvious delight in such a simple thing as a ride in the car. It must be nice, she thought, to get pleasure from something so ordinary.

Dottie retrieved the gasmask from the back seat and put it in her basket on her lap. On the way they passed one of Silas Moon's children walking down the lane with a raggedy lurcher dog in tow.

'Hello Bert, hello Tigger,' called Dottie, waving vigorously, determined not to miss being seen having a ride in the car. The boy waved back and Megan smiled.

'Has Tigger got a gasmask?' asked Dottie.

'Of course not,' said Megan. 'They weren't issued to animals.'

Dottie looked worried. 'What will happen to him when the gas comes?'

'There won't be any gas,' said Megan firmly. But Dottie's remark depressed her. Poor old dog. He'd die if they were gassed, and so would all the other animals. It was not something she'd thought of before. Waves of melancholia suddenly washed over her.

The lane crossed the open heathland of the New Forest for a way before twisting down towards the foreshore of the River Stib as it meandered its way towards the Solent and the open sea. On that hot August day the heather murmured with the constant hum of bees gathering the last of the summer's nectar; butterflies frittered away their short lifespan spreading their multicoloured wings in the warmth, and swifts, swallows and house martins dived across the road before lining up on the telephone wires in readiness for their migration to sunnier climes. Megan began to relax again. The birds still behaved in the same way; war would not stop them from leaving England for Africa. War could not change the rhythm of the seasons.

Crossing the bridge over the inlet which separated one side of the New Forest from Stibbington, she drove into the High Street. A florist's shop crowned the hill. Outside stood two green buckets crammed with coral-coloured gladioli. The brilliance of their colour spread a glowing warmth which reached Megan's heart. On impulse she stopped the car.

'This isn't right.' Dottie looked worried. 'Clarence Stores is down on the quay.'

'I know, but I want some flowers first.' Megan pointed at the gladioli. 'Look at those. Aren't they a wonderful colour? They look as if they are on fire.'

A smiling Miss Cozens, the owner of the shop, came out to greet them. 'Hello, Mrs Lockwood, hello Dottie.' Miss Cozens was of indeterminate age, and was small and frail looking. But her looks belied her strength. Megan had seen her manhandle great boxes and buckets of flowers around, and she'd owned and run the shop in the High Street for as long as anyone could remember. 'You are looking very well today,' she said.

Megan stood on the pavement gazing at the gladioli. 'I feel very well,' she said, suddenly realizing that she actually did. Pointing at the gladioli, she said, 'I'll take all of those.'

Miss Cozens folded her arms across her bony chest and looked surprised. 'All of them?'

'Every single one. I'm feeling extravagant.'

'And why not?' Miss Cozens set about wrapping the long stemmed flowers in shiny blue paper. 'You might as well be extravagant now, while you've got the chance. There won't be many flowers once the war starts.'

'Why not?' Megan was surprised.

'I'm closing the shop. That's why. Flowers are no use against that awful Hitler man. I am doing something more useful than selling flowers. I'm joining up.'

'Joining up?' Megan thought Miss Cozens was probably too old to join anything.

'Yes, I shall join whoever or whatever will have me.' Miss Cozens jutted her jaw out determinedly. 'I might not be in the first flush of youth, but there's plenty of fight left in me yet. I shall drive an ambulance if silly old Colonel Blewitt lets me. He's against women drivers, but he'll be glad to have us when the war starts and all the men disappear.'

'I suppose so,' replied Megan, who hadn't given driving ambulances a thought before.

'Now you open the boot of your car,' said Miss Cozens briskly, 'and I'll put these flowers in.' Megan did as she was told, watched by Dottie.

'I wish I could drive,' said Dottie wistfully. 'Then I could drive an ambulance.'

'You just concentrate on what you're good at. You'll be needed up at Folly House,' said Miss Cozens kindly.

'Yes,' said Megan quickly. 'We couldn't do without you, Dottie, and I shall need you more than ever when I've had the baby. Someone will have to look after it when I'm busy in the office.'

Dottie looked pleased. 'Will you let me take the baby out in his pram?'

'Of course.' Megan wondered whether it was wise to say yes.

Miss Cozens finished packing the flowers in the boot. She looked at Megan. 'What are you planning to do?' she asked.

'I'm already doing something,' Megan replied. 'Henry has made me his estate manager as he is in London now most of the time.'

'Mr Henry does important war work,' said Dottie proudly. 'I know because I heard my mum say so.'

'Civil Defence planning for when the war starts,' explained Megan.

'Good for him,' said Miss Cozens.

'Of course, there's still a chance there might not be a war,' said Megan.

'And pigs might fly,' was Miss Cozens's unequivocal reply. 'I'm glad you are doing something. There will be a great many things an educated young woman like you can do. You'll be in great demand.'

Later, waiting for Dottie to purchase the Kilner jars, she thought about Miss Cozens's remark. *I am an educated woman, but I haven't really bothered to think since I left school. But it's true. I do have the chance now.* Immersed in her thoughts she didn't at first see the two men who emerged from the hotel; they were both dressed in pinstriped suits. She locked the car and crossed the road, intending to help Dottie carry the shopping, but then noticed the two men and realized that one of them was Gerald. He saw her immediately and came across with the other man beside him. On reaching Megan, he put his arm proprietoriarily around her waist.

'This is my new sister-in-law, Megan,' he said, squeezing her in closer. 'Gorgeous, isn't she.' He indicated the other man. 'This is Roderick Williams from the Royal Swallows Bank in London. He's down here doing one or two shady deals with me.' He laughed.

Roderick Williams looked embarrassed. 'Pleased to meet you, Mrs Lockwood,' he said.

Megan nodded a quick acknowledgement and tried to edge away, but Gerald didn't let her go. There was a strong smell of alcohol on his breath, and she turned her head away. But Gerald persisted. 'What is Henry thinking about, staying up in London all the time, and leaving a gorgeous filly like you down here alone?'

'I'm not alone, Gerald,' said Megan firmly, managing to disengage his hand. As she spoke Dottie came out of Clarence Stores, carrying an enormous box of Kilner jars. It was her opportunity. 'Excuse me now, I must get the car and help Dottie. That box is far too heavy for her to carry across the quay.'

'Oh!' Gerald scowled. 'I was going to ask you to take tea with me in Stibbington after Roderick has got the train back to London.'

'Quite impossible,' said Megan briskly, 'but thank you for asking me. Excuse me now, gentlemen, I must get the car.' She indicated to Dottie to wait outside the shop and went to fetch the car.

As she drove away from Clarence Stores she could see Gerald and Roderick Williams going towards Stibbington railway station. Everyone knew Gerald was making money from armaments and obviously the Royal Swallows Bank was financing one of his nefarious deals. What had happened to the Gerald she'd once known? Why was he so obsessed with money? But even as she thought this, a guilty feeling reminded her that she had wanted money too, and had married Henry to get it. But that wasn't so bad, was it?

Dottie, blissfully unaware of Megan's troubled thoughts, enjoyed her afternoon enormously. Especially when Megan took her for tea at the Anchor Hotel which overlooked the Stib estuary; they had tiny cucumber sandwiches, tea and biscuits in a posh hotel, and even better, they sat in the bay window where she could see everything, and where Megan kept a watchful eye out for Gerald.

Later Megan visited the rectory and told Arthur of her encounter with Gerald. 'You want to be careful,' said Arthur, looking worried. 'I have a feeling Gerald could be bad news; he's not to be trusted.'

'I'm sure you're right,' said Megan noncommittally. What would he say if he knew just how untrustworthy Gerald was, or herself come to that?

'I am right. I don't like him,' said Arthur sharply. 'But once the war really starts, all the able-bodied men will be called up, even Gerald.' He hunched his shoulders. 'You'll have to make do with a few puny men like me to hold the fort.'

'You're not puny,' said Megan. 'It's not your fault you caught polio.'

Arthur shrugged again. 'Just me feeling sorry for myself,' he said, adding, 'and you'd better be going unless you want a session with our esteemed housekeeper. She'll be back from shopping soon, and you know she doesn't like visitors interrupting her regime.'

Megan gave a wry smile at the thought. The housekeeper in question was a formidable widow, called Mrs Fox, who was a staunch Salvation Army member. After Megan had married and left the rectory a housekeeper was needed for Arthur and her father. Megan had found Mrs Fox from a notice in the window of the local grocer. Mrs Fox had advertised her services by a card placed in Torbocks' window. Torbocks was the largest grocer in Stibbington and everyone shopped there. Megan made the arrangements, much against her father's wishes.

'I can manage perfectly well with Arthur to help me,' he said.

Arthur had objected too. He didn't care whether the house was tidy or not. All he cared about was playing the piano.

But Megan had insisted. 'No, you can't manage,' she had said looking around at the untidy kitchen, and the even more untidy dining room, which her father had overflowed into and was using as a study. Arthur in the music room was even worse, sheet music was everywhere. 'You both need someone to organize you.'

'We don't want to be organized,' said Arthur.

'No, we don't. I don't want anything moved. I always know exactly where everything is,' said Marcus grumpily. 'You know I hate being organized.'

Megan ignored them both and Mrs Fox duly arrived at the rectory.

Marcus was afraid of Mrs Fox the moment he clapped eyes on her. 'You know I am a Church of England minister,' he said, when he'd reluctantly interviewed her for the position. 'And you are Salvation Army. Where religion is concerned we have very different views on many things.'

'The Lord moves in mysterious ways,' boomed Mrs Fox loudly, and rather ominously Marcus thought. 'He has sent me here to look after you.'

'Well, I'm not sure whether I can offer you the post now, I do have another . . .' Marcus was going to lie and say he had some other women to interview, but Mrs Fox, already primed by Megan, didn't listen. She rose to her feet, opened her handbag with a decisive snap and passed him some letters.

'Here are my references. You'll not find them wanting. I'll go upstairs now and look at the bedrooms and decide which one I'll have. I daresay I'll know which ones are yours and Arthur's. They will be untidy, if the look of downstairs is anything to go by.'

So Mrs Fox moved in, and Marcus Elliot and Arthur had never lived in such a spotless house, nor had they had their meals served so regularly before. Marcus didn't like it, but Arthur took to it like a duck to water. Not having to think about the house left him even more time to play his music. He needed to practise, as Megan had promised she'd try to persuade Henry to finance him at the Royal Academy in London if he could pass the audition.

Mrs Fox believed that cleanliness and organization were the nearest things to godliness, and decreed that meals should be eaten on the dot of twelve noon and 5.30 p.m. in the evening. Marcus hated eating just before evensong; he preferred a leisurely meal after the service. But 5.30 p.m. it was because after that Mrs Fox went off to play the trumpet in the Salvation Army Band as they made their way through the forest villages. They played at various inns, saving souls and collecting money at the same time.

Another problem for Marcus was that she did not allow a drop of alcohol in the house. He had to make do with the dregs of the communion wine, although even that was rationed. Wine taken in the name of the Lord came under Mrs Fox's organizational skills. The church was next door to the vicarage and she considered it part of her remit. She enjoyed working in the beautiful Norman church, which was so different from the tin hut where the Salvation Army worshipped, and she started overseeing the flower rota, which caused Marcus problems with the older ladies of the village.

She also laid out the communion table with the wafers and wine, always measuring just enough wine for the congregation to take a sip. Marcus began looking forward to the mornings when there was an unexpected drop in attendance, then he would drain the chalice on the steps of the altar so that it was always empty before being returned to the vestry where Mrs Fox could get her hands on it, and, to Marcus's horror, would pour the wine left down the sink.

After leaving Arthur Megan drove back to Folly House. The summer of 1939 had been long and hot and the countryside on that late after-noon looked as if a large brush of tawny gold had been splashed over it. Everything was painted in subtle browns and golds and Megan paused at the side of the road to drink in the scene. There was no wind, so the sea had a molten sheen. The tide was out and the mud of the marshes and ancient saltings glinted rose pink in the last rays of the sun.

'Such a peaceful unchanging landscape,' said Megan to herself, suddenly feeling content. So different from London and other cities with their barrage balloons bumbling about in the sky like enormous prehistoric animals, and the ugly brick-and-concrete air-raid shelters with their piles of sandbags at the doorways. That was another world. This world, her world, changed slowly with the tides and seasons; the impact of man on the landscape was imperceptible, and that was how it was meant to be. No hastily thrown up slabs of concrete would disfigure the view here.

Except for the two Anderson shelters dug into the garden of Folly House. Henry had said they were needed, so they were installed with enough room for everyone should they be needed. But Megan had insisted on George planting honeysuckle and clematis on either side, so that next year they would be covered in flowers and hardly visible.

Not that she could envisage that they would ever need them.

CHAPTER FOUR

September 1939

On Friday 1 September 1939 Henry walked slowly down the long corridor of St Thomas's Hospital, where he'd trained and worked all his professional life. This would be the last time for as far as he could see in the turbulent world of 1939. The familiar smells of the hospital, the carbolic disinfectant, the floor polish together with the ever-lingering smell of cooked cabbage had always comforted him; he'd felt at home in the hospital since the very first day he'd stepped inside as a medical student. But now he was about to enter the unknown world of an officer in the Royal Army Medical Corps. He would join his unit after the coming weekend and after that had no idea when he would see Megan or anyone else at Folly House.

The thought caused him to falter. No one there knew he had enlisted. They were in for a shock. Everything had happened at breakneck speed once he'd made his mind up to enlist. The authorities at the hospital had given their blessing to his leaving to enter the army, but somehow he doubted the family at Folly House would be so generous.

'You should at least have told Megan,' Adam had said in surprise.

But he had not. Part of him felt guilty at leaving a pregnant young wife, but he could stand by no longer: he had to do something. Hitler and the Nazis were ruthless in their quest for domination of Europe. Life was going to change for everyone, even those in the New Forest.

But he comforted himself that everything would be fine. Megan had made such progress with the management of the house and farm; there was nothing to be concerned about. But he did wonder if

Megan realized that he was not a wealthy man, and that without his salary and money from his private practice, the land would have to pay for itself. A captain in the army didn't earn as much as a surgeon in London. It was something he had never discussed with her.

When he'd told Adam of his worries Adam had laughed. 'I can't see what's bothering you,' he said. 'You're doing the right thing. Your country needs you more than they do. Anyway, I'll come down to Folly House the first weekend in September, when you tell them, to give you moral support.'

He had spoken to Adam that very morning as soon as he heard the latest radio reports. Hitler's armies and air force had crossed the Polish frontier in a blitzkrieg of bombing, backed up by tanks. 'Will you still be able to come?'

'Yes, although it will probably be for the last time in peacetime; war is sure to be declared now.' Adam sounded excited. 'Soon I'll be able to get at the blighters. I'll blast them out of the sky.'

Henry didn't think war should be approached with such relish, but that was Adam. He loved living on the edge. Henry viewed the forthcoming weekend with a mixture of pleasure at being at Folly House and apprehension at having to tell everyone of his decision. He'd arranged with Silas Moon and George Jones to get the guns and beaters ready for a spot of shooting on the estate. Adam would love that. Megan wouldn't. He sensed she was jealous of Adam and felt slightly guilty because he'd seen far more of Adam lately and knew he had neglected her.

There was no way he could explain why he needed Adam's company more than hers. It was illogical. He couldn't even explain it properly to himself, except that he felt they were closer than brothers. They thought alike on everything: music, politics, literature and the theatre. They were on the same wavelength, seeming to know what the other was thinking without the need to speak sometimes. Conversation was never difficult, they could talk about everything. Whereas with Megan he often felt tongue-tied, needing to think before he spoke, unsure of her sensitivities. Maybe it was because she was a woman. The only disagreement with Adam had been when he married Megan. Adam could not understand Henry's necessity for marriage and an heir to Folly House, which, he'd scathingly remarked, was not a stately home, merely a large country house with a farm attached. In his turn Henry had been disappointed both with Adam for not understanding, and with Megan for not liking Adam. However, Adam's friendship was strong and rare, and one he prized above all else.

He decided that when they arrived at Folly House later that evening, the first thing he would do was to call a meeting of everyone: Megan, Lavinia and the Jones family. Then he would announce that from the following Monday, 4 September, he would be a member of the Royal Army Medical Corps, and would be reporting for duty on that day. He would be known in future as Captain Lockwood RAMC.

So engrossed was he in his thoughts that he arrived at the end of the corridor almost without realizing it. He stopped and looked into the long Nightingale surgical ward. Although he hardly needed to look, he knew everything by heart. The two rows of beds facing each other, all their wheels facing the same way; Sister, a stickler for symmetry, had the young nurses whizzing up and down the ward kicking the wheels straight if one of them so much as dared deviate slightly left or right. He could see his replacement, an older man, too old for military service. He was at the far end doing a ward round followed by a flotilla of nurses and medical students. For a moment he felt sad, but then he turned into his office and picked up the last of his belongings and his medical bag, before leaving the hospital and striding across Westminster Bridge towards Waterloo Station and a waiting Adam.

The concourse was heaving with people, but he easily picked out Adam. He was there, tall and handsome in his blue pilot's uniform, waiting beneath the clock as they'd arranged. No need for words, they fell into step and crossed the concourse, pushing their way through crowds of children and attendant adults towards the barrier where the train for Weymouth stood steaming at the platform.

There were no seats on the train. Even the first class carriage, for which they both had tickets, was filled to bursting point with children and their escorts.

'I'd forgotten this was the first day of the great evacuation from London,' said Henry apologetically. 'I'm afraid it's going to be standing all the way to Stibbington.'

Adam was unfazed. 'No matter. We've got the peace of Folly House to look forward to.' He grinned and pulled a face. 'At least, I presume you won't be flooded out with evacuees.'

'Not if Bertha has her way,' said Henry with a wry smile.

Once they'd crammed themselves into a corridor at the end of the carriage, Adam lit a cigarette for Henry, then one for himself. They were surrounded by tearful, exhausted and dirty children. They were sitting on the floor, on each other, in fact on anywhere they could find a surface to sit on. All were clutching their gasmasks, and shabby little suitcases. Every now and then jam sandwiches were passed along from various teachers in charge of the children, and occasionally bottles of lemonade appeared, to be fiercely fought over.

The train lurched and rattled over the points, past Clapham Junction, on into the darkness of the south west, away from the city and the danger of bombs. 'Poor little sods,' said Henry, looking down at them. 'They don't know what's happening to their world.'

'Might turn out better for some of them. Most of them come from pretty dire circumstances.' Adam puffed at his cigarette. 'You know what they say. It's an ill wind etc. . . .'

Henry thought about Megan and the coming child. At least their child would be born in comfort and away from danger. Not like the children all around him. 'I wonder how all these urchins will cope.'

'Not your worry, old man.' Adam concentrated on blowing a perfect smoke ring, much to the amazement of the nearest child – "Cor!" he could be heard muttering. 'All you've got to do is enjoy the war.'

Henry raised his eyebrows. 'Enjoy it? How can anyone enjoy war?'

Adam laughed. 'Come on! Be honest. Of course you'll enjoy it. You'll be shaking off the marital ties. Seeing a bit of the world and beating the jerries into a pulp at the same time.'

Henry realized yet again that Adam really did mean what he'd said about enjoying the war. 'I've only thought of the death and suffering which is coming,' he said slowly. 'Of the disruption of everyone's lives, and the social changes that will inevitably come as well.'

Adam slung an arm companionably around Henry's shoulders. 'Your trouble is that you are too serious. Of course there'll be change. Change is progress. And as for death, well, everyone has to die sometime. So make the most of life while you have it, eh?'

Henry wished that he could be more like Adam and grab the things he wanted, rather than always doing what was expected of him. Not for the first time the nagging worry of wondering whether he had done the right thing in marrying Megan crept into his head. That was something he could never admit to anyone, especially not to Adam. But she was expecting their baby and that was something to look forward to. A child would surely bond them together, wouldn't it?

The journey was long and tedious because the train stopped at every small station once it had reached the country away from the city, letting off small groups of evacuees who disappeared into the now totally black countryside. The only things visible were dim shaded torches, and the occasional swinging hurricane lamp. To make matters worse the train itself was in almost total darkness. All the light bulbs in the compartments and corridors had been removed because of the blackout regulations, and only a tiny weak blue tinted bulb illuminated the whole corridor. The scene took on Hogarthian nightmarish qualities, made worse now by the sound of wailing children who were hungry and missing their mothers.

'I can't wait to get out of here,' muttered Adam irritably, lighting another cigarette.

The train clanked to a screeching halt and Henry peered out of the window, looking for the sign. 'Beaulieu Road Halt,' he said. 'Thank God. Next stop will be Stibbington, that's ours. George Jones should be there waiting to drive us to Folly House.'

But it was Megan who was waiting for them. She'd driven the large Daimler into Stibbington from Folly House and had enjoyed it, as she didn't get the chance to drive the luxurious car very often as it used too much petrol. It had pre-selector gears on a wheel on the dash-board, and she enjoyed the sophistication of choosing the gears before actually shifting into them. She'd had a battle with George Jones and Lavinia, who'd both said she shouldn't drive, but Megan won that battle.

She felt exultant. But one thing marred her jubilation and that was the dull ache in the pit of her stomach. *I should have eaten something before I left,* she thought, rubbing her aching stomach. But there'd been no time; she didn't want to keep Henry and Adam waiting.

It was pitch dark when she arrived at the station. Only one of the platform gaslights was working and that had a grey shade on it. It made the tiny station look surreal, all dark shadows and black buildings.

'I'm not keen on all this blackout lark,' said Mr Moger, the stationmaster, coming up to Megan when she entered through the iron gates on to the platform. 'Can't say as I think it necessary out here in the country. Hitler don't know where Stibbington is, we won't get no bombs here.'

'Not tonight anyway, as we're not even at war,' said Megan, pulling her jacket closer around her. She shivered; the night air seemed very chilly and was making her stomach ache worse. Maybe she was going to be sick. But she gritted her teeth. *Mind over matter,* she told herself. *I am not going to be sick.*

The stationmaster pushed his cap back and scratched his bald head. 'Not at war yet,' he repeated in a sombre tone. 'But soon will be, mark my words. That's why we've got all these kids coming here tonight.' He'd hardly finished speaking when there was the sound of several bicycles coming along the gravelled road outside the station, then the sound of a car, and other people; in the background Mr Noakes's voice could be heard. 'That'll be the welcoming committee,' said Mr Moger. 'They've come to sort out the children and billet them on those who have agreed to have them.' He turned to Megan. 'How many are you having up at Folly House?'

Megan shook her head. 'I don't think we're having any. Nothing has been said.'

'That'll be Bertha Jones's doing,' said Mr Moger, pulling his cap back down. 'She'll not want the work of extra children. But mark my words. You'll be having them up there sooner or later. We've all got to do our bit when the bombs come.'

'Maybe the bombs won't come,' said Megan.

Mr Moger didn't answer but went to the edge of the platform and stood silent for a moment. 'The train is near,' he said. 'I can hear the rails humming.'

As he spoke the trained rounded the bend in the track and a huge white cloud of steam billowed into the night sky. Then with a roaring hiss and screeching of brakes the large locomotive slid to a halt at Stibbington station. The smell of burning coal and hot steam engulfed the station, and Megan felt sick again.

In the hubbub that followed Megan missed Henry and Adam. Instead she found herself caught up in a whirlwind of grizzling children, anxious adults shouting and trying to keep control, and above it all the voice of Mr Noakes, taking charge as usual. He was in his element.

'Boys this side,' he shouted, 'and girls over there.'

'But I want to stay with my friend,' a small voice wailed.

'You can't separate them like that,' a teacher argued.

'I'm staying with my brother. I'm not going anywhere without him,' another child screamed, close to tears.

'All right! All right! Brothers and sisters in the middle.' Albert Noakes capitulated. He saw Megan. 'Are you taking some?' he asked. 'Who do you want?'

Megan backed away from the scrum. 'No, no,' she shook her head. 'We're not taking evacuees. Not this time,' she added, trying to make good her escape. A small girl caught her hand.

'Am I coming with you?' she asked. 'I don't have no brothers and no sisters either. There's just me. I'll be no trouble.'

A little face, smeared with grime from the train journey, looked up at her. White streaks tracked the course of recent tears down her cheeks. Suddenly Megan's heart was touched, and for the first time the real misery of the situation struck home. The coming war, which she'd tried not to acknowledge, abruptly forced its way into her consciousness. These children surging around her on the platform were the first in England to be picked up and tossed hither and thither like leaves before the storm. Not knowing what the next day might bring, and unable to choose their future. The chaos would touch them all; with a shiver she knew that even Folly House would be affected.

'Who is having this child?' she asked Albert Noakes.

He bent down and looked at the label attached to the child's thin cotton coat. 'Rosie Barnes,' he muttered, looking through the sheaf of papers in his hand. He looked up. 'Here we are, Rosie Barnes, seven years old and a cripple.' He looked at Megan. 'She's a problem, this one. No one wants her 'cause she's no use to work on the land on account of her club foot, and that's what most folk round here want them for. Another pair of hands on the farm.'

'I'm not a cripple,' said Rosie, her childish voice high in indignation. 'I've just got one leg shorter that the other and a club foot, but I can do everything all the others can. Look, I can even skip.' She gave a little hop to demonstrate.

'You going to take her?' Mr Noakes looked at Megan, pencil poised above his list.

'Yes,' said Megan impulsively. The moment the word was out of her mouth she wondered what on earth had made her say it.

'Then sign here.' Mr Noakes thrust a piece of paper into her hand and before she could stop and think Megan found herself signing for Rosie Barnes, of 23 Gasworks Street, Hackney. As soon as she'd signed Mr Noakes dashed off to begin allocating other children to the assembled crowd.

She was left standing in the gloom of the station lamp looking at Rosie, and Rosie looked back, a wide smile now spreading across her small face. 'I won't be no trouble, I promise,' she said. 'My mum said she'd kill me if I was sent back, and it's not true what he said,' she nodded towards Albert Noakes, now surrounded by children and the inhabitants of Stibbington. 'I can work. I knows how to wash up, scrub floors, and I can black grates, and white steps as well.' Her smile faded and her pale, pinched features took on an anxious look. 'I can really.'

Megan found herself smiling down at her. 'I don't think we shall need you to do any of that, Rosie,' she said.

'But what will I do all day?' Rosie looked worried.

'Go to school, of course,' said Megan. 'Come on,' she picked up

Rosie's small cardboard suitcase, and held out her hand.

After a moment's hesitation Rosie put her small hand in Megan's. 'I've got to look after that,' she said indicating the suitcase. 'It's brand new. My mum bought it in Woolworth's special for me.'

By the time Megan got back to the Daimler, where an irritated Henry and Adam were now standing, she had found out that Rosie rarely went to school because her mother had another sickly infant at home and wasn't well herself. From what Megan could deduce Rosie was to all intents and purposes the housewife running the little family. Her father was unemployed and according to Rosie was in the Kings Head most of the time during the day, only returning at night if he could find his way home. She didn't say he was drunk or violent, but reading between the lines Megan guessed he was probably both.

'Who have you got there?' said Henry as soon as he'd spotted Rosie.

'This is Rosie,' said Megan. 'She's an evacuee from London and she will be staying with us while the war is on.' Unlocking the Daimler she put Rosie's case in the boot. 'Do you mind?'

'Not at all,' said Henry, putting his own case in the boot and making room for Adam's as well. He caught Adam's eye and knew what he was thinking. This would make it easier for him to tell everyone that he was leaving to be an officer in the RAMC. An evacuee made the prospect of war much more real.

Megan sat in the back of the car with Rosie as Henry drove back to Folly House. The child peered curiously out of the window into the darkness. 'The blackout is good here,' she said. 'I can't see any lights. Our street has one light still on, but it's dim. My dad says that our light will be bombed first because we're near the gasworks. I wish we didn't have any lights at all, like here.'

'There are no lights here because it's the country,' said Megan. 'We don't have streetlights.'

'None at all?' Rosie was amazed. 'But where are the houses? They must have very good blackout too.'

'There are not many houses either,' said Megan. 'Just one or two, here and there.'

Rosie digested this information in silence, and Megan leaned back in her seat, looking at Adam and Henry in the front. She noticed Henry had a new haircut, very short, rather like Adam's. It suited him, and Adam was looking even more handsome in the blue uniform of the Royal Air Force. They were talking quietly together. She tried not to feel jealous; it was ridiculous to feel jealous of one of Henry's friends. Then she thought about Henry's reaction to Rosie. She'd expected him to be irritated and hostile, but he'd just accepted it.

Rosie suddenly slipped a cold little hand into hers and squeezed it. Megan guessed that despite her cocky self-confident air she was nervous, and hoped Bertha and Lavinia would be kind and not be put out by the arrival of an evacuee.

Suddenly the dull ache in her stomach increased in intensity, and involuntarily she grasped Rosie's hand tightly. 'Sorry,' she said hastily. 'I had a sudden pain in my stomach and it made me jump.'

'What you need,' said Rosie, nodding her head knowledgeably, 'is a good drop of gin and a hot bath. My mum always has that when she's got a pain in her stomach. Of course she can only have a hot bath if my dad brings the bath in from the yard, but he don't always bother, so she don't get it.'

'Really,' said Megan, wondering if Rosie knew that gin and hot baths were supposed to bring on a miscarriage.

There was a moment's silence, then Rosie added wistfully, 'I loves a bath, especially when we've got a bit of soap.'

'You can have one when we get to Folly House,' said Megan, steeling herself against the increasing pain. 'I'll get Bertha to run one for you.' The pain got worse, coming in regular violent spasms. Was this what it was like to have a baby? But it was months too soon, so it couldn't be that.

'Who is Bertha?' asked Rosie.

But Megan didn't answer. She couldn't. The pain was tearing at her insides, she was hot and sweaty and at the same time shivering violently.

Henry turned the car through the iron gates of Folly House. Home at last thought Megan feverishly and tried to get out of the car. But her legs crumpled beneath her and suddenly she felt the cold gritty stones of the gravel against her face.

There were lights, lights everywhere, Rosie was still holding her hand, and then disappeared. Henry was shouting, the house swirled in a kaleidoscope of colours, and she felt a hot sticky wetness engulf her. Then there was blackness, and pain, only pain.

'Megan!'

From far away she heard Henry calling, but it was too difficult to get through the blackness. It was easier to let go and float away into the black night away from the gut-wrenching pain.

'Sorry old chap.' Dr Crozier flung himself down on the chesterfield at the side of the gold room, and tossed back a hot toddy Henry passed him. 'Not a good homecoming, but you know yourself that these things happen. I've left Lavinia up there; she's going to stay with her for a while. But Megan's young and healthy. She'll get over it and have plenty more babies.'

'Exactly,' said Adam, flicking his lighter into life as he lit yet another cigarette. 'I never understand why people make so much fuss over a miscarriage. It's not as if it's really a child.

Henry made a toddy for himself and gazed out into the darkness of the garden. In the distance he could see the red port light of a cargo ship making its way along the Solent towards Southampton. The last few hours seemed unreal; the nightmare journey from London; the dramatic event of Megan's collapse; finally, the bloodied mess that should have been their baby. 'I suppose you're right,' he said slowly. 'There will be other babies.'

'Of course there will. It's not the end of the world.' Dr Crozier shrugged himself into his overcoat. He paused a moment, then put his hand on Henry's shoulder. 'Of course, we know it's not the end of the world, but I'm afraid Megan may not see it like that. She'll need plenty of support in the coming days.'

Henry escorted the doctor through to the large front door which opened out on to the portico. Dr Crozier paused, and Henry held out his hand. 'Thank you for all your help.'

'Just wish I could have saved the little blighter,' Dr Crozier muttered gruffly.

Henry didn't reply, and when the doctor had gone leaned against the closed door and shut his eyes. How could he tell Megan that he was leaving? But he *had* to. Although not tonight, that was impossible. But it would have to be tomorrow, Saturday, because he was leaving on Sunday evening. He wished he'd not left it so late, but knew the answer. It was because he was a moral coward; always hoping that difficult things would somehow resolve themselves. Of course they never did.

'Please sir,' a small voice interrupted his troubled thoughts. 'What shall I do? I don't know where to go.'

Opening his eyes Henry looked down. It was Rosie, still clutching her gasmask and cardboard suitcase. In the melée of the past events he had entirely forgotten about her.

'Has nobody taken care of you?' he asked.

'No sir.' Rosie looked worried. 'I hid in the big cupboard there, underneath the stairs. I didn't know what else to do. I always hide under the stairs when I don't know what to do. Is Miss Megan all right now?'

'Yes she's all right now.'

'And the baby? Is that all right?'

Henry looked at her. Her small face had wisdom far beyond her years. He had no doubt she knew about suffering and dead babies. 'No, the baby is not all right.'

'You'll be wanting to send me back now, I suppose.' It was not so much a question as a resigned statement.

Henry gave himself a mental shake. He'd just lost a child, but life had to go on. Megan had befriended this small evacuee, maybe it would help her in the coming days. It would give her something else to think about if she had the responsibility of a child. 'No, we shall not be sending you back. In fact I am very sorry you haven't been taken care of. However, I shall rectify that now. Come with me.'

He strode across the hall with Rosie stumbling along behind him, encumbered by her suitcase and gasmask.

'Lordy, what have we got here,' was Bertha's reaction when he opened the kitchen door and ushered in his small charge. Bertha, George and Dottie were sitting at the kitchen table drinking tea and looking very miserable. Dottie was crying. Tilly came in at the sound of Bertha's voice and looked as if she'd been crying as well.

'This is Rosie. An evacuee from London,' said Henry. 'Megan took charge of her at the station, and then I'm afraid she got forgotten after we arrived and Megan collapsed.'

'Well, that's not surprising,' was Bertha's only comment. She didn't offer her sympathy to him in words, but she cared. They all cared and he knew that. It was comforting.

'Will you take care of Rosie until Megan is better? Then she can take charge.'

'Of course.' Bertha bustled round the table and looked more closely at Rosie. 'Poor little lamb,' she muttered. 'London's no place to live these days, not with what's going on up there.' She nodded towards the radio which Dottie had switched off when Henry arrived. 'Been listening to the news. It's terrible.' She picked up Rosie's suitcase and untangled the gasmask box's cord from around her neck. 'There now,' she said. 'Where do you want her to sleep? Has she had anything to eat?' She peered closer. 'She looks as if she needs a good bath.'

'I hadn't thought about sleeping,' Henry said, 'and I suppose she should have a bath . . .'

'A bath,' squealed Rosie. Everything forgotten in an ecstasy of delight. 'I'd love a bath, especially if there's smelly soap. We never have smelly soap, only carbolic.'

'I think we can organize smelly soap,' said Henry with a smile. He thought quickly, the Joneses didn't have a bathroom but still used a tin bath in the outside scullery once a week. It was something he'd meant to get changed but somehow he'd never got around to it. 'Use the bathroom on the top floor at the back of the house for tonight, and as for sleeping, I think . . .' he hesitated, unused to making domestic decisions.

'She can sleep in the box room along the corridor from the bathroom. It's not far from Dottie's room in the attic,' interrupted Bertha, making the decision for him. 'But I'll give the mite a bite of supper first, and then we'll see about the bath.' She put Rosie's belongings in the corner of the kitchen and indicated a chair at the table.

Rosie scrambled on to it eagerly, beaming from ear to ear. 'Thank you,' she said.

Henry left the kitchen, suddenly feeling more cheerful. Rosie would be fine with the Joneses looking after her, and Megan would also enjoy organizing Rosie's life. He returned to the gold room where Adam was sitting, moodily smoking and staring out into the dark garden.

'I hope it's OK but I've persuaded Lavinia to sleep in her old bedroom tonight,' he said. 'She came down from Megan's room while you were away, and I thought it too late for her to walk back to the dower house. I hope that's all right. She'll be down in a moment to have supper with us.'

'Of course it's all right,' said Henry. 'Thanks for organizing it.'

He sensed that Adam was feeling excluded from the family crisis and was unhappy that tomorrow's shoot would probably not happen. But for all their closeness he suddenly realized that the loss of what would have been his first-born was not something he could talk about with Adam. To Adam it was not a child, it was an *'it'* something that had never existed. Now there was a chasm between them, something Henry had thought would never happen.

The supper gong sounded in the rose room. Adam got up and walked across to Henry. 'Is the shooting still on for tomorrow?' he asked. 'I hope so. I promised the CO at Biggin Hill I'd bring him back a brace of pheasant.'

'Well, I'm not sure.' Henry hesitated. 'It depends on how Megan is.'

Lavinia entered the room. 'Megan will be fine,' she said firmly. 'The sooner she gets back to normality the sooner she'll recover from this episode. All she needs is a few days' rest and she'll be as right as rain. You and Adam should go shooting while you have the chance. Tomorrow is going to be a lovely day.'

Episode! thought Henry. *Episode!* Even Lavinia thought it a minor matter. He wondered what Megan was thinking, but knew he could never ask her. They were not close enough to talk about such things. They would each mourn alone for the flicker of life that had been snuffed out before it had a chance to get a foothold in the world.

*

The following morning Megan woke to sunlight streaming in through the window. She was in a side room, not the bedroom she shared with Henry; someone had been up and drawn back the curtains, and she was warm and comfortable snuggled in crisp white sheets. The previous night was a distant memory of pain and darkness, but apart from that, nothing. She put her hands on her stomach. It felt bruised and sore, but it was flat and there were a few drops of blood on her nightdress. Blood: yes, she remembered now. She'd been bleeding when she fell from the car. She felt well now, but more than that she felt relieved. The baby had gone. It didn't matter now who the father might have been. The next baby would definitely be Henry's.

In the distance she heard dogs barking and the sound of footsteps on the gravel. That must be Henry and Adam going out shooting, and those were Silas Moon's dogs, excited at the thought of retrieving plump birds from the undergrowth.

She smiled. Bertha would be pleased with some game birds to cook, and if they got a few partridge as well she'd make one of her famous game pies.

She stretched luxuriously. Whatever it was that Dr Crozier had dosed her with last night had the effect of making her feel pleasantly relaxed and carefree.

The door to the bedroom opened quietly and Lavinia tiptoed in carrying a teapot, followed by Bertha with a heavy tray. 'We've brought a light breakfast, dear,' Lavinia said.

Bertha put the tray on the bedside table. There was half a grapefruit with a cherry stuck in the middle, some golden-brown toast, a large pat of butter and a jar of marmalade, as well as the tea and milk.

Megan pushed herself into an upright position. 'The breakfast looks lovely,' she said. She put her hand on her stomach, 'What happened?' she asked. She needed confirmation that the baby was no more.

'You lost the baby last night,' said Lavinia sombrely. She leaned forward and took Megan's hand. 'You mustn't be too upset. Dr Crozier said you are young, there's plenty of time for more babies.

53

The important thing is that you are all right.'

The feeling of relief when Lavinia confirmed that the baby had gone was so immense that she had difficulty in not smiling. She looked at Lavinia's sad face. Everyone was expecting her to be sad: yes, to be sad and upset. Squeezing Lavinia's hand she gave what she hoped was a wan smile. 'Yes,' she said slowly. 'There's plenty of time. Henry and I have our whole lives ahead of us.'

It was true, and the next baby would be Henry's. She was never going to betray him again.

CHAPTER FIVE

Saturday 2 September 1939

As a compromise to Lavinia's concern Megan rested all day but on the Saturday evening she dressed and came downstairs to dinner.

It was the custom to have a sherry before dinner and Megan sat with Lavinia in the gold room. Outside the late summer evening was drawing to a close, the warm scent of approaching autumn wafting in through the open windows. As she sat absorbing the sights and sounds two figures came across the lawn from the direction of the folly. It was two girls, one was Dottie and the other was. . . ? Uncertain, she peered into the slowly darkening evening and suddenly realized that the other was a very small girl. It was the child she had agreed to take in as an evacuee the night before. What was her name? Rosie. Yes, that was it, she remembered now. Rosie Barnes. It seemed a lifetime ago that she had met her on the draughty railway station.

Lavinia followed her gaze and saw the girls too. 'That little Rosie has settled in here incredibly well,' she said. 'Bertha told me that others in the village haven't been so lucky. Some of them have turned out to be infested with lice, and most of them wet their beds last night. At least Rosie is clean and toilet trained. The only thing wrong is her clothes. She is dressed respectably enough, but her winter coat is so thin you could shoot peas through it, as Bertha always says, and her shoes were padded out with cardboard. They will disintegrate at the first shower of rain.'

'Oh dear, then I must take her into Southampton as soon as possible and get her kitted out in something suitable,' said Megan.

'No need.' Lavinia looked self-satisfied. 'I did it myself this morning. I got George to drive me into Southampton with Rosie. I had a bit of trouble with the shoes because of her club foot, but we compromised for the time being. I'm having a special pair made up for her in Ganges, the shoe shop at the bottom of the town near the docks. They specialize in handmade shoes.'

From her expression Megan could see that Lavinia had enjoyed every moment of her shopping trip. But the cost bothered her. 'I'm not being mean,' she said, 'but it might make things difficult for her mother. She's probably having trouble paying for things as it is.'

Lavinia nodded. 'From what little I've gleaned from the child, she can't afford anything, and Rosie was anxious about the cost of everything, especially the shoes. But I set the child's mind at rest. I told her that while she's with us we are in *loco parentis* and she will, therefore, be treated as one of our own.' Lavinia looked sharply at Megan. 'I hope that's what you had in mind; you weren't going to treat her like a servant, were you?'

'Of course not,' said Megan indignantly. 'She will be my temporary daughter.'

So that was it. Rosie Barnes was seamlessly absorbed into the family and was adopted as a daughter of Folly House.

The gong sounded for dinner and the two women rose and joined Henry and Adam who were already waiting in the rose dining room. Henry, looking serious, was standing in his place at the head of the table and Adam was by his side. Megan took her place at the opposite end of the table. Tradition decreed that, as Henry's wife she should sit there; something Megan thought faintly ridiculous, having to sit miles away from her husband. But tradition was tradition, and she had acquiesced and now always sat there. Lavinia took her place at the side and Rosie was steered into a seat opposite her by Dottie, who then left and went back to the kitchen. The little girl, her big brown eyes round and solemn, sat very still, looking rather scared. This was the first time she had eaten with the Lockwood family and she would have rather been in the kitchen with Dottie. But she obediently did as she was told and sat at the table which was resplendent with a snowy-white damask tablecloth, gleaming silver cutlery and sparkling crystal glasses. She thought the whole room looked like something out of a fairly tale.

Once they were seated Bertha and Tilly began to leave ready to bring in the soup tureens and plates for the first course. As they went to the door Henry raised his hand. 'Bertha, before you start to serve, would you go and get George and Dottie, and bring them in here. I have something to say.' He looked at Tilly, who looked startled. 'You wait here, Tilly; you also need to hear what I have to say.'

Lavinia frowned. 'Good heavens, Henry,' she said. 'You are being very dramatic.' She sniffed. 'It's a pity Mr Chamberlain can't be a bit dramatic and take us into the war once and for all, now that Germany has invaded Poland.'

Henry didn't reply but waited until everyone was assembled; he glanced down at Adam who was looking straight down the table at Megan. It seemed to her that there was a glint of triumph in his eyes, and she shivered.

'Maybe I am being a little dramatic,' said Henry. 'But I have something to say which will affect you all, especially you, Megan.' His clear blue eyes looked at her. What was he going to say? She clasped her hands tightly beneath the tablecloth. 'I have been accepted as a captain in the Royal Army Medical Corps, and I join my unit, tomorrow, Sunday 3 of September. I shall be at Millbank in London for two days next week, after that I expect to be posted to the training camp at Catterick, Yorkshire.'

Megan was stunned. 'Tomorrow?' she said. 'Why didn't you tell me before?' As she spoke she was sure she saw a glimmer of a smile pass across Adam's face and knew it was not a surprise to him. The thought made her angry. Surely as Henry's wife she should be the one to share his confidences, not Adam.

'I did intend to,' said Henry swiftly. 'Truly I did. But I didn't want to write a letter or tell you over the telephone, I wanted to tell you myself. But then you collapsed last night, and there hasn't been an opportunity until this moment, and now there's not much time before I leave.'

Megan didn't reply. There has been time, she thought rebelliously. Plenty of time. You could have come to Folly House earlier, you needn't have gone shooting today, you could have found time to be with me alone. But you didn't. You chose to be with Adam. It's always Adam.

But she sat still as stone and said nothing.

Lavinia came round and grasped Megan's hands in hers. 'It's true, my dear. You were in no fit state to hear news of this kind before this evening. I know it's a shock. But now with war so close there must be many wives suddenly facing the prospect of life without their husbands for a while.'

'Only while the war lasts,' said Henry.

'And it won't last long,' said Adam smoothly, lighting another cigarette. 'Henry and I will be back in civvy street before you've had time to miss us. You should be proud, Megan. Your husband is now an officer and a gentleman.' He inhaled deeply and smiled.

Megan wanted to hit him, which she knew was illogical, but all the same the impulse was almost overwhelming. So Adam *had* been in on the secret, and what was more she knew he was pleased about it. He and Henry were together again, in a man's world from which she was excluded. She felt angry and powerless at the same time, but she was not going to let Adam know it.

Instead she lifted her head and looked straight at Henry. 'Of course I'm proud of you, darling,' she said firmly, then, looking towards the assembled room, she continued, 'and I'm sure everyone here at Folly House wishes you godspeed and good luck. We shall all be counting the days until you return.'

'Yes, and that's the truth of it, sir,' said Bertha taking a step forward. In her uncomplicated way she could feel the conflicting emotions swirling around and didn't like it. She wanted to get back to the plane she was familiar with, one of food and housework. 'Shall I go and bring the soup in now?'

Glad to have got the announcement over and done with, Henry sat down. 'Yes please, Bertha,' he said.

It was a silent meal that night. Rosie sat wide-eyed and drank her soup and ate her poached salmon, and roast lamb without comment. Megan noticed that she waited until everyone else had started before picking up the correct knife and fork; she could see Lavinia smiling in approval at their small evacuee's common sense. Strange, she reflected, in one night she had lost one child and acquired another; suddenly she felt more cheerful. What other surprises had life got in store for her?

The wireless was kept on after dinner and more or less continuously during the night. The whole country was listening to accounts of uproar in parliament as MPs tried to force Prime Minister Chamberlain to take the decision and confront Hitler.

Megan left the room early and took Rosie upstairs to put her to bed. She found Bertha and Lavinia had gone to a great deal of trouble to make the room welcoming. The bed was covered with a patchwork quilt in various shades of pink, and some of Gerald's and Henry's old toys had been retrieved from the attic and set out in a row under the window. At the far end of the room stood a rather battered, but still beautiful, black wooden rocking horse. One eye was missing and his mane was a little threadbare, but he was still an imperious-looking creature. On entering the room Rosie rushed towards the horse and threw her arms around his neck.

'He's called Black Beauty,' she said. 'Bertha told me.'

Megan smiled at her enthusiasm. She looked around at the room, the walls could do with another coat of paint, but even so it was warm and cosy, perfect for a little girl. 'Do you like your room?' she asked.

Rosie turned a rapturous face towards her. 'Like it?' she said. 'I *love* it. And I don't have to share it with no one.'

'Anyone,' corrected Megan automatically.

'Yes, that's right, no one,' said Rosie, adding, 'can I have another bath tonight?' Then she looked doubtful. 'But Bertha told me too many baths make you weak. She said that when I told her I'd like a bath every night.'

Megan laughed. 'I'm afraid I don't agree with Bertha on that score. On the contrary, being clean makes you strong. Come along then.' She led the way towards the bathroom at the end of the corridor.

Rosie trotted behind Megan, smiling gleefully. 'What does contrary mean? she asked.

*

By Sunday morning everyone knew that their fate, and that of the civilized world, would be decided by 11.00 a.m. that morning. Hitler had received an ultimatum from the British Government at nine o' clock that morning; unless Germany withdrew its troops from Poland, war would be declared. The ultimatum expired at eleven o' clock.

Just before eleven o'clock Henry, Megan, Lavinia, Rosie and Adam, together with Gerald and Violet who had driven over from Brinkley Hall to share the news with the rest of the Lockwoods, had gathered in the gold room and turned on the wireless. Arthur and Marcus arrived in a rush, having hurried over from a shortened matins service. The Jones family and Tilly were also invited, and stood a little apart in a nervous huddle.

Henry sat with Megan by the window, staring with unseeing eyes at the sunlit garden. No matter how much Adam told him it wasn't important he was still uneasy about the way he'd broken the news of his enlistment to her. They'd been married for nearly six months, but if the truth be told, Henry still felt as remote and ill at ease with the young woman he'd married as he had on his wedding night. Her pregnancy so early in their marriage had given a good excuse for not having sex too often and, of course, this weekend had made it out of the question. It was not that he didn't want sex or was inexperienced: he and Adam had shared a string of beautiful young actresses, but having sex with someone he didn't care about was easy; he didn't have to pretend he wanted anything other than sexual release. But with Megan it was different; she was his wife, he loved her. Or at least he thought he did, and he had expected something different from their shared intimacy. He'd expected it to develop into something more than just sex. But it hadn't, and it wasn't even good sex, and apart from their shared interest in the house and farm they had nothing in common: something Adam was always reminding him about.

He glanced sideways at Megan. She was young and very beautiful, and deserved a good husband. Maybe when he came back from the war he'd feel differently and everything would fall into place.

Megan felt his glance upon her, but steadfastly didn't turn to look at him. She was still numb with the shock of his announcement. Common sense told her she was being ridiculous, after all it was inevitable that he would have been drafted into the services sooner or later anyway. Britain was sliding inexorably into war, men all over the country were getting their call-up papers, and priceless treasures from the London museums were being hidden away in caves in the country. Children too, like Rosie, were being taken from London, to escape the bombs which surely now would soon come.

Last night when they were alone together in their bedroom she had expected Henry to tell her more about his plans. But he said nothing; only whispered that everything would be all right. But that was all. He said nothing about the loss of the baby. Their last night together before he left for war had been one of long silences, and Megan felt it was as if they had just met. Long after he'd fallen asleep she lay beside him, stiff and uncomfortable. Was marriage supposed to be like this? Surely they should be wrapped in a warm embrace?

In the morning she'd tried to summon up courage to throw her arms around him and tell him she loved him. But she hadn't, and now the moment had passed. They sat side by side, in a room full of people, but Megan felt alone.

Rosie crept forward and settled herself at Megan's feet, then reached up and took hold of her hand. It was warm and living, quite different from the coldness in Megan's heart.

Violet sat with Lavinia. She was dressed in a beautiful pale blue silk dress with a long lacy-knit matching cashmere cardigan over it; the outfit shrieked money, but somehow Violet managed to look quite plain. Her mouse-blonde hair was stylishly cut, unlike Megan's mass of dark curls. Like Megan she wore no make-up, but whereas Megan's face was healthily tanned from her outside life, Violet was pale and had a large bruise on her forehead.

'How did you manage to hurt your head?' she whispered to Violet.

Violet raised a hand to her brow. 'Oh, I crashed it on one of the kitchen cupboards while I was putting china away.'

'What on earth were you doing putting china away? That's a maid's job,' said Lavinia.

Violet looked unhappier than ever. 'The servants have all left.'

'Again,' said Lavinia acidly.

Violet seemed to shrink even further back in the chair. 'Gerald is getting some more from London. He says there are plenty of people wanting to leave London and work in the country.'

'Hmm, maybe,' said Lavinia sharply. 'But will they be willing to work for Gerald?'

Megan looked at Gerald. He was leaning on the mantelpiece, by the side of the wireless, and smoking one of his usual cigars. A heavy gold chain glinted across his waistcoat, attached to a gold-encrusted pocket watch which he was studying. 'It's nearly time we learned your fate, Henry. Are we going to war and will you fight the Nazis, or will we join up with Hitler and become a really organized country like Germany?'

'How can you say that, Gerald? To even think such a thing is wrong. Hitler is evil. England will never join the Nazis.'

Megan was surprised at the sudden ferocity of Violet's voice. She looked at her with a new respect. 'I agree with you, Violet,' she said, adding, 'Maybe you, Gerald, will be called up to join the army as well.'

Gerald laughed, but the laughter didn't reach his eyes. He glowered at both Megan and Violet. 'No chance, Megan,' he said smoothly. 'I am excused, like Arthur, on the grounds of my health. He can't walk, and I have a chest condition.'

'First I've heard of it.' Henry lit a cigarette and Megan knew he was angry. His hand was shaking. 'You've never done anything you didn't want to, Gerald. You've always managed to escape any real responsibilities.'

'Then how do you explain the fact that my financial position is far superior to yours, and I didn't inherit a house?'

Only Megan heard Violet's softly spoken words. 'No, you married me.'

'Anyway, someone has got to stay behind and run the country,' said Gerald.

'All you care about is making money,' said Henry angrily.

'It's the only thing worth caring about,' Gerald snapped back.

Megan stared at him. Surely he didn't really mean that. But as she looked at his handsome face she realized with disquiet that he did. There was an arrogant hardness about him that she'd never noticed before.

'Be quiet, the pair of you,' said Lavinia. She stalked across the room to the wireless and turned up the volume.

Bertha and George Jones looked uncomfortable at the family quarrel. Luckily at that moment the wireless crackled into life with the announcer's voice, then a few moments later, at 11.15, the metallic voice of Chamberlain was heard echoing around the room as he announced over the wireless that his work for peace had failed and that as a result of Germany not replying to the ultimatum, Britain was now at war with Germany.

'This country is now at war with Germany. We are ready.' Neville Chamberlain's words dropped like pebbles into the stillness of the room.

Outside a sudden gust of wind blew up and a swirl of brown leaves eddied across the lawn, scattering in all directions at the far end of the garden. Megan shivered. Where would they all be at the end of the war? Would they be picked up and tossed hither and thither by the winds of war? Or would everything remain the same? She'd always thought nothing would ever change in the New Forest or the village of East End, but suddenly she was not so sure.

The Sunday sunshine poured into the room, and Lavinia heaved a sigh of relief, as she snapped the radio off. 'Well, that's that,' she said. 'Now we know, we can make proper plans. We will be ready for whatever comes.'

Bertha stepped forward. 'I'll be getting back to the kitchen if that's all right with you, Mr Henry. Lunch will be at one o'clock; its roast leg of lamb with mint sauce, baked potatoes, runner beans, and carrots.'

Henry smiled. 'I couldn't ask for a better send-off, Bertha. It will be a meal to remember.'

By that evening, just before Henry and Adam departed it was announced that France had also declared war on Germany as well. A joint Anglo/French statement was issued saying that the two governments would avoid bombing civilians and did not intend using poison gas or germ warfare.

Megan was not allowed to drive Henry and Adam to the railway station. Lavinia forbade it pronouncing her not fit enough to drive, and Megan didn't demur. So their final goodbyes were said at the front of the house before the assembled crowd.

'I'll write,' whispered Henry as he kissed her.

'So will I,' said Megan. 'Be safe.'

'Of course he'll be safe,' Adam interrupted with a laugh. 'We're off to give the Jerries a good hiding, and have some adventures at the same time.'

That's all it is to you, thought Megan resentfully, an adventure. But she said nothing.

But Lavinia said, 'That's what they said at the beginning of the last war, but it didn't turn out quite like that.

Seven months later: March 1940

Silas Moon stood in the small room off the hall of Folly House, which now served as Megan's office, twisting his greasy old cap in his hands. Round and round it went as he shuffled his feet uncomfortably.

'I just don't know what to do,' he said. 'Sometimes I thinks I ought give up altogether and retire, and let Mr Gerald take over running the farm. He's always telling me he wants to do it.'

'Never! Not while I'm in charge,' said Megan sharply.

'But how can I manage now? All the young men have disappeared. My last labourer, Charlie Sims, got his papers yesterday morning. He's going in the Navy.' Silas paused, still twisting his cap round and round in his hands. 'Although what use he'll be in the Navy I can't think. He can't swim, or even row a boat on the Stib.'

Megan hid a smile. 'I don't think he'll be doing much rowing. He'll be on some enormous battleship.'

'Anyway,' Silas went on, 'I was wondering if you could write to Mr Henry and ask him what we should do?'

Megan bit her lip in exasperation. Surely she'd proved by now that she knew how to run the farm and Folly House. But apparently not as far as Silas was concerned. Holding back her annoyance, she said, 'Henry is much too busy to be bothered with matters here. I am dealing with it, Silas, and I've already decided what to do. We are taking on two land girls.' She picked up a sheaf of papers and waved them at a startled Silas.

'Land girls!' gasped Silas in horror. 'I've heard about these girls. They comes down from London, or some other city up north, they don't know nothing about farming, they 'as painted nails and fancy hairdos, and they thinks they can work on a farm!'

'They are war workers; they are doing their bit the same as everyone else,' said Megan firmly, ignoring Silas's scowl. 'And what they don't know you can teach them. I am making arrangements for two to join East End farm next week.'

'Where they going to live then?' demanded Silas. 'They can't stay with me and the missus, and Charlie Sims rents the only tied cottage we got, and his wife and little 'uns will need that even though he 'as gone to war.'

'I've thought of that,' said Megan. 'There are the groom's old quarters above the stables. I looked at them yesterday. Two rooms, a kitchen with a fireplace and a toilet. It only needs a lick of paint and some furniture. I'll see to that. It will be fine.'

A very disgruntled Silas left, muttering that he didn't want no women on his land. Megan watched his retreating back and then wrote a long letter to Henry, telling him of the latest events at Folly House. It was early evening before she'd finished the letter and put it in the tray ready for Tilly to take to the post office the next day.

Then it was time to hang up the blackout curtains in the gold room and the rose room. Megan often thought the evening ritual of struggling to put up the blackout a waste of time. It was seven months now since the declaration of war, and not one single bomb had fallen in England. Throughout most of the house the task was simple, as they'd rigged up blinds which could be pulled down by one person, but the windows in the gold and rose rooms were too tall and wide for blinds, so thick black squares of heavy material was hoisted on to the brass curtain rails every night,. Megan thought them ugly and refused to let them hang there during the day, so they were stowed under the stairs, hence the evening ritual of hanging them each evening.

She grumbled about it to Tilly, who was helping her. 'I really don't think this is necessary. Why can't the Government just get on with the job of finishing off the Germans before they have a chance to drop bombs?'

'Yes,' said Tilly, adding, 'but it's a disappointment there being no bombs yet.'

Megan stopped halfway up the stepladder. 'Disappointing?' she echoed in astonishment. 'I'm not sure I'd say that.'

'Well, yes. It is disappointing to me. I've made up my mind to join the ATS so I'm hoping the war won't stop before I get there.'

Megan looked at her in dismay. 'Oh, Tilly, don't you desert us as well. It's bad enough all the young men in the village being away, don't *you* go as well. However will we manage?' She hooked the heavy black material over the end of the curtain pole with a vicious twist. 'I don't know. Life seems to get more and more difficult, even without being bombed. Everything is rationed: food, petrol, and to make matters worse we're spied on by that bumptious little air-raid warden, Albert Noakes, the whole time.'

Tilly laughed. 'Everyone in the village says he's got very big-headed since he got his arm band and tin hat with ARW written on it.'

Megan clambered back down the stepladder. 'Do you want to leave, Tilly? Don't you like it here?'

Tilly sighed. 'Well, it's like this. I feels I got to do my bit. Most of the girls in the village are doing war work now. They're not just housemaids like me. They're doing something important.'

'You are not *just* a housemaid. You are an important part of Folly House.'

Tilly put out a hand and touched Megan's arm diffidently. 'I'm not really important here, you know that. But I'll come back when the war is over, if you'll have me.'

Megan shook her head. 'No you won't. By then you'll have found yourself a husband, or a better job. But you're right I suppose. You've got to go.'

'Then it's all right if I leave next week?' said Tilly eagerly. 'I've been to the recruiting office in Southampton and I can start training next week. I've done all the paperwork, and made arrangements for half my army pay to be sent to my mother. I've got to tell them by tomorrow for definite.'

The words came out in a rush and Megan realized that Tilly had been dreading having to tell her. She hastened to reassure her. 'Of course it's all right. It's your life. You must do what you want to do.'

Tilly took the steps to put them away. 'Thank you. I knew you'd understand. My friend Doreen says it's time for us girls to move on.' She paused and clasped the steps to her chest, adding in an excited voice. 'Just think. Doreen says we might even get sent to foreign countries. Oh, I've always wanted to go abroad.'

Time to move on. Foreign countries. The words rang through Megan's head. 'Yes,' she said, 'I suppose it is time to move on. For all of us.'

Suddenly she envied Tilly. Tilly's horizons were opening up in a way that would have been unimaginable a year ago. Whereas she was staying put at Folly House, the place she'd known all her life. Which was what she'd always wanted. Wasn't it?

CHAPTER SIX

March 1940

Coming up from the underground at Piccadilly, Henry stood for a moment waiting for his eyes to adjust to the blackout. He missed the twinkling array of lights and the floodlit buildings of pre-war London. Tonight the only illumination came from a slim sickle moon. He could see a couple of barrage balloons silhouetted against the night sky like two huge elephants bumbling about.

Carrying his kitbag on his back Henry made his way down Haymarket, passing the queues of people filing into the two theatres on either side of the road and on to Trafalgar Square, where Nelson stood on duty on the top of his column. In Nelson's time, thought Henry, civilians stayed at home and were not involved in a war, but this time everyone would be drawn into the conflict. Already throughout Europe people were dying every day. How would England cope if it was invaded by the Nazis? The thought was disquieting and Henry pushed it from his mind. He had other responsibilities, as tomorrow he was due to meet his unit at Victoria Station; he knew they were going to France, but the men did not.

But tonight, his last night in England after being briefed for the expeditionary force he was accompanying to France, he had the evening to himself and was meeting Adam. Trust Adam to manage to wangle a weekend's leave in London, and also manage to borrow a friend's flat near Admiralty Arch. He'd told Henry it was the last word in luxury and had invited Henry to stay as well, instead of staying in the officers' mess at Millbank. They'd arranged to meet at a new officers' club in Chelsea.

Walking along the embankment Henry could hear the Thames but could only just make out the bridges across it. He found the club, a tall white house with a discreet shaded lamp by a door at the bottom of steps down from the pavement.

Once inside Henry saw Adam at once. He was holding court as usual. For a moment Henry felt irritated. Once Adam had an audience he was always loath to let it go, and he'd been looking forward to a quiet evening's chat. Adam saw him and waved. The club was crowded with officers from all three services, making it difficult for Henry to weave his way through them towards Adam.

'This is Henry,' said Adam. 'He's off to France tomorrow to patch people up after they've finished beating up the Jerries. Buy him a drink, someone; he needs cheering up.'

Someone thrust a brimming pint glass into Henry's hand. 'Don't broadcast the fact that I'm going to France, it's supposed to be a secret,' said Henry.

Adam made a face. 'We're all on the same side in here,' he said. 'Don't worry so much.'

A honky-tonk piano began playing and the assembled company started singing. Henry began to wish he'd taken the train back to Folly House and the peace of Hampshire, which was what he knew he should have done. But too late now, he was here, and Adam was in party mood. He seemed to have a formed a close friendship with the naval officer at his side. Henry noticed that the man, whom Adam had introduced as 'Mike, works on minesweepers you know,' hung on Adam's every word. As the evening wore on more and more alcohol was consumed by everyone, Henry began to feel bad-tempered; he didn't want to drink himself into oblivion, not when he had to be up at the crack of dawn and take charge of a unit of men.

There was a lull in the piano-playing and Henry took the opportunity to have a quiet word with Adam. 'Don't you think it's about time we went back to the flat? I've got a long day ahead of me tomorrow, and God knows when I'll next sleep in a bed again.'

'Eat drink and be merry,' laughed Adam, 'for tomorrow we die.'

'Hear, hear,' slurred his new friend Mike. He flopped across the bar, and fumbled in his pockets, then produced a set of keys. 'Here, go on, you two,' he said. 'Use my room here in the club. You don't need to go back to the flat.' He winked at Henry. 'Adam already knows where it is, don't you?'

'Shush,' said Adam, and laughed. 'You'll get us into trouble.'

Henry stared at both of them. He didn't want to think what he was thinking; he picked up his kitbag and slung the heavy canvas across his shoulder. 'Perhaps I'll go back to my room at Millbank,' he said. 'Goodnight.'

He turned and fought his way through the throng of bodies towards the exit. Once outside he ran up the steps and stood outside, breathing in the cool air. What a fool Adam was getting mixed up with a man like that.

There was a touch on his shoulder. It was Adam. He was smiling and jangling the keys in his hand. 'Why run away? Let's go upstairs. You know you want to.' He slid his arm round Henry's shoulder.

Henry flinched away. 'Don't be stupid. What's the bloody game? You've had too much to drink. I'm not a homosexual, Adam, and I didn't think you were either.'

'Oh, for God's sake, Henry, don't be so stuffy. I've always been AC DC. I'm the same as you, except you've never had the courage to admit it. Come on, come with me and let's make a proper man of you. You don't know what you're missing.' He reached out and grasped Henry's arm again.

Snatching his arm away Henry turned on him with fury. 'I am not, never have been, and never will be a homosexual. It's against the law. Surely you know that?'

'Against the law!' Adam mimicked Henry's voice. 'It's against the natural order of things to deny your true feelings. You love me, surely you know that; not that milk-faced girl you're married to. It's always been you for me. Always. Ever since that day we hid in the showers at school after rugger. I still remember your lovely long white thighs. I wanted you then, and I want you now.' He lunged forward and tried to fling his arms around Henry's neck.

Without stopping to think Henry swung his heavy kitbag around and hit Adam full square on, felling him with one blow. Adam started groaning. Switching on his pocket torch Henry bent over him.

There was blood pouring from Adam's nose, but apart from that he appeared all right.

'Go and get your friend Mike to mop you up.' He could hardly speak because of his anger, the words were spat out. 'I never want to see you again.' Flinging his kitbag over his shoulder he marched back towards Millbank.

'I love you, you bloody fool,' Adam's voice echoed along the empty street, bouncing eerily off the Embankment wall. 'Don't think you can get away from me. I need you, and you need me.'

When he arrived at Millbank Henry had two large whiskies in the officers' mess before going up to his room. He couldn't sleep; the scene with Adam replayed in his head over and over again, and he knew it would haunt him for the rest of his life. How could he have been so blind? Did other people know? Did they think they were a pair of . . . he could hardly bring himself to even think the word homosexual.

At last he fell asleep thinking about Megan. He needed to cling on to thoughts of her. She was his reality. She was his wife. He made up his mind to telephone her in the morning to say goodbye and tell her how much he loved her.

Dunkirk – The Beaches June 1940

England, and any other life they'd ever had was on another planet as far as Henry and his men were concerned. They were bogged down in the ghastly mess that was war. They had seen horrors they had never imagined existed before they came to France. Seen men turned from civilized human beings into rabid animals.

Now, Henry realized the inevitable, they would have to leave their vehicles. It was too dangerous and slow to continue trying to use the lumbering noisy trucks which fell down potholes and bomb craters every few yards, quite apart from the fact that they were running out of fuel. They were fleeing France and were, for the moment, just ahead of the enemy on the roads. He gave the order to abandon the vehicles. Only a whispered command, for who knew who might be there lurking in the surrounding fields and ditches in the dark? He felt as if he was in a terrible nightmare, it was surreal, but there was no waking from it. He knew that. What was he, Henry Lockwood, a surgeon, doing leading a band of men through the darkness towards a beach on the northern coast of France? He was a doctor, not a commander of men. But fate had dictated that he should lead. He was the only officer in the little unit he was with who was still alive. The men needed an officer; they looked to him for reassurance and safety.

Henry looked around. There was a murky canal to their left, and although it was dark he could see jagged shapes lying in the water. Other units had jettisoned their vehicles there before seeking refuge on the beaches.

'Get rid of these.' He tapped the sides of their two trucks, knowing they needed to leave the narrow road clear for other army units coming along behind them, and also to prevent the enemy from being able to put their vehicles to use.

The men set to work with a will, smashing their vehicles up with whatever they could lay their hands on, before rolling them over and into the canal where they slid partially below the water's surface with a dull, sucking sound.

'Shall I call the roll, sir?' Corporal Taylor, his medical orderly and ever-present shadow, was by his side.

As soon as Henry had assumed leadership, Corporal Taylor had assumed the role of sergeant. No one complained, no one cared. All they wanted was to get the hell out of France. Henry knew that. It was a sentiment he shared. As part of the ill-fated British Expeditionary Force into France all any of them wanted was to get home. For a split second Henry felt angry. What a waste of lives this expedition had been. Bad planning and appalling back-up had sacrificed more than half the men in his unit. His momentary spurt of anger gave him the strength to go on. Somehow he had to get these men through the next village, down the dunes and on to the beach and then, he hoped, on to a boat to safety.

'Yes, call the roll,' he said, 'and be quick about it.'

It was a weird scene: the men forming up along the roadside, Corporal Taylor ticking their names off his list by torchlight, the answers being whispered back from the darkness. All were present and Henry gave the order to march forward. They crossed a small bridge spanning the canal and entered a village on the other side. Henry had no idea of its name and didn't care. They were going in the right direction towards Dunkirk, the sea and salvation.

As they passed by skeletal walls of bombed buildings, shadows flitted in and out of broken windows and doorways. Henry guessed they were stray inhabitants cut off by the fighting; having to survive in whatever shelter they could find, and probably looters too, on the lookout for anything saleable in the ruins.

He thought of Folly House. It would be slumbering now in peaceful darkness. In his mind's eye he could see the thin veil of mist creeping across the fields and between the trees. The only movements would be Silas Moon's cows, gently blowing through their nostrils into the damp night air and munching on the soft spring grass. East End and the New Forest were a world away from this god-forsaken spot and he longed to be there. For a split second he allowed himself to remember the ordered chaos of Bertha's kitchen on baking day; a favourite place of his as a child. But the moment flew, and he concentrated on the narrow road ahead filled with trudging, despondent troops.

Once through the village their road merged with another, and they began to meet groups of men coming from different directions but all marching the same route towards the coast and Dunkirk. Every now and then a voice would call out.

'Is that you, Bill?'

'It's B Company here, sir.'

'Fred, over this way. Come on, mate.'

'Keep together lads.'

'You can do it. Not far to go.'

It was difficult keeping together in the darkness as more and more men swelled the ranks of marching soldiers, all orderly, none pushing or shoving, but all desperate to get to the beaches.

Henry and Corporal Taylor managed to keep their men together. As they entered the dunes the sand rose like dark elephantine humps making the gloom seem even more impenetrable. Every second or so explosions lit up the sky, silhouetting the twisted shapes of abandoned vehicles half sunk in the sand. It was difficult to walk, but somehow they did, slipping and sliding knee-deep in sand towards the angry red glare in the sky, which they knew was Dunkirk. The place they had been ordered to get to.

'Not much fun is it, sir,' grunted Corporal Taylor, struggling up a steep incline beside Henry. 'I prefer Margate.'

Henry paused a moment on the summit. He could see their destination now. Dunkirk was in sight. He could see the gaunt skeletons of what had once been the fashionable, sought-after promenade of hotels and houses, now all worthless shells. The whole sea-front was one long tongue of flame, orange smoke pouring skywards disappearing into blackness. *The fires of hell, like a medieval painting* thought Henry. 'No, not much fun,' he replied, suddenly thinking of Adam and his declaration that they would have adventures once they went to war. Adam and his fun! The thought of their last encounter still caused him to wince mentally with pain. But there was no time to think now. All he needed to think about was hanging on to life, for himself and his men.

Behind them the men followed wearily to the top of the dunes, over the straggly clumps of marram grass at the top and then down towards the beach below. There was no talking. Everyone was too exhausted to waste what little breath they had left.

Henry could see the tide was out, and he could just about see that there were dark masses of soldiers moving in an orderly fashion towards the sea. Once in the water the men formed black lines, looking like so many breakwaters in the darkness. They were waiting patiently, waist-deep in the water, for their turn to be loaded into small boats and then on to the waiting warships and larger vessels out in deep water.

Henry tried to find their field regiment, which they were supposed to link up with, but the heavy shelling began crashing down masonry from the promenade on to their heads. 'We'll go down on to the beach,' he told his men. 'It will be safer there.'

But down on the beach it was no safer. Small aircraft were flying overhead strafing the men on the beach with machine-gun fire. Shells were exploding everywhere as they stepped across dead and dying men, some of whom, Henry could tell from the stench, had been lying there for days. He, who had seen many deaths in his career as a doctor, had never before felt the evil of it. But now, with death surrounding him on all sides, he felt as if it were a physical being, trying to claw at them all, dragging them down to join the mutilated flesh lying rotting on the beach.

A wounded man called out. 'Sir,' and reached out towards Henry in the gloom.

One look and Henry could see there was no hope for him. Half his body was missing. 'Are you thirsty?' he said, kneeling beside the man

'Sir, we must keep going,' Corporal Taylor's agitated voice cut in.

'Yes, go on. Get the men into line and into the water. Don't wait.'

'But sir—'

'Go, goddamn you,' shouted Henry, and, kneeling beside the dying man, held his water bottle to his lips. 'Drink,' he said gently. 'You'll feel better.'

'I'm cold.' The man shivered violently.

Henry took off his jacket, and wrapped the man's dying remains in it.

'Sir, you must come now.' Corporal Taylor ran back, more agitated than ever.

'I said go. Look out for the men.'

Corporal Taylor hesitated for a split second, then ran down the beach. Henry put the water bottle to the man's lips once more.

The water spilled from his mouth, running in rivulets down his chin. 'Don't leave me,' he whispered.

'I won't,' replied Henry.

That was the last thing he remembered. After that was blackness.

Everyone was talking about the disaster at Dunkirk. The government was trying to persuade everyone that a glorious victory was snatched from the jaws of defeat. But people knew the truth. The Germans had driven the British and French into the sea and many lives had been lost. Men and women all over Britain lay awake at night praying that their sons and husbands were not among the hundreds machine-gunned down on the beaches of Dunkirk.

Megan was among them. She had heard nothing for weeks. Had

Henry been at Dunkirk? No one knew and everyone at Folly House prayed that somehow word would come that he had survived.

It seemed a lifetime since Henry had been at Folly House, and since he'd left for France Megan had heard just once. In an obviously hastily written letter from somewhere in France – it had been censored – he'd said he'd just eaten some delicious Camembert, which that day made even war seem bearable. He'd also said that he'd managed to visit the farmhouse in Normandy where he'd once spent a summer camping holiday with friends from school. Megan had written back, care of the battalion headquarters, hoping that somehow it would reach him. Then, like everyone else, she concentrated on the jobs in hand. For East End it was the annual summer fête held at Folly House.

Lavinia was dead against holding the fête. 'There's a war on,' she kept saying.

But war or no war, the village fête committee decided that they'd have a fête and it would be as good, if not better, than in previous years. As the chatelaine of Folly House it was inevitable that Megan became heavily involved.

Lavinia changed her mind when she found that no one was taking any notice of her. Now she was in danger of taking over the whole event.

As for Megan, she worked from dawn till dusk, and early on the morning of the fête, when she looked out into the garden, she knew it was going to be a lovely day. The sun was rising, spreading long fingers of golden light across the lawn; the dew sparkled like diamonds, and the pink climbing roses that framed her bedroom window filled her nostrils with a heady perfume. She could see the tide was out and the beach and mudflats glistened in the distance; beyond them, shimmering against the skyline, were the blue hills of the Isle of Wight.

Megan ran downstairs, suddenly feeling light-hearted and happy. Of course Henry would be all right. He knew how to care for himself because he was a doctor and he'd know what to do even if he did get hurt. She didn't allow the thought that he might get killed even to enter her head. After a very quick breakfast she went out into the garden, still munching on a piece of toast. George Jones and Silas

Moon and some older men from the village were already there, setting up the stalls and the big marquee.

The Women's Institute had a stall and were there, filling it with eggless fruitcakes and sugar-free jam. 'Goodness only knows what everything will taste like,' Lavinia had said to Megan. 'I do like things to be made in the traditional way. I know we've got this wretched rationing, but surely they could have saved up some of their butter and sugar, and everyone has got a chicken or two to provide eggs.'

'People need the small amount of butter and sugar they get on ration,' Megan pointed out. 'They haven't much to spare for fête cakes.'

Lavinia had sighed. 'Yes, I do know that, dear. But nothing tastes the same these days. It's like that dreadful Camp coffee Bertha will insist on serving up for breakfast.'

Megan didn't reply because she actually rather liked the Camp coffee. It had always been drunk at the vicarage because it was much cheaper, so when beans disappeared she hadn't really missed them,

She joined Silas Moon, who had constructed a sturdy pen and was now setting up a bowling alley on the flattest part of the lawn. 'For the pig,' he said, nodding his head towards the pen.

'But I thought we couldn't do it because of the regulations,' Megan began, 'and Albert Noakes . . .'

Silas laughed. ''Tis a pity old Albert has gone down with a bit of stomach trouble and a terrible headache today.'

'Oh.' Megan was suspicious. There was something too smug about Silas's voice.

Silas laughed again. 'We all had a drink at the East End Arms last night, everyone buying Albert drinks on account of him being made fête supervisor. A drop of the cider might have been a bit off.' He raised his bushy eyebrows expressively. 'I'm thinking he won't be straying far from the privy today. So we can have bowling for the pig like always. It's one of Wally Pragnell's, a piglet, the runt of the litter, but with a bit of care it'll fatten up nicely for Christmas.'

An over-excited Rosie joined Megan, with Dottie in faithful attendance. She was already in her maypole dress of white with red and blue ribbons sewn on it by Lavinia. Megan had noticed that

Lavinia was completely besotted with Rosie; helping her with her homework, attending to her every need, and informing Megan that the little girl had a very good brain and would go far if given the chance.

Rosie and Dottie danced around the men erecting the maypole under George's instructions until they were banished before the pole should fall on them and flatten them both.

Megan took them and let them help sorting out the bottle stall. There was ginger beer, lots of home-made cordial and, what the girls liked most, tiny bottles of perfume. Little blue bottles of Evening in Paris, and a whole box of green dimpled bottles of Devon Violets, plus one or two tiny bottles of pure perfume left over from before the war. The bottle stall kept them quiet for the rest of the morning.

When everything was ready the Folly House party had a picnic lunch on the lawn before the official opening. Gerald and Violet came and Gerald manoeuvred himself so that he ended up sitting by Megan. 'Heard from Henry yet?' he asked casually.

Megan pretended not to hear and waved at Arthur, who was sitting on the other side of the family circle. 'Come and keep me company,' she called.

'A crippled brother is not the answer. You need other company.' Gerald's voice was low, and he touched her bare arm with his hand. Megan flinched away. 'Henry wants an heir for Folly House, and here's a man right here who could give you one.'

'Don't be ridiculous,' whispered Megan.

'I'd be only too willing.' Gerald laughed and caught her hand in his.

'Go away. I'm married to Henry.' Megan turned and looked into his dark eyes. He was smiling but the smile didn't reach his eyes. Megan shivered and snatched her hand away.

'That's not what you said the last time, my mistress of Folly.' He stood up as Arthur wheeled himself over, and said, 'Park yourself there, old chap. I'll go and join my wife.'

From the relative safety of sitting beside Arthur, Megan watched him talking with Violet. Gerald held a dangerous fascination for her, and she knew she must be careful. She kept silent, only nodding at

Arthur's query asking if she was all right.

Later Lavinia made a short opening speech, and Marcus gave a prayer for the success of the fête, for the success of England in the war, and for the safe return of all the sons of East End as well as everyone else in the world who was caught up in the conflict.

Then the fête started in earnest as the stalls were open for business. At half past three East End Primary School gave a display of maypole dancing. Miss Cousins, the head teacher, had wanted to exclude Rosie because of her clubfoot and limp, but Megan had insisted she should be included. Now as she watched how hard Rosie tried, and how well she kept up with everyone else, she was proud of her.

'You know, Rosie is one of the prettiest girls there,' remarked Lavinia to Megan. 'You'd hardly know she's got a clubfoot. When she dances she doesn't limp at all.'

Megan smiled and felt relaxed. Their plan for the fête to make everyone forget the war for a few hours was working. She and Lavinia retired to two seats near the East End brass band, which started playing a medley of patriotic tunes when the dancing finished. They were applauded enthusiastically, no one minding the occasional squeak from the saxophonist; elderly Mr Miller was playing the instrument in place of his son who was away at war, and obviously needed a little more practice.

Dottie brought them both a cup of tea and some home-made seedy cake, and Rosie joined them still in her maypole dress. 'Can we have a go on the bottle stall now?' she asked. 'I've got two sixpences saved, that's two goes at getting a bottle, and Dottie's got sixpence as well.'

'Of course,' said Megan.

The band struck up the tune: *There'll always be an England*.

To Megan's surprise Lavinia suddenly looked tearful. 'There will, you know,' she said softly. 'There will always be an England, no matter what happens. And Henry *will* come back. I'm sure of it.'

Megan leaned forward and took Lavinia's hand in hers. Something she'd never done before. Never dared to, but Lavinia had never sounded old and vulnerable before. 'I know he will,' she said. 'All will be well.'

She was rewarded by a radiant smile from Lavinia and as if on cue the band started playing *The White Cliffs of Dover.*

They were interrupted by a whoop of joy from Rosie who practically threw herself at Megan, brandishing a small green bottle decorated with a purple ribbon. 'Look what I've got. I've got a bottle of Devon Violets and Dottie has got Evening in Paris.'

Dottie waved her dark-blue bottle and proceeded to try and unscrew it.

'Wonderful,' said Megan. 'What lucky girls you are.'

'Yes, this has been a lucky day for all of us.' Lavinia stood up. 'Now we've finished our tea I think we should patronize all the stalls once more before the afternoon ends. And Dottie, you'd better give me that perfume before you spill all of it.'

'Can I bowl for the pig?' asked Rosie, as Dottie reluctantly handed her bottle over to Lavinia.

'Why not?' Megan stood and was about to move towards the pig pen when her father came rushing up, closely followed by Arthur propelling himself along in his wheelchair.

'Megan.' Her father was breathless. 'Here's a telegram for you.' He thrust a small buff envelope towards Megan. It had the letters OHMS stamped across the top.

Megan knew what it meant. They all did. Some of the people near by had seen the envelope, and they drew closer. They were quiet, all looking at Megan expectantly. She was aware of Gerald and Violet moving across to join their group, and it seemed to her that the sun had suddenly gone behind a dark cloud. She shivered, and her hand trembled as she took the envelope.

'Shall I open it for you?' her father asked.

'No. I must do it.' But her fingers were shaking so much she couldn't peel open the envelope.

Lavinia moved to her side. 'We'll open it together,' she said quietly, taking the envelope from Megan's nerveless fingers.

The envelope opened, she passed the paper with its faint tickertape message across to Megan. 'It says,' said Megan, and then stopped. 'It says,' she began again, her voice wavering with the effort of keeping it under control. 'Captain Henry Lockwood of the Royal Army Medical Corps is missing presumed killed in action.'

CHAPTER SEVEN

Christmas 1940

When a bomb dropped on the village of East End no one was surprised. In fact it was a surprise that it hadn't happened earlier as they were not far from Southampton which had been bombed almost daily. The rumbling German Heinkels came from occupied France, bombed Southampton, and then swung round over the New Forest on their way back to their German bases.

Megan didn't have much time to worry about bombs. Life was one incessant rush; there were things to be done on the farm, in the house, and on top of everything else Christmas was coming. Henry was still missing presumed killed; sometimes Megan had difficulty in visualizing him, it was as if he had never been. There was no time to mourn or even think of it, as since Tilly's departure she'd taken on her share of the housework; there was only so much Bertha and Dottie could do. She reflected wryly back to the days at the vicarage when she'd thought she was hard done by with only one maid/cook for the whole house. Now, she had to work on the land as well. Her hands, once soft and manicured, were now calloused and red, roughened from her manual work. Rosie, who was her shadow when she wasn't at school, tried her best to help, and Megan couldn't imagine life without her, neither could she imagine life without the two land girls. They were now valued members of the team, even Silas Moon approved of them.

Molly Fox was tall, slender and blonde, with a penchant for smoking cigarettes in a long cigarette holder, and Pat Humby, plain, dumpy, with a jolly disposition had the strength of two men. They slotted into life on the farm and the village as if they had always been there, and Molly Fox was in demand for the darts team at the East End Arms on account of her unerring aim.

In the middle of December there was a sudden cold snap on the day they'd been due to harvest the carrots from the lower field at East End, and transfer them to the clamp so that they'd last the rest of the winter.

Megan went with the two girls to the field. Molly kicked at a furrow with a booted foot. 'Like cast iron,' she announced. 'Maybe we'd better pick the sprouts instead of doing the carrots.

Pat dug her spade into the hard earth and managed to shift some. 'Look, it's softer underneath. Maybe we can do it. What do you think Megan?'

Megan thought. 'The sprouts will keep,' she said slowly. 'Silas says sprouts taste better when they've had a few frosts, and if we have more cold nights this earth really will be like iron, then we'll never get at the carrots.'

'OK, so we'll go to it,' answered Pat and willingly began to dig.

Molly slid her cigarette packet back into her jodhpurs and picked up her spade as well. 'OK, but you'll owe us a round at the East End Arms this evening.'

'Done,' replied Megan with a grin. 'Now I've got to get back to some office work.'

Back in the office she started on the monthly accounts for November, cursing the fact that she was so far behind. Normally she managed to keep everything up to date and was not faced with the pile of post she had in front of her. She shuffled through the brown envelopes – all Ministry Forms, thought Megan irritably, as she dropped half a dozen. An official form for everything under the sun, she thought. As she stacked the pile she came across a blue envelope addressed to her, Mrs Henry Lockwood, in unfamiliar handwriting.

Inside was a brief note.

Dear Mrs Lockwood,

I am writing on behalf of Squadron Leader Adam Myers who is enquiring the whereabouts of his friend, Captain Henry Lockwood. He is unable to write himself at the moment as he has been injured and is in hospital, but he asked me to send this letter to you. Perhaps you can let him know the current address of your husband so that he can correspond with him.

Yours in grateful anticipation
Maureen O'Malley (Nurse)

The address was a hospital in Surrey. Megan put the letter aside. She hadn't given Adam a thought for a long time, but suddenly all the old uncertainties came back and with it the unreasonable jealousy. Then common sense prevailed. She'd reply later when she had more time. Adam couldn't influence Henry now. No one could.

Later that night she was awoken by Bertha hammering on her door.

'The siren is going. Shall I take Rosie to the shelter?'

'Yes,' shouted Megan, and threw on an old sweater and jodhpurs before grabbing some warm clothes and a blanket for Rosie and making for the Anderson shelter in the garden.

Then the all-clear siren started; the warning had obviously been a mistake. As the long, drawn-out howl of the all-clear speared the cold night air Megan began helping a very sleepy Rosie back up the steps from the shelter. They were in the garden when a tremendous explosion shook the ground, the house and everything around. With a frightened cry, Rosie clung unto Megan as the sky was lit by a brilliant orange flash coming from the direction of the village.

'A bomb has landed in East End,' shouted Bertha, stating the obvious.

Megan didn't reply. East End was such a small place; she prayed that the bomb had landed harmlessly in a nearby field.

George clambered out of the shelter behind Bertha. He had on his tin hat, which shone eerily in the increasingly intense orange glow. 'I'm going there now,' he shouted, scrambling across the garden in the direction of the shed. 'See what I can do.' He dragged his bicycle out and pedalled away.

'I ought to go,' said Megan. 'They must need some help. By the look of it the bomb must have been an incendiary.'

'You are not going anywhere,' Lavinia appeared out of the darkness of the garden in her dressing-gown and grabbed hold of Megan determinedly. 'Your place is here with us. We need you here.'

'Quite right.' Bertha came across with a frightened Dottie close behind her. 'Let's go into the house now and I'll make a cup of tea.' She looked up at the sky from where came the faint throbbing sound of an engine. 'That bomb must have come from a stray plane left behind.' She shook her fist at the darkness of the night sky. 'How dare you bomb us,' she shouted.

Despite everything Megan and Lavinia looked at each other and smiled. 'Bertha would take on the Luftwaffe single-handed if she could,' said Lavinia.

The sound of the plane's engines faded into the distance, leaving the night silent save for the roaring sound from the fire blazing in East End.

Bertha set about making tea for the crowd in the kitchen. Rosie cuddled up to Lavinia, and Dottie cuddled up to Rosie. Megan laid out the cups and saucers, but was worrying about the fire in the village.

'Not those,' said Bertha, when she saw the plain white cups and saucers on the table. 'Get out the bone-china ones.'

'For goodness sake, Bertha,' said Megan. 'This is an emergency; we certainly don't need to bother with best china tonight.' She paused a moment, then said, 'think about all those families, the ones who have been bombed tonight. They will have no china at all.' Putting down the last cup on the table she made up her mind. 'I have to go. I can't stay here drinking tea.'

The words were hardly out of her mouth when the kitchen door to the yard burst open, and an excited Albert Noakes, supporting a very blackened and dishevelled Marcus, staggered in.

'The vicarage took a direct hit,' announced Albert dramatically.

'Arthur, where's Arthur?' Megan rushed towards them, hearing her own voice high with fear.

Her father collapsed on to a chair. 'He's safe. He's playing the piano over at Buriton village hall tonight,' he muttered, then slid unconscious to the floor.

On her knees beside him Megan grabbed Lavinia's smelling salts from her hand, and, with Bertha splashing cold water on his face as well as the smelling salts beneath his nose, Marcus began to cough and splutter and recover consciousness. 'We must call Dr Crozier,' said Megan.

But Marcus refused. 'I'm just a bit battered and shocked.'

'He must stay here,' Lavinia said firmly. 'He can sleep in one of the front bedrooms.'

'Not like that he can't,' said Bertha. 'He looks like a chimney sweep. He'll spoil a set of good linen. I'd never get the soot stains out.'

'It doesn't matter about the linen,' said Lavinia in exasperation.

Bertha didn't argue but her mouth set in a straight determined line and both Lavinia and Megan knew there'd be no budging her.

So Marcus was taken up into one of the bathrooms, where Albert Noakes helped him remove his blackened, torn clothes, and ran a bath.

'You can borrow one of Mr Henry's dressing-gowns and a pair of his pyjamas,' said Bertha.

Neither Megan nor Lavinia argued. Bertha had temporarily assumed charge.

Marcus didn't argue either and with Albert's assistance struggled into Henry's pyjamas which were too small; and then, after drinking a cup of hot cocoa, he collapsed into bed and slept.

'There's not much left of the vicarage,' Albert Noakes told Megan when he returned downstairs. 'Two of the walls have been completely blown away; anyone can walk into the house. Mind you, the furniture and stuff that's left will be safe. No one from the village will let any outsider loot the vicarage. But I'll go over and keep a lookout just to make sure.

'Will you stay there until Arthur comes back from the social, and then make sure someone brings him back here?' Megan was torn between staying with her father and going to look for her brother.

Albert put a hand on her arm and squeezed it. ''Course I will, my dear,' he said gruffly. 'I'll make sure he gets here safely. You don't need to worry about him. You just look after yourself.'

Unexpected tears filled Megan's eyes. 'Thank you.' She wasn't sure whether the tears were for Arthur, her father or herself, or because

Albert Noakes had suddenly shown that he had compassion and wasn't always a bad-tempered old man.

Arthur arrived at Folly House at gone midnight. Megan and Lavinia joined Bertha in the kitchen, which was warm from the stove, wrapped themselves in their dressing-gowns and drank watery cocoa. Bertha had given Marcus the last decent cup.

Eventually, after many explanations, Arthur was safely tucked up in another spare bedroom and it was time for all of them to go to bed for the remainder of the night. Lavinia put up in the boxroom for the rest of the night; it was hardly worth going back to the Dower House, besides she was nervous. The boxroom was the one Adam had always slept in. It reminded Megan of the letter, but she didn't mention it to Lavinia.

'Well, one good thing has come from that stray bomb,' remarked Lavinia as she and Megan mounted the stairs.

Megan, who couldn't think of a single good thing, said, 'What?'

'All the bedrooms are in use, except for the boxroom which I'm using for tonight.' She saw Megan's puzzled expression. 'Don't you see? Now that Marcus and Arthur will have to live here the War Office can't possible requisition Folly House. We're safe. They can't turn all of us out; they'd have nowhere to put us.'

Megan smiled wearily. 'The thought of finding somewhere else to live would be more than I could bear. But surely they wouldn't really turn us out?'

'Oh yes,' said Lavinia, pausing as she reached the corridor leading to her room, and leaning forward confidentially. 'I was hearing only the other day that the War Office is looking for rooms to put up more Army and Navy engineers from America. Everyone says they may requisition somewhere near here to build something very, very secret. But I dare say our boxroom wouldn't be suitable because it's too small.'

Megan laughed at Lavinia's hush-hush expression. 'It would only be suitable for a very small engineer,' she said. 'And it can't be very secret if everyone is talking about it.'

'Hmmm,' Lavinia looked thoughtful. 'If the worst comes to the worst and they do try and inflict someone on us, you'd better stake a firm claim to your office. Your father will need to use it now to write his sermons, when you're not using it. You can't afford to let anyone else lay claim to it.'

The house now was permanently full of people and sometimes Megan longed for solitude. The only place she could find it was in her office, and even there she was interrupted. And every time she was in the office it seemed that the letter from Nurse O'Malley jumped up at her. It troubled her; she couldn't get rid of the irrational fear that Adam was dangerous to herself and Henry. But eventually she could put if off no longer and wrote a short letter to Nurse O'Malley saying that Henry was missing presumed dead.

As she sealed the envelope she suddenly remembered Adam's last laughing words, *It will be an adventure,* and was overwhelmed for sadness for him. Adam was injured, and she wondered how he would take the news about Henry now that the great adventure had turned so bitter.

She was still lost in thought when the door opened and Gerald walked in, startling her.

'Most people knock,' said Megan, trying to hide the discomfiture she always felt in his presence.

'I'm not most people,' replied Gerald. He leaned across the desk towards her, putting a finger under her chin and tipping her face towards him. 'I'm your one-time lover, remember?'

Flinching away, Megan stood up.

Gerald kicked the door shut with his foot and held out a manilla envelope. 'Read it,' he said.

Megan slipped the folded sheets from the envelope and read them in silence. As she read she became more and more angry, but at the same time she was afraid. Did Gerald really find her attractive or was she just another route to his acquiring Folly House? The closely written sheets were couched in legal language, but Megan knew exactly what it meant. Gerald was halfway to realizing his ambition of taking over Folly House and the farm at East End. He was assuming that Henry was dead and wanted to step in immediately to *maximise the business possibilities of the estate,* it said as a summing-up.

'Does Lavinia know about this?' she said, trying to stall for time while she collected her thoughts.

'It's nothing to do with Lavinia. She will continue to live in the dower house as she does now, and will remain there until her death, when it will revert back and become part of the estate.'

Megan put down the papers. There, in the legal speak of the London solicitors whom Gerald had engaged, Randall & Randall of High Holborn, London, was the end of her dreams. The end of her life at Folly House because it stated that in the event of Henry's death *(as written in Sir Richard Lockwood's will)* if he had not fathered a son or daughter, the house, gardens, and East End Farm together with the estate cottages and dower house would be in the sole charge and ownership of Gerald Lockwood.

Of course Megan had always known that if they'd had no children the estate would revert to Gerald on Henry's death. But she and Henry had thought they would have children. Now it was different. If Henry didn't return she would be at the mercy of Gerald. Megan took a deep breath. She hadn't become the mistress of Folly House to give it up so easily. She had to play Gerald at his own game, a tactical one of bluff and counter-bluff. She looked at Gerald, determined not to show her fear.

'All it needs is your signature, then I'll take over immediately.' Gerald made a broad gesture with his hand and smiled. 'I'll let you stay in the house for the time being. Maybe we can come to some arrangement.'

'I'm not signing anything,' said Megan icily. 'Henry is not dead. I know he'll be found and will come back. Then we'll have a child and there'll be no need for any of this.' Shoving the papers back into the envelope she thrust it at Gerald, then walked across and opened the door. 'Please go now. I have a lot of work to get through.'

Gerald's dark eyes flashed in exasperation. 'Don't be ridiculous, Megan. Of course he's dead.' He pushed the door shut again.

'I don't think we have anything to discuss, let alone anything for me to sign. If you won't leave my office then I will.'

As she tried to pass him Gerald grabbed her and pushed her back against the desk. 'Uncle Richard should have left this place to me,' he hissed, his voice rough with anger. 'And I think he would have done except for Lavinia, who persuaded him to leave it to Henry, who was never interested in it. Medicine, that's all he ever thought about. That, and his fancy friend, Adam. He was never interested in you, either. If you want another baby, you'd better come to me. I'll give you a baby, but it won't help you get your hands on Folly House, not unless you stay with me.' His heavy body pressed against her. 'Don't pretend you don't want me, because I won't believe you.'

His face was close to hers and reeked of sour whisky. She felt angry; how dare he try to force himself on her. She turned her face away and tried to escape, but he was too strong. Clasping her around the waist, he twisted her head back with his other hand so that she was forced to look at him. 'You thought you could do better than me, didn't you. A jumped-up vicar's daughter trying to be a lady. You slept your way into Folly House, you wanted Henry for that reason, and that reason alone. But you made a mistake when you stopped off along the way with me. And now,' he jerked her head back and pulled her so close she could feel his arousal through her skirt. 'And now, I fancy having you again. Why try and stop me? Once I've started you know you'll enjoy it.'

'Let me go.' In vain she twisted and pushed, but he was too strong.

Tightening his grip on her, Gerald forced his mouth on hers, prising her teeth apart, filling her mouth with his tongue. Megan could hear his hoarse breathing and grunting as he fumbled at the front of her dress, searching for her breast; then with a satisfied groan, he found it. The pain as he cruelly pinched her nipple was excruciating, and involuntarily Megan raised one knee and thrust it as hard as she could into his groin. She knew she'd found her mark as he gave a short agonized yelp and loosened his hold. Needing no second opportunity Megan pushed him with all her might and Gerald staggered back, hunched and clutching his groin. Megan put the table between herself and Gerald and picked up the heavy glass paperweight on the desk. 'Get out,' she screamed, 'get out of Folly House, and don't ever come here again.'

'You'll not get rid of me that easily, you bitch,' shouted Gerald, still bent double. 'I'll come again. I've every right to come. I'm a

Lockwood by birth. Folly House is mine by right, as you'll find out when it's confirmed that your feeble husband has ended up as cannon fodder.'

'Get out,' Megan screamed, and threw the paperweight with all her might. It narrowly missed Gerald's head and smashed to smithereens against the wall.

'I'll go now, but I'll be back. You can count on it.' He wrenched open the door and crashed straight into Arthur's wheelchair in the hall. 'Out of my way, you bloody cripple,' he snarled. The whole house reverberated as the heavy front door crashed shut behind him.

There was a moment's silence. 'What was that all about,' said Arthur quietly.

Megan wiped her mouth with her handkerchief, then stuttered, 'It's Gerald. He wants Folly House. He . . . he, tried to . . .' words failed her.

'I'll kill him.' Arthur gripped the sides of his chair and tried to lever himself up. Despite everything Megan managed a ghost of a smile. 'You're no match for him, Arthur, neither am I. Not physically anyway. I need to be clever. That's the way to defeat him, and I'll do it. I *will* do it.' Megan drew in a breath and straightened her shoulders.

'Not alone you can't,' said Arthur, taking her hand in his. 'I know I'm in a wheelchair, but I've got a brain and I'm no fool. We'll tackle him together.'

'It's not your problem.' Megan was reluctant to involve Arthur.

'Anything to do with you is my problem. That's what a brother is for.'

Megan shivered. 'I don't think I can talk about it now.'

'Tomorrow then,' said Arthur firmly. Megan nodded reluctantly and Arthur said quietly, 'You'd better button up your blouse; we don't want anyone to know what Gerald has been up to.'

Megan didn't reply, but did as Arthur said. What would Arthur say if he knew they had once been lovers? A moment of madness on a dark night long ago that now seemed destined to haunt her fo rever.

True to her word Megan did discuss Gerald with Arthur. But she skated over the truth, merely saying that Gerald had wanted to marry her, had coveted Folly House ever since they'd all been children, and now saw a way of grasping it for himself; because unless Henry returned and she had a child to inherit Folly House, everything would revert to Gerald. But he did not want to wait, and was demanding that Megan sign an agreement now.

'I don't know what to do,' said Megan. 'Supposing Henry never comes back? Supposing we never know what has happened to him.'

Arthur, however, was pragmatic about the situation. 'First of all,' he said, 'we don't know that Henry is dead. He may well come back. Second, when he does, you are sure to have a baby, and third, we will put up a hell of a fight to stop Gerald laying claim to the estate. Anyway, what does he want it for? He's married to Violet and has got Brinkley Hall as well as pots of money, which is more than can be said for you. I know Henry was never that wealthy because he told me. He was worried about how you'd manage on his army salary while he was away, and now, since he's missing, you don't even have that.'

His words did comfort Megan a little, but she couldn't tell Arthur she was afraid of Gerald, and afraid of the strange power that Gerald had over her. It wasn't affection, she was sure of that. It was an irrational lust for each other as well as for Folly House. It didn't make sense. Why should the ownership of an old house be so important? She had no answer.

A week before Christmas and Arthur and Marcus were firmly settled in Folly House since the vicarage had been bombed beyond early repair. They helped Rosie and Dottie decorate the house with mistletoe and holly collected from the hedgerows.

'Berries everywhere,' grumbled Bertha, but she didn't stop the girls decorating everything so that the house glowed with a profusion of dark-green foliage and red and white berries.

The two land girls gave them white candles wrapped in silver cigarette paper for the tables at Folly House. They were to spend their Christmas Day at the Moons once they'd finished on the farm. The gold room smelled of pine needles as George and Silas had dug up last year's Christmas tree and it now stood in the bay window. Rosie and Dottie decorated it with ancient glass balls and paper angels, which

Lavinia produced, as she did every Christmas, from a box in the attic.

'Cor, it do look lovely,' breathed Dottie when it was finished and the lights were switched on.

Bertha made the ritual trip to East End farm and made Silas parade the birds destined for the Christmas dinner table in front of her. She chose the biggest for Folly House, the second biggest for Gerald and Violet, Silas had the next in size for his family which included the two land girls. It had been decided, when they were being reared, that if they all survived the foxes, the last two should be divided between a charity in Southampton for the homeless, and a prize for a raffle to be held in Mr Shepherd's butcher's shop in Stibbington. Albert Noakes tried to put a spoke in the plan, saying that as food was rationed it was against the law to raffle a turkey. Everyone ignored him as usual, and in the end even he bought a ticket. But he didn't win. Mrs Rousel won it. She was head of the Rousel clan, a bunch of gypsies who always descended on Stibbington to set up camp in the winter.

Mr Shepherd said, 'Good luck to them. Christmas is a time of goodwill.' Albert Noakes didn't agree as, in his opinion, gypsies always cheated and ought not even to be allowed to buy tickets. As usual he was ignored.

Megan decreed that the turkey should be shared by all the inhabitants of Folly House, including the Joneses, and that the capon which had been fattened up in the kitchen garden should be shared by everyone for New Year's Day.

'Sharing with the Jones' family is a good idea,' said Marcus. 'I didn't know you had such socialist tendencies.'

'Not socialist but practical. I've got to watch the pennies,' said Megan.

Her father was concerned. 'Are you short of money? Arthur and I must increase our allowance towards the running of the house.'

'No need for that,' said Megan. 'Not yet anyway.' No point, she thought, in telling anyone she *was* worried about the finances. After Christmas she intended to step up sales from the farm shop and also see if she could get orders for local produce from Leckford House, which had been commandeered by the War Department and was now full of Army and Navy personnel. A visit to the quartermaster was on her schedule for the New Year.

Just before Christmas the bishop ordered Marcus to cancel midnight mass on Christmas Eve on safety grounds. The year before Marcus had persisted with the midnight service and several villagers had fallen into ditches in the blackout. 'Not so much the blackout as too much sherry,' grumbled Marcus, but he had to obey the bishop, and he decided to have early evensong.

At the very last minute, on Christmas Eve, he called upon Arthur to play the organ as Miss Lander, the usual organist, had the flu. Arthur wanted to practise in the morning and Megan agreed to use some of her precious petrol ration to drop him off at the church, and then pick him up at lunchtime.

At lunchtime it was still bitterly cold; a hoar frost glistened white on the gravestones, riming the dead heads of cow parsley so that they looked as if they had been dipped in icing sugar. Pausing a moment at the lych gate, drinking in the frozen beauty of the ancient churchyard, Megan prayed. Not something she did often; for although brought up as a parson's daughter, religion had passed her by, and she'd never felt a spiritual need. But lately she'd felt lost, caught in a vicious spiral of conflicting emotions, not knowing where or who to turn to. She prayed for guidance for herself, and for Henry to return home.

Closing her eyes she gave herself up to the peace of the winter morning. Then suddenly the stillness was pierced by the clear trumpet notes of Bach's prelude in A Minor. The achingly beautiful sound rang around, echoing from gravestone to gravestone, and for a moment Megan felt that the very beings lying in the cold dark earth would rise up and join the living in the sheer exuberance of the music.

The music gave wings to her feet and she flew up the flintstone path and in through the open door of the church. There was a stranger sitting at the organ, a man with dark hair that fell across his forehead, and a serious face; he was bending over the keys as if his life depended on it. He didn't notice her; neither did Arthur, who was sitting mesmerized beside him. Megan stayed where she was in the shadow by the door, waiting, watching and listening.

When the last throbbing note had died away the man turned towards Arthur and smiled. Megan caught her breath. It was as if someone had switched on a light inside him, and she found herself smiling as well, although he wasn't smiling at her.

Arthur must have heard her footsteps on the stone flags leading to the organ because he turned. 'Megan,' he called. 'Come and meet Jim.'

The dark stranger stepped down from the organ loft and came towards her, hand outstretched. 'Hi,' he said. 'I'm Jim Byrne. I guess you must be Arthur's sister, Megan.' His gentle voice had an attractive American drawl.

He was smiling at her now, and as Megan moved towards him she felt as if she was being swept along in a strong current; she was unable to go in any direction other than towards him.

'Yes, I'm Megan,' she said as he took her hand.

'Jim's here on some secret work up at Leckford House,' said Arthur.

Jim was still holding her hand and smiling. 'Yes, I'm living in that splendidly massive house, but would you believe it, there's no piano or organ? So I went looking for a little local church and found St Nicholas's and Arthur playing the organ. And of course, I just had to come in.'

Reluctantly Megan slipped her hand from his. 'You're a musician?'

Shaking his head, he turned and helped Arthur move his wheelchair down the wooden ramp from the organ loft. 'Not professionally; I'm an engineer by profession, which is why I'm here.'

'I've told Jim he can come to Folly House and use our piano whenever he wants,' said Arthur. 'I didn't think anyone would mind.'

'Of course not. It will be a pleasure to hear the piano more often. It doesn't get used enough.' Megan crossed to Arthur and took the handles of his wheelchair.

Jim stepped over and took the chair handles from her. 'Let me wheel Arthur down to your car,' he said.

'Stay to lunch,' said Arthur as they bumped down the flinty path.

'Unfortunately I can't. I have a meeting scheduled this afternoon starting at one o'clock. In fact I should be there now preparing my papers.'

'Another time then,' said Megan, holding out her hand. 'We'd be pleased to see you.'

He took her hand and smiled and Megan smiled back. What was it that was special about him? Even Arthur was smiling from ear to ear; something about this Jim Byrne was making him happy.

'Yes, another time,' she repeated. 'Why not tomorrow? Christmas Day, we have plenty of food.'

'But what about the rationing?' he queried.

'We have a farm,' said Arthur. 'We can kill the fatted calf any time we like.'

Jim looked surprised and Megan shook her head. 'Not strictly true,' she said, tucking Arthur's coat into the car. 'But we have killed the fatted turkey, and we'd be pleased to share that with you.'

'I'd love to come,' he said quickly. 'To tell you the truth I wasn't looking forward much to tomorrow. Most of the other guys at Leckford House will be away with friends and families, but my family is an ocean away.'

So Jim came for Christmas Day, and won over Bertha's heart by bringing with him a pound of lard and a pound of butter. She was flushed and almost girlishly coquettish as she clutched it to her bosom. 'I can't thank you enough,' she spluttered before rushing back to the kitchen.

Rosie and Dottie stood side by side staring curiously at this man with the strange accent. 'I've brought a bag of cookies for you,' said Jim. 'Arthur told me there were two young girls here.'

Dottie held the bag and Rosie read the label. 'Chocolate Cookies,' she said curiously. 'What are cookies?'

'We call them biscuits,' said Lavinia. 'But you certainly won't get anything as luxurious as chocolate biscuits at Torbocks' shop in Stibbington. Not these days.'

So Jim was welcomed into Folly House and slipped seamlessly into the family. His free time he spent playing the piano or turning his hand to anything that needed doing in the house or garden.

Bertha worshipped the ground he walked on, and even George admitted that 'For a furriner he's not too bad.'

Megan loved hearing the piano and was always happy when he was around. To her he was like another brother.

CHAPTER EIGHT

Summer 1943

Henry gave up trying to work out what the time was, or how many years, months, days it had been since he'd been pulled from the bottom of a boat after Dunkirk. He'd been more dead than alive, they told him. But even the word Dunkirk had no meaning. They told him it was in France and that he was lucky to be alive. He said nothing. Was he lucky to be alive? He didn't know. What did alive mean? He had no point of reference. He knew he was English, at least he presumed he was as he could speak fluent English, but apart from that there was nothing.

He'd been told that they thought he'd been blown up, because he was virtually naked when he'd been rescued, with no identification on him at all. He was their mystery man and they'd named him Rob Roy, as that was the name of the fishing-boat that had brought him back to England. But all this meant nothing to Henry, as he could remember nothing. Now he lived each day following a routine to which he had become accustomed, gradually becoming able to do a few things for himself. He got up, was washed and shaved by a nurse, fed at regular intervals during the day, and then put to bed at night. But nothing had any meaning as he could see nothing. He knew no one. Could see no one. Life consisted of a dark, meaningless void: no past, no present, no future. They told him he had been like this for nearly three years. But what did three years mean?

But one thing did give him pleasure, and that was music. Henry gradually became able to tune his radio to the stations he liked. Sometimes he listened to the news, but that depressed him. It was always about the war. He'd been in the war, but remembered nothing.

'Probably just as well, dear,' said his nurse. 'The men we've got here who can remember have terrible nightmares. At least you are spared that.'

Henry wanted to ask what a nightmare was, but said nothing. It would only involve another long explanation, which he wouldn't understand.

On sunny days he was wheeled out in a wheelchair, settled in a sunny spot out of the wind, and wrapped in a warm rug. Little by little Henry got his strength back and became able to walk a few steps. More aware of his surroundings he knew when the sun was shining as he felt the warmth on his hands and face. He knew, too that he was near the sea. He began to imagine the sea, and saw moving images in his mind: water ebbing and flowing, and sometimes he thought he could hear it. There was a faint smell in the air, which he knew was the sea. It was familiar. Perhaps he'd lived by the sea. But no matter how hard he tried the memories of another life remained firmly locked away. He shivered.

'What's the matter, dear? Are you cold?'

He felt the rug being tucked firmly around his knees and knew it was his nurse Jenny speaking. 'No,' he said, and then asked, 'Where am I now. What is this place?'

'You're in the Royal Victoria Hospital at Netley. It's a military hospital with more than a thousand patients set in lovely spacious grounds on the edge of Southampton Water.'

'Water? What do you mean, water?' queried Henry. 'It smells to me like the sea.'

Jenny patted his hand. 'There, you've remembered something. It is the sea, but it's called Southampton Water.'

Henry slowly smiled. 'I knew it was the sea. I could smell it.' He drew in a breath, savouring the saltiness, then said, 'How long will I stay here?'

'Probably until you get your memory back, or we find out who you are, and when you are stronger, of course.'

'And if I don't get my memory back, and you never find out who I am?'

He heard her sigh. 'I don't know.' She squeezed his hands in hers. 'But you will get it back. These things take time.'

'But no chance of getting my sight back.' Henry didn't ask, rather made a statement.

Jenny squeezed his hands again. 'No.'

Sitting in the fresh air, still imprisoned in the dark world he now inhabited but now visualizing the sea made him feel restless. Had he grown up by the sea? Memories were pushing at the dark boundaries of his mind, trying to emerge. Who was he? Where did he belong?

At East End the summer of 1943 proceeded like all the other summers of the war. Rationing was harder than ever, food, clothes, petrol, even paper. The land and animals always needed tending and some-times Megan was so tired she could hardly put one foot before the other. But she thanked God for the two land girls, as they were worth their weight in gold. During the long summer days they worked hard, sometimes only stopping when it grew too dark to continue. Bertha, after her initial hostility, had taken them under her wing and showed her admiration for them in the only way she knew how. She cooked for them. Most evenings Dottie and Rosie were given some-thing, either a casserole, or some chops or pies and plates of buttery potatoes to carry over and put in the kitchen of the rooms the girls shared above the stables. Molly and Pat were grateful not to have to cook at the end of a long day in the fields, but Molly felt guilty and tackled Bertha about the butter she used for them.

'You really must take our ration books,' she told Bertha one day, holding out their brown paper books filled with their coupons for food. 'You are giving us more and more and you must need our coupons for everything we're eating.'

'No,' Bertha was firm. 'You need your ration books for your day to day things from Torbocks'.'

'But what about the butter?' said Molly. 'We only get two ounces a week and you are giving us more than that. We don't want Megan and the family to go without.'

'They'll not go without,' said Bertha firmly, 'because every day

Dottie, and sometimes Rosie, sit down there on the kitchen step and, come rain or shine, turn the butter churn with the milk I've kept back from the day's milking.' She nodded at the ration books still in Molly's hand. 'Now you put those away until they're next needed, and we'll say no more about it.'

'Still, we both wish there was some way we could repay you,' said Pat.

Bertha wrinkled her forehead. 'Can either of you shoot?' Both girls shook their heads, and a wide smile creased Bertha's face. 'There's the answer then. I'll get George to teach you. He's getting a bit rheumaticky for crawling through the damp grass hunting rabbits. He's not bringing many back home these days. Now if you could shoot a few for the pot we'd all be grateful.'

George was not keen on teaching two city girls to shoot, but was overruled by Bertha. Pat especially proved to have a really good eye, and soon there were always a couple of rabbits hanging on the back of the larder door; strung up by the hind legs, their heads in brown paper bags, their underbellies pegged open with a wooden stake. Rabbit stew was regularly on the menu.

By now Lavinia had moved into Folly House as the WD had requisitioned the dower house and put three naval officers in there, as Leckford House was bulging at the seams with all the extra personnel who'd been drafted into the area.

Lavinia grumbled. 'Even the forest seems to be getting crowded these days. Wherever you look there are soldiers, sailors and airmen.'

It was true. The fields attached to the enclosures, normally kept for herding cattle, started sprouting neat rows of camouflaged tents, then soldiers moved in and set up camp, and guards were posted on the gates. Great patches of heathland were concreted over and turned into runways for the aircraft which began to arrive. Everything was camouflaged. Posters were displayed in Stibbington post office, the library and all the banks saying: CARELESS TALK COSTS LIVES, and there was a general air of secrecy and anticipation. Mrs Fox now cleaned for the naval officers in the dower house, and then was engaged for the rest of the time cleaning at Leckford House.

'You'd think she was a general herself,' scoffed Bertha. 'Giving herself such airs and graces, telling everyone she meets that she is bound by the Official Secrets Act.'

'Perhaps she is,' said Lavinia.

'What, a general?' joked Arthur.

'No, bound by the Official Secrets Act. There's a lot of very hush-hush stuff going on up there.' She turned to Megan. 'Doesn't Jim ever say what he does there?'

Megan shook her head. 'Not to me,' she said.

'Nor me,' echoed Arthur.

They all now regarded Jim as part of the family. It was as if there had never been a time without him. Megan couldn't imagine life without him. He was teaching Rosie the piano, and she was a very apt pupil.

'I think Rosie is exceptionally gifted,' he told Megan. 'In fact, I think she may well be good enough eventually to be a professional musician. When I leave here, you must promise to make Arthur continue to teach her.'

Megan added that task to the long list of things to do, although somehow she couldn't imagine Jim ever leaving. But of course he would, as would all the people camped around them, together with the equipment and the boats being mustered in the river Stib. Yes, they would go once the war in Europe really started. But for the moment she was happy that they were there, since she was supplying HMS *Mason*, as Leckford House was now called, with fruit, vegetables and milk, and it all boosted Folly House's income.

Jim was a frequent visitor, letting himself into Folly House to play the piano whenever he could get away. When she was deep into marking up the official returns for the Food Office, a job she hated, she would pause and listen, then smile. With music in her ears even the hated Food Office returns didn't seem so bad.

The previous summer, in the long evenings, when Rosie was in bed and supper was over, Megan and Jim had started riding the two ancient hunters, Major and Lady Penny, out into the depths of the forest. Henry had put the two old horses out to pasture at the beginning of the war despite Silas Moon's suggestion they be sent to the knackers' yard, but now they were enjoying their new lease of life.

Both Megan and Jim found a new pleasure when riding through the forest; there the circle of life was unchanging; it was another world far away from the stresses of war.

Two years passed and they got to know each other well as while they rode they talked. Megan told Jim about growing up in the rectory with her father and brother, and how she'd always wanted to live in Folly House; a dream come true when she married Henry. But she didn't mention that her marriage had been a disappointment, or that Gerald had forced himself on her on the wedding night. Those dark guilty secrets she kept to herself.

She learned that Jim came from Sandwich in Massachusetts, New England, and that he wasn't married but was engaged to his child-hood sweetheart, a primary schoolteacher called Betty. He showed her pictures of his fiancée. She was small and blonde, standing outside her parent's home, a white-painted clapboard house on the edge of a creek by the sea.

'It all looks very neat and tidy,' said Megan.

Jim Laughed. 'It is. We have a few old houses in Sandwich, but there is no house like Folly House, rambling and odd-shaped because of all the bits and pieces added on over the centuries. That's what I love about England and the English villages, their sense of timelessness.'

Jim told her that in peacetime he'd taught engineering at Boston University, although he'd always dreamed of becoming a concert pianist, but Betty hadn't thought that a very secure career; she approved of engineering.

Later, when the war started, he'd decided he couldn't stay on the sidelines in America and watch Europe, which he loved, being destroyed by the Nazis, so he'd volunteered to work as a design engineer for the British at Leckford House. Betty hadn't approved, but he'd come anyway.

'I was like Betty in the beginning,' said Megan. 'I didn't want to hear about the troubles in Europe. I blocked my ears and thought if I didn't think about it everything bad would go away and that we'd remain here untouched by the war. I was selfish. I know that now.'

'Poor Megan,' said Jim. 'But it has touched you, hasn't it? You've lost your husband.'

Megan didn't reply. She couldn't tell him that although part of her wanted Henry to be alive and well, she wasn't missing him as much as a wife should. In fact, when she was riding out with Jim it seemed that it had always been like that, that just the two of them existed, and that Henry had never been part of her life. She also knew that slowly, little by little in their snatched hours together, she was falling love with Jim. She loved everything about him. The way he tilted his head when talking, his gentle laugh, the touch of his hand. But she wasn't free to love him, nor he her, and so Megan didn't allow herself to think about the future. She just lived for their brief moments together.

One evening they went further than usual and reached a sheltered hollow right in the middle of the forest, where the grass was short and springy, nibbled down to a green carpet by rabbits and deer. A small New Forest brown trout stream meandered through the hollow, reflecting golden splashes of light on to the leaves of the trees bending low over the water.

Jim jumped down and lightly tethered Major to a nearby black-thorn bush, already laden with sloes almost ready for picking. He held out his hand and Megan put hers in his and slid down from her mount to stand beside him. Jim tethered Lady Penny beside Major and, still holding Megan's hand, drew her down on the bank beside the stream.

'I've been thinking,' he said. 'About what will happen to us when this war is over.'

Megan shivered and took her hand from his. Suddenly the sunny glade seemed chilly. 'I don't want to think about it,' she said. 'I want us to go on like this for ever.' The words were blurted out before she could stop them.

Gently Jim took back her hand and raised it to his lips. 'Look at me,' he said softly. 'You know we can't go on for ever like this, don't you? Fate has thrown us together, but now we have to decide what happens next.'

Later, Megan was never quite sure who made the first move or even how it happened. But one moment they were looking at each other, and the next moment she was in his arms and they were kissing. They made love. Gently, tenderly at first and then with increasing passion, and Megan suddenly realized that she had been waiting all her life for this man. It all seemed so right, their bodies moved in harmony, fused together in ecstasy, and when at last they lay quiet in each other's arms it was Megan who spoke first.

'I didn't know it could be so wonderful.'

Jim stroked her hair, and kissed her bare shoulder. 'Nor did I, my darling.' He was quiet for a moment and then said, 'I do love you, you know. More than I can ever say.'

'I love you too,' Megan whispered. 'But I have a husband and you have a fianceé.'

Jim sighed, rolled over and positioned her more comfortably in the crook of his shoulder. He kissed her slowly, then said, 'Betty wrote me last week. She's found another man. A man who is staying in America and not running off to fight a foreign war. That's what she says.'

Megan propped herself up to turn and look at him. 'You sound as if you don't mind.'

Jim sighed again. 'I fell out of love with her a long time ago, but I didn't want to hurt her. We were both too young to get engaged, and now we're grown up. Both of us. I'm glad she's found someone to love, especially since I've fallen in love with you. I didn't plan this, I didn't even want to, but I couldn't help myself.'

'I think I fell a little bit in love with you the very first day I met you,' said Megan. 'I suppose I married too young as well. But now I feel guilty. I don't know what to do. I don't know whether Henry is alive or dead.' She paused, then said softly, 'It's wicked, I know, to hope that he never comes back.' There was silence, then she repeated, 'I don't know what to do.'

Jim sat up and began to pull his shirt back on. 'There's nothing we can do at the moment,' he said. 'I'll wait for you, and you will have to wait and find out whether Henry is coming back. We both have to wait until the war is over.' He took both her hands in his and looked very serious. 'I will have to leave here eventually and go on active war service, I can't tell you when or where, but when I come back we will decide what to do. If you still love me, and can bear to leave Folly House, we can make a life together.'

Leave Folly House. Megan hadn't thought of that before. It was an unwelcome thought. Of course, leaving Henry would mean leaving Folly House. But she didn't need to make that decision yet. For the moment she could love Jim and stay at Folly House.

After that their evening rides inevitably led to the same sheltered glade, and the horses hardly needed guiding to the sloe-laden bushes, where they stood silently, not even needing tethering. If anyone at Folly House suspected, they kept their own counsel, and let the lovers disappear into the forest while the weather stayed warm.

Lavinia did remonstrate with Megan one evening. 'You are neglecting Rosie a little. The child is missing you. Cannot you stay in a little longer in the evenings and read to her once she is in bed?'

Megan felt guilty and did as she suggested. But she worried that Lavinia might suspect something. Part of her wanted to tell Lavinia about Jim as she'd persuaded herself that Henry must be dead, because they'd heard nothing. She knew most people, including Gerald, thought he was dead; that then brought up the problem of Folly House. She dreamed that she could keep Folly House and live with Jim there when the war was over. A pipe dream; Gerald would never let that happen, and anyway common sense told her that Jim would probably want to go back to teaching in Boston. There was never going to be an easy answer. Such dreams were unlikely to come true.

CHAPTER NINE

December 1943

Just before Christmas 1943 the news gave everyone hope that the war might soon be over as Italy surrendered to the allies, then declared war on Germany.

'Never could trust those Eyeties,' muttered George as he and Silas plucked the Christmas turkeys.

'They're good workers though,' Silas pointed out.

They now had six extra farm labourers, all Italian prisoners of war, teenagers all of them but willing workers. Pat said it was because they were glad to be away from the war and had never wanted to fight anyone.

'Huh! And the pity of it is that we're losing them now. Don't know where they're sending them, no one ever tells us anything.' George lit a match and started singeing the bird he'd just plucked.

Rosie was especially happy to receive a Christmas five-shilling postal order from her mother, although she was not quite so happy when she read the accompanying letter, which said she'd soon be able to go back home.

'I've been here four years now,' she told Dottie. 'I like it here, it's better than London.'

'What's your London house like?' asked Dottie. She'd seen pictures of London on a newsreel at the cinema and knew it was big, and that lots of houses had been bombed.

'Our house is very small and we share a lavatory with five other houses. We've got a scullery downstairs, and two little rooms upstairs. I share a bedroom with my baby brother.' Dottie was silent, and thought Rosie sounded very unhappy.

Megan too was unhappy when she read the letter, although she pretended to be pleased for Rosie's sake. 'It will be lovely to see your real mother again,' she said. She didn't mention that Rosie's mother had never once visited her, not even when they offered to pay her rail fare.

Rosie didn't answer. She went to her room and put the postal order in the little bag she'd won at the fête, and didn't mention the letter or her mother again.

'I mustn't be possessive,' Megan said to Lavinia. 'But that letter made me realize just how much Rosie has become part of our lives. She is the daughter I've never had.'

To her surprise Lavinia was near to tears at the news. She hugged Megan and said, 'I know. I feel the same. But it's only natural her mother wants her back, and when the time comes we will have to let her go, but I shall insist she continues with her piano lessons. I'll pay for her tuition in London.'

The thought that this might be Rosie's last Christmas at Folly House took away all the pleasurable anticipation for Megan. Added to that was the fact that Jim was preoccupied with his work, and the only times he came was to teach Rosie the piece she was learning for the Christmas concert that Arthur was arranging at the church. Megan could hear the piano as she sat in her office and knew Jim was near. Rosie was trying to master a simplified version of Debussy's *Girl with the Flaxen Hair,* it sounded melancholy and sadness overwhelmed her. Soon Rosie would be gone, and so would Jim; he'd told her that the time was near when he'd have to leave, although he couldn't say more. Life without them loomed ahead, empty and meaningless. The war had picked them up and thrown them into her life, filling it with an unexpected joy, but when they went she'd be alone again. Not a mother, not a wife, not a widow. Nothing. Usually she fought off negative thoughts but that evening she let despair swamp her and the tears came, only to be interrupted by Gerald barging in without knocking. He was wearing his captain's uniform, complete with revolver in a leather holster at the belt. He'd taken to wearing it ever since he'd been promoted to the rank of captain in the local Home Guard. Everyone thought he was very pretentious. 'After all, he ain't a proper solder,' as Albert Noakes remarked. This time nobody corrected him; they all thought the same.

'Leave the door open,' said Megan quickly, trying to keep her voice firm and not to show she'd been weeping. 'I feel safer with the door open.'

'How's the merry widow?' he asked sarcastically.

'What do you want?' She made a show of blowing her nose while surreptitiously wiping away her tears.

'You know what I want. I want you and I want this house.'

'Neither is available.' Megan sat still. Trying to escape was useless; he was bigger and stronger than she was, and was in front of the door.

'I'm not good enough for you, eh? But lover-boy in there on the piano is.'

Megan felt her cheeks burn. Did he know, or was it just an educated guess? 'I'm a married woman, and—'

'You're a bloody widow,' Gerald interrupted. 'Why can't you admit that? Everyone knows Henry won't be coming back. His remains are lying festering somewhere in a muddy ditch in France, and the sooner you accept that fact the sooner we can come to a proper arrangement about where you will live when I move into this place.'

'Megan is not leaving Folly House because Henry *is* coming back. I know it.' Lavinia appeared in the doorway, ashen-faced and shaking with anger. 'How dare you come here, Gerald, and threaten Megan.'

But even as she was uttering the words about Henry returning Megan knew she didn't want them to be true. She wanted Jim, but she couldn't tell Lavinia that.

Gerald turned to Lavinia. 'Have it your way. But you know the terms of your own husband's will as well as I do, and if no heir is produced for Folly House then all this comes to me. Henry is dead. There is no heir. You are both only putting off the day of reckoning.'

'Get out,' said Lavinia. 'And with regard to Folly House, I'll have you know that I've already got some London lawyers working on Richard's will. As Henry's widow they think Megan will stand a good chance of inheriting Folly House, heir or no heir, because you also have no heir, and you have Brinkley Hall through marriage. You don't need Folly House.'

'It doesn't matter what I need, it's what I want that's important.' Gerald spat the words out menacingly and pushed past Lavinia just as Jim appeared in the doorway. 'Hello, lover-boy,' he said and disappeared.

'What was that all about?' Jim looked serious.

'Nothing, Jim,' replied Lavinia. 'Just Gerald being objectionable again.' She turned to Megan. 'Shall I put Rosie to bed now that she's finished the piano lesson?'

Megan nodded, hoping that Lavinia wouldn't notice her burning cheeks. 'I'll be up in a moment to read to her before she goes to sleep.'

When they were alone Jim pushed the door shut. He reached out and drew Megan to him. He kissed her briefly.

'I think Gerald knows about us,' Megan whispered.

'Probably.' He kissed her again. 'But don't worry, everyone will know about us eventually. I'm pretty sure Lavinia does.'

Megan threaded her arms around his neck and laid her head against his chest. His rough woollen sweater had a comforting smell of aftershave and cigarette smoke. It reminded her of their secret trysts in the forest back in the summer. 'What are we going to do?' she asked.

'I know what I'm going to do,' he said, disentangling her arms and getting down on one knee. Then, holding her two hands in his, he looked up at her very seriously. 'I love you, Megan. Will you marry me?'

Megan looked at him in silence, knowing that this moment would be imprinted on her memory for ever. His dark hair, always a little untidy, the tender expression in his brown eyes, the gentle curve of his mouth; yes, this moment would always be with her.

'Well,' he said softly. 'Do you want to marry me?'

'The answer is, yes, yes, yes, of course I want to. But I don't know how we can, because I'm not free.'

He got to his feet and drew her back into his arms. 'You will be,' he said softly. 'I shall be going away soon, probably in the spring, and when I come back we will sort it all out. I promise.'

They stood still, just holding each other close, and Megan relaxed. Yes, Henry must be dead, everyone thought so, and when it was officially announced she would be free to marry Jim. Afterwards, with Lavinia's help, then perhaps she would even get to keep Folly House. Suddenly the future seemed bright. There was nothing to be afraid of.

The concert at the church on the Sunday before Christmas was a great success. Jim played the organ and Arthur played the piano. And the highlight, for the audience from Folly House, was Rosie's rendition of the Debussy piece.

Afterwards Megan saw Jim talking to a tall silver-haired man in army uniform. He beckoned Megan to join them. 'This is Colonel Young,' said Jim. 'He is in charge of the Royal Victoria Military Hospital at Netley, the other side of Southampton. He would like us to play for the patients one evening this week.'

'On Wednesday the twenty-third of December, if that's possible,' said the Colonel. 'I understand from Jim here that the delightful little girl who played so beautifully is in your charge. Do you think you could let her come and play that evening? I know it will be late for her, but school must be finished now for the Christmas holidays.'

And so it was arranged. Both Arthur and Rosie were very excited at the thought of performing in front of several hundred soldiers. The concert was to be in the big chapel at Netley, which was right in the middle of the hospital facing Southampton Water.

Jim organized a jeep to take them there. 'Official army business,' he said with a grin.

Rosie went to bed the night before with her hair tied in rag rollers, and the following day Lavinia brushed it into glossy ringlets. They set off with Arthur's wheelchair stowed in the back of the jeep, Megan and Jim in the front and Arthur and Rosie securely strapped into the back. It was a cold and draughty ride in the windowless jeep across the River Test and into the ruins of Southampton, and then across the River Itchen on the floating bridge. That was the part Rosie liked best.

'It's like being on a boat,' she cried in delight, 'and look, there is another boat.'

To their right lay a big grey ship.

'That's a minesweeper put in for repairs,' said Jim, 'and those over there are landing craft.' He pointed to a group of small flat-bottomed boats tied together. 'They'll be in use soon.' He sounded serious and Megan guessed he was thinking of what lay ahead. It was only rumours but the whispers were getting louder every day, that one day soon the Allies would invade Europe. He had never mentioned it but Megan was certain that Jim was involved in the invasion, and she was worried.

Once off the floating bridge it was not long before they arrived at the big gates guarding the entrance to Netley Hospital. Waved through by uniformed guards they then drove past a long building with many windows, all in darkness. 'The hospital is a quarter of a mile in length,' Jim told them. Then they came to a large building with a cupola-shaped dome situated bang in the middle of the building. 'The chapel,' said Jim

Megan waited with Rosie and Arthur in a small anteroom at the side of the stage while Jim went to inspect the piano and organ. The plan was that when the performers were on stage Megan would have a seat in the front row. The hum of the assembling audience penetrated their small room, and against Megan's instructions Rosie opened the door a crack so that she could see into the auditorium.

'They've all got blue trousers on,' she squeaked.

'Wounded soldiers in hospital always wear that uniform. Regulation dress on top and blue trousers,' Arthur told her.

Megan went to close the door and stood behind Rosie. She caught a glimpse of the audience. Most were already sitting down, but some were being escorted to their seats. Suddenly she saw him. Her heart lurched violently and she gasped. It couldn't be. But it was. A nurse was holding his left elbow, helping him along, and in his right hand he held a white stick.

Arthur heard her gasp. 'What's the matter?' he asked anxiously.

Megan shut the door and leaned against it. She couldn't get her breath, and gasped for air. Panic-stricken thoughts ricocheted around in her head. It couldn't be him. If it was, why hadn't he told them? Did the white stick mean he was blind? Hot tears scalded down her cheeks, and from far away she could hear great hiccuping sobs. For a moment she wondered what it was, then realized it was herself making the noise.

'Megan, what is it?' She could hear Arthur shouting as if from a great distance, then suddenly Jim pushed open the door and was there.

Concerned and puzzled he put his arms around her and Megan clung to him as a drowning man clings to a spar at sea. 'What is it? What's the matter,' he asked urgently.

At last she managed to speak. 'It's Henry,' she sobbed. 'Henry is there in the front row. He's a patient.'

Christmas passed in a blur for Megan. Henry went back to Folly House for Christmas day, but it was a strained and difficult occasion for everyone, including Henry. The doctors thought familiar surroundings might jolt his memory, but he remembered nothing and no one. Eventually he said very quietly that he'd like to go back to his room at the hospital.

Megan went with him in Jim's jeep. She held his hand. 'You don't have to hold my hand,' he said politely.

'I want to,' she said, and hated herself for not being truthful: she didn't want to. She wanted him to disappear. She could just make out Jim's profile in the dark. It looked stern. Turning back to Henry, she said, 'I was hoping that you might remember something now that you know who you are, and where you lived.'

'No,' he replied in a toneless voice. 'I only know what you told me, but it's not real. I feel like a stranger. I don't belong there. I don't belong anywhere.' He slid his hand from Megan's and put it in his lap.

It was a long silent journey to the hospital in the darkness and Megan was glad when they'd delivered Henry back into the care of his nurse, Jenny.

'How did it go?' Jenny asked brightly. 'Did you have a lovely Christmas Day? Did it jog your memory?'

'No,' replied Henry tersely. 'I didn't remember a bloody thing.'

'Well, early days,' she said in the same bright tone, while making a face at Megan and Jim. 'A few more visits home and it will all come back to you.'

Megan watched Henry's retreating back as he was assisted down the long corridor towards his room. The lighting was dim as most of the patients were already asleep. The whole place smelled of disinfectant mixed with a faint odour of cooking. Megan hated it and felt depressed.

'Do you think he will ever remember?' she asked Jim as they walked back together to where the jeep was parked beneath bare trees by the water's edge.

Jim pulled her to him and held her close. 'God alone knows,' was his answer. He didn't kiss her, and Megan knew why. It seemed wrong to kiss, but he went on holding her.

At last Megan pulled away. 'We must get back,' she said, and climbed into the jeep. On the way back she sat with her head on his shoulder. As they turned to drive through the forest towards East End, they passed another convoy of armoured vehicles making their way to some secret destination along the shore near Leckford House. More men for the war, thought Megan miserably. More lives to be ruined. She took a deep breath. 'You know I can't possibly divorce Henry now,' she said. 'And even if he gets his memory back, I don't think I'll be able to. It would be too cruel.'

Jim didn't answer. Megan sat up to look at his face but couldn't see it in the darkness. She put up her hand to caress his cheek. It was wet with tears.

After Christmas in the New Year of 1944 Henry was discharged from hospital. The doctors said that from the physical point of view he was now as fully recovered as he was likely to be. His blindness was permanent, but they thought his amnesia was more likely to be cured if he was among familiar people and things.

Megan found his presence a terrible strain. He was Henry, and yet he was not. The man inhabiting his body was a total stranger, and also his physical presence in the house was a barrier between herself and Jim because they both felt guilty. It hadn't been that way when he was missing. They hadn't made love for weeks now and the subject of marriage was never mentioned again.

Sharing a bed with Henry was another difficulty. She felt that she was sharing with a total stranger and suspected Henry felt the same.

But there was no option as far as the sleeping arrangements were concerned, as the rest of the family occupied all the bedrooms now, and as Lavinia said, 'Someone has to keep an eye on Henry, and who better than his wife?'

Then to Megan's worry Gerald started nurturing a friendship with Henry. What was he planning? She tackled Gerald about it one day.

'Don't think you can bamboozle Henry into signing his inheritance away,' she said.

But Gerald merely laughed. 'You can't stop me being friends with my own brother. I'm taking him to a mess dinner at the Salisbury Plain camp. He's still a captain in the RAMC, he'll enjoy it.'

Lavinia had also noticed and tried to reassure Megan. 'While Henry has amnesia he cannot sign any legal document,' she told Megan.

So Megan watched and worried, and Gerald regularly took Henry out to official army dinners. Gerald as a captain in the Home Guard was basking in the reflected glory of his brother's position. Henry was a passive passenger in life; he just did as he was told making no comment on anything.

One night they were very late back, and staggered in through the big front door of the house. They were both drunk, and collapsed on the leather chesterfield which stood against the wall.

'How dare you bring him back drunk,' hissed Megan furiously, dragging Henry up and pointing him in the direction of the stairs. 'Shut the door on your way out,' she said over her shoulder to Gerald.

Upstairs in their bedroom Henry hung on to her as she struggled to get him out of his uniform and into bed. 'Shall we make love?' he mumbled as she tugged his trousers from his legs and over his ankles.

Megan stopped and froze with horror. She could think of nothing to say.

'Gerald says we should be making love every night to make up for lost time. He says . . .' Henry stopped. 'Oh shit. I've forgotten what he bloody well said.' He collapsed back on the bed, his trousers still around his ankles.

Megan bent down and slipped them off. Then she said quietly, 'Is that what you want?'

'No. No!' the answer came back immediately. He sat up and began to weep. 'I don't even know how to start to make love to a woman. The bloody bomb must have blown to pieces all my feelings and senses. I don't want anything. I don't know anything. I'm a meaningless void. I wish I were dead.' Tears streamed unheeded down his cheeks.

'Oh Henry.' Megan put her arms around him and held him as one would a small child. 'I wish I could help. Truly I do.' Compassion overwhelmed her as she held him. She stayed, comforting him like a mother until at last he finally fell asleep. Then she laid him down and covered him with the bedspread. Later, she lay down beside the wreck of the man who was her husband.

Winter crept into spring. The first snowdrops drifted across the lawn sloping down to the water, then the daffodils appeared, great yellow banks of colour hugging the edges of the tamarisk bushes around the garden. Usually Megan felt joyful at the first sign of spring, but not this year. Jim came less and less frequently as his work at Leckford House increased; he even passed over his piano tutorial duties for Rosie to Arthur. The whole area around Folly House, along the coast and up along the River Stib became a no go area for anyone who did not live there. All the residents now needed permits that allowed them to travel in and out of the area.

More and more soldiers appeared every week and soon every field was commandeered as a temporary army camp. The heathland areas that had been cleared now hummed each day with the sound of aircraft, large and small.

Bertha grumbled about the permits as George was always forgetting to carry his and having to return to the house to collect it. 'Everything takes him twice as long now,' she said.

But Jim, on one of his now rare visits to Folly House, said, 'Soon the war will be over, Bertha, and you will all be free to resume your lives as they were before.'

Bertha had looked at him and then at Megan, standing by his side. 'Some people's lives will never be the same again,' she said quietly.

The words hung in the air alongside other unspoken thoughts. Megan could hardly bear it. Nothing would ever be the same again.

To stop herself from thinking too much Megan immersed herself even more in work. Then, on top of everything else, the farm shop started losing money. Sales were drastically down as their usual customers were unable to get permits to visit the forest. Megan decided the only solution was for the farm shop to go to their customers, so she started up a weekly greengrocery round. Petrol was in even shorter supply, so a surprised Horace, the pony, was taken out of retirement to pull the trap again on a regular basis.

'It will give you your figure back,' said Megan, slapping the fat pony's flanks, when he objected a little to being put between the shafts of the trap.

Rosie polished some horse brasses and hung them on his bridle. 'You look very beautiful,' she said, kissing his velvety nose.

On a warm Saturday in March she and Megan set off on their first expedition to sell vegetables. They came back with an empty cart, and the round became a permanent fixture every Friday and Saturday. Rosie loved it because she was allowed to hold the reins, and to her surprise Megan found a measure of peace sitting behind Horace's fat rump as he plodded along the lanes. She looked forward to every weekend.

But her trips at the weekend with Rosie came to an abrupt halt one day when an official from the town hall in Stibbington arrived at Folly House with the news that Rosie's mother had decided that it was now time for her to return to London.

It was the day Megan had been dreading. 'But couldn't she stay here until the end of the war?' she asked, trying to keep back her tears.

The official, a Mrs Lee, shook her head. 'No, it has been decided by the authorities that it is safe for Rosie to return. Furthermore, a place has been reserved for her at Hackney Wick School, near her home. If she goes now she will have the whole term to settle in before she moves on to secondary school.'

Rosie wept bitterly. 'I don't want to go back,' she cried.

Mrs Lee looked at her sternly. 'Your mother needs you,' she said.

'Apparently your father is no longer part of the family, and your mother needs your help.'

'She doesn't want me. She just wants to put me to work,' said Rosie angrily.

But officialdom had its way and Rosie was packed up and taken to the railway station, where Mrs Lee put her on a train for London. 'A Mrs Portman will be waiting for her at Waterloo,' she informed a worried Megan.

Rosie clung to Megan until the very last minute when Mrs Lee brusquely separated them and thrust Rosie into the railway compartment. Megan stood on the platform holding on to the top of the carriage window.

'I shall always be here for you,' she said. 'Remember that. Whatever happens there is a home for you at Folly House. You can come back in your holidays, and I'll come up to London to see you.'

'I don't think that would be wise,' Mrs Lee snapped. 'Rosie belongs with her own family; Folly House was just a temporary measure.'

Megan didn't reply but stood in silence, enveloped in steam as the train drew slowly out of the station, remembering the first time she had seen the tiny little girl all those years ago, never knowing that love could be such pain and pleasure. When the last vestige of the train and steam had disappeared round the bend in the track she turned and walked slowly back to the trap. Horace whinnied softly, and scraped his hoof impatiently in the dust of the road, his brasses, so lovingly polished by Rosie that morning, shone in the afternoon sunlight.

Megan wept all the way back to Folly House. Little by little all the things she loved most were being taken away. Rosie first, then Jim soon and, once gone, who knew if she would ever see either of them again. There was Henry, too. Taken by the war and thrown back an empty husk of a man. How stupid she'd been to think that war was something that happened in a faraway land. She knew now that the girl who'd married Henry that Easter Saturday in 1939 had been shallow and ignorant. All she had wanted was to become mistress of Folly House and in that she'd succeeded. But folly was the name and nature of what she had desired. Now there was no going back. Her path was forward to whatever the future might hold.

CHAPTER TEN

Spring/Summer 1944

After the drunken episode Henry began to get his memory back. Not all at once, but in little bits and pieces. Megan felt closer to him now, not like a wife but like a good friend, and when snippets of memory came back she tried to help him as much as possible.

The rumours and gossip along the south coast had subtly changed now. People no longer said *if,* but *when* Europe was invaded. The invasion force was building up in the countryside and couldn't be missed from the ground. But from the air the local inhabitants knew it must look different, as everything was hung with camouflage tarpaulins and green netting. Troops, tanks and jeeps were everywhere. The river Stib was crammed with flat-bottomed barges and naval vessels small and large. Talk about this was discouraged: CARELESS TALK COSTS LIVES, the posters said, but people talked nevertheless.

Jim never spoke of it and Megan never asked. Their time together was too valuable to talk about things beyond their control. Now the weather was warmer they'd started their forest rides together; it was not often, but their snatched moments were precious, although their love was tinged with sadness as well as guilt now.

Henry began to change, revelling in the warmth of the spring sun on his face and hearing the sound of the sea. Slowly he found his way around Folly House and the gardens, and as he did so he felt the mist in his brain slowly but surely shifting a little. He liked Megan and felt comfortable with her; although she was like a sister, not a wife. As he got to know her better he realized how hard she worked, and knew too that she was grieving over Rosie's absence. He missed the little girl himself. He missed her lively chatter and never-ending questions.

One morning he started getting flashes of a scene in church. Was it of his own wedding? Megan was the obvious person to ask, so he made his way to her office and sat beside her. 'Did Lavinia wear lavender and purple at our wedding?'

'Yes.' Realizing it was another small piece of his memory returning she tried to help him. 'Can you tell me about her hat?'

'Big, with feathers,' said Henry with a smile as the vision appeared in his mind's eye. 'Adam was there too,' he added softly. 'Yes, I can see Adam clearly. He was wearing his Air Force uniform and looked very handsome.' He paused and frowned. What was it about Adam that bothered him? Why did he have such an uneasy feeling? 'Where is Adam now?' he asked. 'He's never been to see me.'

'The last time I heard he was in a hospital at East Grinstead because he'd been shot down and injured,' said Megan. 'I'll get his address,' she promised.

'Yes, do that if you can. Maybe seeing him will trip the blockage in my brain. See, I already remember something. I know he was in the Air Force, that he was a pilot. Maybe he's recovered and is still flying.' But the uneasy feeling persisted although Henry didn't mention it. What could he say? He couldn't remember why he should feel this way. Perhaps Adam could tell him.

He stood up and made his way across the room to the open door, then surprised Megan by turning suddenly and saying. 'Was our marriage a happy one?'

How could she answer? The truth, thought Megan, was that she didn't really know what constituted a happy marriage. Had she been happy before she met Jim?

Not really, but then she hadn't been unhappy either. 'I think we were as happy as most people,' she said carefully.

Henry didn't answer, merely nodded and left the room.

Megan wrote the letter to East Grinstead enquiring the

whereabouts of Squadron Leader Adam Myers. It had been a difficult letter to write as half of her didn't want Henry to get in touch with Adam again. Not because she was still jealous of Adam, but because meeting Adam might give Henry all his memory back, and if that happened would he want her for his proper wife again? What would she do if he did? Now, after Jim, she was not sure that she could ever make love with another man. He was her one and would be her only love, of that she was certain. She didn't post the letter but kept it in her jacket pocket. Why did life have to be such a muddle? She prayed that night for an answer, but none came.

The following Saturday morning, while harnessing Horace ready for his vegetable round, she was startled by Jim arriving on his bicycle. He gave her a letter. There was no stamp on it, and the address on the back was The Priory Hospital, Larchwood, New Forest. Megan knew of it. Previously it had been a small private hospital but had been requisitioned by the WD and now treated wounded servicemen who needed further surgery and long-term convalescence.

'How did you get this? she asked curiously, turning the envelope over in her hand.

'A nurse driving a car through East End stopped and asked me the way to Folly House. When I told that was where I was going, she gave me this letter and asked me to deliver it. She said it was important.'

Megan looked at the envelope in her hand. The writing was spidery and she didn't recognize it. 'I wonder who it's from?'

'Open it,' suggested Jim with a smile, 'and then you will know.'

Megan opened it. Inside was a letter and a smaller envelope addressed to Captain Henry Lockwood. 'It's from Adam,' she told Jim, and passed the letter across for him to read. It was short and to the point.

Dear Megan,

I was told that Henry was missing, but I'm writing this hoping that perhaps by now you know where he is. The enclosed letter is very personal and I'd like you to make sure it is delivered to Henry if possible. If Henry is dead, please tell me and send the letter back to me at the Priory Hospital where I am a patient now.

Yours sincerely,
Adam Myers

'Well,' said Jim. 'What are you going to do? Read the letter to Henry?'

'He says it's very personal,' said Megan, stuffing the letter and envelope into her pocket. 'I'll think abut it, but now,' she put her arms around Jim's neck, 'don't let's think about that. There's no one here except Horace, and he won't talk. Am I allowed a kiss?'

'I thought you'd never ask,' said Jim, bending his head to hers.

Horace blew out noisily through his nostrils and stamped a hoof, shaking his horse brasses. 'He wants to get going,' said Megan, breaking away from their embrace, 'and I must go if I'm to do all my rounds. I haven't even loaded the vegetables on to the cart yet.'

'I'll help today,' said Jim. 'I thought you'd like some company as I've got the day off.'

The letter burnt a hole in Megan's pocket all day, but by tacit agreement neither of them mentioned either the letter or Henry.

Not until that night, when she was alone in her office after supper, did Megan open the letter addressed to Henry. She had her doubts, as it was marked personal, but reasoned that as Henry was blind she'd have to read it to him anyway, so she might as well read it first. But she was totally unprepared for its contents. As she read on she found it hard to breathe and eventually her nerveless fingers dropped the letter to the floor.

She felt shocked, horrified and guilty, each emotion struggling for supremacy in her dazed mind. She wished she had never read the letter. But she had, and now there was no going back. Still trembling, she reached down and picked it up, read it again, hoping vainly that she'd been mistaken the first time. But the words were still the same, and the shock was also still the same. The spidery handwriting leapt off the page, the words searing themselves into her brain.

My dear, darling boy

I must admit that at first I was furious with you when you rejected me that night when I needed you so much. But I can't say I was furious with you for long because I love you. You must know that. I've always loved you since that first day at school when we both hid in the showers in order to escape rugger practice. I can still see your blond hair flecked with sparkling drops of water, and the shape of your beautiful body; as I've said before your long white thighs drove me mad with desire that very first day. But I was unsure of myself in those days so did not reveal my true feelings. However, now, as you know, I can. There is nothing to be ashamed of; one man loving another is as natural a form of love as that between a man and a woman. I don't believe you love Megan more than me. I know you love me more. But now you are married I have to get used to sharing you. Stay married to Megan, have your family if you must, but please, please stay steadfast to me, I beg you.

Your one true love,
Always waiting for you,
Adam

There it was in black and white. A love letter. Adam loved her husband. But did Henry love Adam? The letter spoke about rejection. Had Henry rejected Adam in favour of her? But had they been lovers before? She'd heard about such love, but everything in her upbringing made her recoil from it. She didn't know what to do, whom to speak to. There was no one. The subject was taboo in the society she moved in; not only taboo, but criminal. Imprisonment was the fate of men who declared their love openly.

Folding the letter carefully she slipped it back into the envelope, then made her decision. She would seal it carefully, then return the letter to Adam and swear it had not been opened. She thought of lying and saying she did not know of Henry's whereabouts, but the Priory Hospital was near, someone might talk, and then she'd have some difficult explaining to do. She decided that she would take

121

Henry to visit Adam, and watch what happened between them. What she would do after that she had no idea.

The visit to Priory Hospital was arranged. Henry showed no emotion when told he'd be seeing Adam, as he hadn't remembered who Adam was. Megan said nothing about the letter and had resealed it, intending to give back to Adam as if it had not been opened. She'd stopped feeling muddled and guilty and now felt angry instead. What right had Adam to write a love letter to her husband? The anger gave her added confidence. She would confront Adam when they met and not be afraid of the coldness in his eyes. Now she knew why: he'd always been jealous of her just as she had always jealous of him. As for Henry, if he eventually decided he preferred Adam to her then she'd be free to marry Jim. But even that thought didn't help much. She felt she was living in a nightmare; life was a mess. She'd not seen Jim for more than a week, and the last time they'd been together he'd been in a world of his own, absorbed by thoughts of the coming conflict. He was nervous, she sensed it, and she was haunted by the fear that something dreadful would happen to him.

But today she had other worries; the meeting of Henry and Adam. They arrived at the appointed time. The Priory was a long, single-storey building, its ecclesiastical history evident from the structure. It had whitewashed walls with small windows set into them at regular intervals and the whole building curved round to one side, where there were open cloisters, that looked out across a steeply wooded valley. At the end of the cloisters was a squat building which looked as if it had been a Norman chapel. It had a huge heavy oak door, studded with great iron nails; the whole place gave a sense of antiquity and peace. Megan and Henry entered through the great door into the matron's office.

The matron, an elderly woman with thick grey hair drawn back in a bun which nestled beneath her frilly white cap, greeted them. She wore a dark-blue uniform, cinched in at the waist beneath her ample bosom by a navy-blue belt with a large silver buckle. She came straight to the point. 'I must warn you both,' she said, 'that Squadron Leader Myers is very disfigured by the burns he received when his plane went down.'

'It will make no difference to me,' said Henry. 'I'm blind.'

But, although warned, Megan was shocked to the core. It was difficult to equate the figure in the bed to a man, let alone Adam Myers, the once handsome heartthrob of the theatre. A hunched creature lay there with clawlike, red-raw hands, looking at the world from a skeletal face with staring eyes. He had no ears, just red holes on either side of his head. His eyes were the same, the hard brilliant eyes she'd always feared, but now they peered at the world through tattered, frilly fleshy folds. His face was a patchwork of different-coloured pieces of flesh, white, brown and scarlet, with no trace of his lips, just the skin finishing in a lopsided ragged line over his teeth, giving the appearance of a perpetual leering smile. When he spoke his voice was different. It was hoarse, and every now and then he stopped and gulped back air that was almost visible as it passed down his throat because the flesh was stretched so tightly across his larynx. Megan did her best to hide her horror, but it wasn't easy.

Once she had greeted Adam and explained Henry's situation and settled him beside the bed, she said, 'I'll leave you two to talk. We are hoping, Adam, that you will be able to help Henry get his memory back. Maybe you can talk over old times.'

'One thing's for certain, we're hardly likely to talk about the bloody future,' Adam replied harshly. 'We haven't got one. Either of us.'

There was nothing to say to that bitter truth, and Megan left the room. At the door she paused and looked back. Adam had taken Henry's hand and raised it to his jagged, scarred lips, and the expression on his grotesque face was so full of love that Megan turned away quickly, not wanting to intrude. Once outside hot tears welled up, and she leaned against the rough stone wall and closed her eyes. *Nothing in my life has prepared me for any of this*, she thought. *Everything is wrong. We all love the wrong people and I don't know what to do.*

Hunching her shoulders miserably she walked through the cloisters to a wooden seat in the garden. As she sat down she felt the crackle of paper. It was the letter she'd intended to return. She'd forgotten about it in the shock of seeing Adam, but when, full of trepidation, she handed Adam the letter on her return, and told the lie she'd prepared, he was not interested.

He crumpled the envelope containing the letter and threw it in the waste-paper bin at the side of his bed. 'It's not important,' he said. 'Henry doesn't know me now. I've lost him.'

Megan understood. 'He's lost to both of us now,' she said, and the myriad of emotions she had felt about Adam all dispersed into nothingness, submerged by the tragic truth of what the war had done to both men.

Marcus was summoned to a Church of England meeting at Lambeth Palace. Not something he'd expected, as he was an unimportant parish priest.

'Old Jeremy Pointer over at Burley told me it's to prepare us old ones to face the chop after the war,' he said gloomily. 'When all the servicemen come back they won't want us any more.'

'Well, you'll get a pension,' said Lavinia brightly. 'It won't be so bad.'

But Marcus refused to be cheered and didn't want to go. 'Supposing I get bombed?' he said. 'London is a dangerous place.'

'Rubbish,' said Lavinia. 'We haven't had any bombs for ages now. You are going to go, and for a treat Megan and I will come to London with you. It will do Megan good to have a day off. We can go out for a meal; the London restaurants always have plenty of food, and maybe we can pop over to Hackney and see Rosie while we're up there.'

So it was settled. They took the train from Stibbington to Southampton, and from there up to Waterloo. Megan was excited at the thought of seeing Rosie again.

But the visit was a disaster. Mrs Barnes, Rosie's mother, was far from welcoming, and was in fact very hostile.

'I don't want my Rosie seeing you again,' she told Megan. 'You've been giving her ideas above her station. Piano lessons indeed! And all this reading! She can't waste her time reading storybooks. She's going to work in Woolworths as soon as she's fourteen. My friend has got a job lined up for her. Already she's started doing Saturdays to get her hand in.'

'But she's only a child,' cried Megan.

'And she's a gifted pianist,' said Lavinia.

They were both horrified at the thought of Rosie working. But there was nothing they could do to persuade Mrs Barnes, who shut the door in their faces. They didn't even get a glimpse of Rosie.

'Maybe when she's older and free of her mother she will contact us,' said Lavinia hopefully. 'Until then we'll have to try and forget her.'

'I'm going to keep in touch,' Megan replied stubbornly. 'No matter what her mother says.'

The meal in Lyons Corner House with the piano tinkling in the background didn't cheer either of them, and eventually a very despondent Megan and Lavinia met an equally despondent Marcus and caught the train home. They sat in silence most of the way.

After passing Winchester Marcus spoke. 'Jeremy Pointer was right,' he said morosely. 'As soon as they can get a younger man for the parish I'm being put out to pasture. I don't know how I'll manage. The pension I'll get won't feed a grasshopper, let alone Arthur and me.'

'You don't have to worry about Arthur,' said Megan. 'He's earning a little money with his concerts and piano lessons, and that should continue.' For a moment she thought back to the days when she'd dreamed of being able to persuade Henry to fund Arthur at the Royal Academy of Music. The war had changed all that.

'And I'm sure Henry and Megan won't want any rent from you for living at Folly House,' said Lavinia, 'and if they do, you can always move in with me when I go back to the dower house after the war.'

'That would provide gossip for the village,' said Marcus, cheering up a little.

But would they still be at Folly House? Lavinia said it was illogical for Megan to worry about not having an heir, as Gerald and Violet didn't have a child either, and the whole purpose of the original will was to keep Folly House in the family. But that didn't comfort Megan. Logic wouldn't stand in Gerald's way. He wanted Folly House and that was that.

At the end of May Megan hadn't seen Jim for nearly two weeks. The weather was bad: clouds, rain and high winds every day. Silas and George had made up their minds to try and get in the first crop of hay, but no sooner had they cut and baled it than heavy thunderclouds came over and soaked everything. Megan worked with them, desperately trying to cover the bales with as many sheets of old tarpaulin as she could find. Buying new was impossible; the WD had commandeered everything for camouflage. She worried about the hay; if it got too wet they'd be in trouble when the winter came and they needed it for feed. The longer days meant everyone at Folly House who could, worked, picking the first of the peas, digging the early potatoes as well as helping with the hay whenever it stopped raining. Even Lavinia did her share of pea-picking.

By now it was impossible to move without bumping into battalions of soldiers, and moving around in the area became more and more difficult. Even Megan was not allowed to venture far with her vegetable round; military exercises were taking place day and night all along the coast. The invasion of fortress Europe must surely be near, thought Megan. She wondered where Jim was and worried.

'I feel so useless,' said Arthur miserably. 'Here we are in the middle of an army, and there's nothing I can do.'

Henry nodded. 'I feel the same. Adam is keeping me up to date as he can read the newspapers. We both wish we could do something.'

Megan kept silent, but she felt sick with worry about Jim. She'd organized a rota to take Henry to the Priory Hospital to visit Adam, and sometimes she thought he didn't enjoy the visits, although he never said anything, and his memory remained as elusive as ever.

As each day passed she knew that the time Jim must leave was coming nearer and nearer, and still they hadn't been able to meet. Their last day came on Friday, 1 June. Jim arrived in the late afternoon, as clouds were rolling in from the west and a strong wind was blowing. She was in the stables giving Horace a much needed grooming.

He looked weary and came straight to the point. 'It's time to say goodbye.'

Megan paused, her hand resting on Horace's warm flank. 'When do you leave?'

Gently Jim took the grooming brush from her hand and started brushing Horace in slow rhythmic strokes. 'I can't tell you that.' He kept his eyes averted. 'But this is the last time I shall come here. I've made arrangements with Captain Eugene Morgan at HMS *Mason* to let you know if . . .' He stopped and drew a photograph from his pocket. 'I've got one of you on the beach,' he said, 'and this is me. In case you forget.'

Megan flung herself into his arms. 'Don't say that,' she cried. 'I'll never forget, never, never. Oh God, I can't bear it.'

'You must.' Jim's voice was firm. 'We all must because it's the only way.' He tipped her face to his. 'Let's saddle the horses and go out into the forest. Let's go to our special place one more time.'

Megan made her excuses at Folly House. It wasn't difficult. Henry was at The Priory, and Lavinia and Marcus were in the church, organizing the flowers for the Sunday service. The horses were saddled and together they sought the solace of the broadleaf forest. As if to celebrate the sun came out from behind the storm clouds; late evening bees hummed amongst the brilliant broom flowers, and silly young baby rabbits scattered before the horses as they made their way into the depths of the forest.

Their secret place was waiting, unsullied by soldiers' boots scrambling through on military exercises. It was tranquil, and the horses knew where to stand, not even needing tethering.

They made love slowly, gently, savouring every moment. Words were not necessary. The knowledge that this might be the last time lay unspoken, too painful to be put into words. Not even when the final goodbye came. After stabling the horses, they walked to the edge of the garden where the forest began, and touched hands briefly, then Jim walked away into the night.

On the six o'clock news on Tuesday night, 6 June, it was officially announced that Allied naval forces, supported by strong air forces, had begun landing Allied armies that morning on the northern coast of France. Mr Churchill, the Prime Minister, said that the operation 'is proceeding in a thoroughly satisfactory manner. Many dangers and difficulties which appeared extremely formidable are now behind us.'

There was no mention of casualties, but everyone knew there must be many, and everyone at Folly House thought of Jim who they knew was somewhere in France.

That night Megan opened the bedroom window and looked out across the dark sea. It was just light enough to see the outline of the hills on the Isle of Wight against a grey, cloud-strewn sky. A strong breeze was blowing, dashing the shingle against the breakwaters. It was a cold, lonely sound, as if someone was down on the beach sighing heavily.

'God help them,' said Henry, who was sitting on the edge of the bed. 'They will need every bit of help they can get.'

Megan suddenly remembered that Henry had been in the disastrous evacuation of 1940. She went and sat beside him. 'It must be terrible,' she said.

Henry reached out and grasped her hand. 'That's the bloody awful part. I can't damn well remember. There's still a bloody great hole where my memory ought to be.'

CHAPTER ELEVEN

Summer 1944

The morning after he'd told Megan he still couldn't remember anything about the war Henry awoke with a strange feeling. He lay beside the still sleeping Megan and wondered what it was that was different. Then suddenly it began. A series of brilliant colours all jumbled together which slowly formed into different pictures. As he lay there Henry realized that his memory was coming back in a series of vignettes, like an amazing movie newsreel. Scenes from his life. Not the brief flashes he'd had before, but longer now and more complex: memories of his thoughts about Megan, his brother, the house. Then quite suddenly he felt exhausted and fell asleep.

Later, when he awoke again, he realized he still retained some of the memories, but nothing new came. At first he was bitterly disappointed, but then consoled himself with the thought that the memories were definitely there. Maybe it was just a case of relaxing and letting them come. He decided to say nothing; he would wait until more came and he was sure that they wouldn't disappear again.

A week after the D-day invasion it seemed perhaps that the war might finish soon and Henry began to worry. What was the future for the family at Folly House? Memory was not the blessing he'd thought it would be, because now he started to understand just how little money he actually had; and worry about the fact that he'd given Gerald permission to reinvest what shares he'd had left in different foreign investments. Was it really true that his original investments had been unsound? However, he didn't mention either his memory or his doubts to anyone. Not even Megan.

Without mentioning it to anyone at the house he took a taxi into Stibbington on the pretext of having a medical check-up, but in reality visiting his old friend, an accountant named Angus Penny.

After their meeting, Angus, with Henry's signed permission, undertook a thorough overhaul of Henry's investment portfolio. But it was too late. Gerald had made the changes and there was nothing Angus could do. He suspected that the present bonds were worthless and forced a confrontation between Gerald and Henry in his office. Gerald then admitted that the bonds had now been declared worthless. His excuse was that the Eastern European countries involved had now been absorbed into the Soviet Union, as the Russian army pushed across Europe. Everything had been frozen or the assets removed to Russia.

'There's nothing anyone can do. It's the luck of the draw. You gambled and lost,' said Gerald, and left the meeting.

Angus Penny advised Henry to tell the rest of the family. The loss of his small inheritance would affect everyone. They had to decide what to do for the future.

As Angus wryly pointed out to Henry, 'Materially the Lockwood family is still rich, but you can't eat bricks and mortar, or pay the bills with poultry, cattle and carrots.'

When Henry asked Megan to call a family get-together because he wanted to discuss the organization of their finances, Megan was surprised. He'd never taken any interest in how things were run before; why could he not just talk to her?

'Yes, everyone,' Henry said firmly. 'And that includes your father Marcus, and brother Arthur.' He waited for more questions, but Megan remained silent. 'Perhaps I'd better tell you that I've got my memory back,' he said. 'I remember everything now.'

So that was it. The moment Megan had been dreading. She looked across at the tall man sitting opposite her. A stranger compared to the man who had left Folly House to go to war. Then he'd been so broad and handsome in his captain's uniform. This man was thin with deep lines in his face and the once shining blond hair was sparse and tinged with grey. His flickering blind eyes were hidden behind dark glasses, and gave an air of blankness, which she couldn't penetrate.

This was not the man she had married, but then, neither was she the young woman he had married. Then she'd been selfish and naive, thinking she could manipulate everything in their lives in the way she wanted. Now she knew that life itself picked people up and tossed them around, so that certainties became uncertain and nothing was the same as before.

Eventually she blurted out, 'Then you remember me as your wife, not just Megan, the woman you met Christmas 1943.'

Henry smiled hesitantly. 'Yes, I remember the young wife, the child we lost, and the fact that we hardly knew each other before I went away to war. Looking back, I don't think I was a very romantic husband. If I remember correctly, I was too tied up with my work in London to pay much attention to you.'

'Yes, with work and with friends like Adam.' Megan couldn't refrain from mentioning Adam. She watched his reaction.

'Yes, work and friends like Adam,' replied Henry carefully. He knew he would have to deal with Adam, especially since he now remembered that last awful quarrel before either of them got injured. But at the moment the problem of money had to be dealt with first.

The meeting was arranged for the following afternoon, and Gerald would be present. Henry heard Megan make a small surprised sound and raised a hand to silence her. 'Gerald has to be there. He is very involved.'

'Hmm, Gerald involved,' Lavinia observed when Megan told her of the meeting. 'It won't be good news for us if Gerald has anything to do with it.'

The whole Lockwood family sat around the oval dining table in the rose room. On the table before them was an assortment of box files, piles of paper and bank statements, all brought in by Angus Penny who was also in attendance.

Bertha's head popped round the door. 'Shall I bring the tea in now, madam?' She addressed Lavinia.

'Yes, bring it in quickly and leave it. We will serve ourselves.'

'Certainly, madam.' Bertha sounded a little put out. She wasn't used to Lavinia sounding officious. Quickly, she'd said, but Bertha wanted to linger. Like everyone in Folly House she sensed there was something going on between Gerald and Henry, and that Lady Lavinia and Megan didn't like it. Bertha wanted to know what it was.

'I think it's something to do with money,' Bertha told anyone who would listen that afternoon. She was making a late lunch for Molly and Pat, who'd come in from a morning's shoot with a couple of young rabbits, and four pigeons. They were laid out on the butcher's block ready for cleaning.

'If it's to do with money, then it's no business of ours.' George emerged from behind his newspaper, his old cherry pipe sticking out of the corner of his mouth. 'You shouldn't even talk about it.'

'Rubbish,' retorted Bertha. George glowered at her. In his opinion, she'd grown far too bold in her relationship with the Lockwoods since the war. 'If they run out of money,' went on Bertha, warming to her theme, 'we'll be out on our ear. It happens to people, you know.'

'I don't think you need ever worry about that.' Molly slit open a rabbit's underbelly with practised ease and, slipping her hands inside pulled out the innards. 'Do you want the kidneys now, or shall I leave them in?'

'I'll have them now. I'll sauté them for Mr Henry's break-fast tomorrow,' said Bertha, then returned to her theme of money. 'Personally,' she announced firmly, 'I don't trust Mr Gerald as far as I could throw him. Never have done. He always managed to get what he wanted as a child. The only thing denied him was this house, and he's still after that. And Miss Megan,' she added as an afterthought. 'He's always been after her an' all.'

This was too much for George. Throwing the paper down on the kitchen table he sat bolt upright and took his pipe from his mouth. 'Enough of that talk, my girl,' he said. 'It's not right and proper to talk about the family like that.'

Pat and Molly raised their eyebrows at each other. They had never been in awe of any of the Lockwoods, because as far as they were concerned they were just ordinary people who paid their wages. The fact that they had more money than most people they knew didn't change anything. Pat was about to say this when an article in George's newspaper caught her eye.

'What's this?' she cried. 'Hitler's got a new weapon.' Picking up the paper she peered at the article and announced, 'In Germany it's called the *vergeltungswaffe* which means reprisal weapon, and it can fly at four hundred miles an hour and is pilotless.' She flung down the paper and continued plucking one of the pigeons. 'Fancy that! Just when I thought we were beginning to win the war, what with the landings in France and all.'

George picked his paper and settled back in his chair. 'There'll be no end to this war until Hitler is dead and buried,' he pronounced, and then disappeared behind the newspaper with a puff of smoke.

Bertha, as usual, had the last word. 'Well, I'd still like to know what's going on in there.' She jerked her head in the direction of the rose room.

After Bertha had left and closed the door the family sat in uneasy silence until Lavinia spoke to Gerald. 'Now, according to Angus Penny, you've been manipulating Henry's investments, and it appears from these statements here that you've lost him a lot of money. In fact, nearly all of it.'

'I didn't exactly lose it. I invested it, and the investment went sour. These things happen,' said Gerald defensively.

'My fault, I suppose,' said Henry. 'I did ask Gerald to manage my money. He told me he would reinvest it and I agreed. But that was before I got my memory back and really knew what was what.'

'You took advantage of Henry.' Megan turned angrily towards Gerald.

'You should know all about that. Taking advantage, I mean,' sneered Gerald.

Angus tapped the table with his pen. 'I must point out that Henry did, quite freely of his own will, allow Gerald to manage his money.'

'Why didn't you ask me to manage your money?' demanded Megan, turning towards Henry.

'Because, my dear sister-in-law, you are a country vicar's daughter and know nothing of the world of high finance,' said Gerald before Henry could answer. 'You may have climbed up the social ladder and become the lady of Folly House, but it hasn't given you the knowledge to deal in complex financial matters.'

'Well, with all your knowledge, it seems you haven't been able to deal in complex financial matters either,' Megan shot back.

'Perhaps I should have included you, Megan,' Henry said quietly. 'But I didn't tell you because I wanted to do something myself. I'm tired of being a useless blind man. You have enough responsibilities running the house and farm, something I never envisaged for you. Getting my memory back made it worse in a way, because now I know that I always thought you'd have the life of a county lady, like Lavinia. But when Gerald read me all my statements, I found the interest I was getting from the stocks and shares was minimal. Even before I got my memory back I knew we couldn't live on what I had in the bank. So I decided, with Gerald's help, to make more money. I get a very small pension from the army, and nothing at all for the years I worked in the hospital. Therefore we needed to make what little money I had work for us.'

'But I've never thought there was a problem.' Megan blurted the words out without thinking, then immediately regretted them. 'I've loved making the farm efficient, although I've always thought of the farm money as being extra to your fortune in the bank in London, which I thought we'd have after the war. I thought the Lockwoods were rich.'

'And that's why you married him, isn't it?' Gerald leaned forward as he spoke and spat the words out. 'That and the house.'

'Gerald!' said Lavinia sharply.

A hot flush crept over Megan's cheeks. It was true. She had wanted both the house and the money. She was glad Henry couldn't see her guilty expression.

But Henry went on talking almost as if nothing had been said. 'I remember now that in those days I was a very well-paid private practitioner; the hospital paid less but I thought I had years ahead of me. I never thought about the future.'

'I didn't think about the future either,' said Megan guiltily. 'It never occurred to me that one day you might . . .'

'Be a useless blind man,' interrupted Henry bitterly

'Be short of money,' said Megan.

'But when you went off to war surely you thought perhaps you might not come back,' said Lavinia. 'Did you not think of Megan's future?'

Henry gave a bark of a laugh. 'Of course I thought I might get killed, so I took out a good life insurance policy, which I still have. So that if that had happened Megan and the house would have been well taken care of.' He turned towards where Megan was at his side. 'Ironic, isn't it. As I still have the insurance you'd be better off now if I were dead.'

'Don't say that.' Reaching out she took his hand. More guilt washed over her; it was more ironic than Henry knew. If he were dead then she'd be free to marry Jim. Except of course, it might be Jim who was dead. There'd been no news.

A tense silence filled the room. Lavinia got up and began to pour the tea. She looked at Gerald. 'You'd better come up with a good explanation for this,' she said sharply.

Gerald shrugged his shoulders, took a sheaf of papers from Angus spread them out across the table. 'See for yourselves,' he said. 'I put a lot of money in with the Baltic states, and other Eastern European states. I admit it was a gamble, but the money should have flowed into my account in Switzerland and I'd have made a killing with the sales of armaments. Everyone was buying, even Germany. All through neutral Switzerland. But unknown to me, they were double-dealing criminals, and in fact Henry has ended up owing money.'

Everyone gasped, and Lavinia said, 'This is disgraceful. Surely Henry can't owe money?'

Angus Penny interrupted quickly. 'The good thing is,' he said calmly, 'that because they are criminals and are wanted throughout Europe they dare not pursue anyone for the money which is owed.' He looked severely at Gerald. 'I understand you got off comparatively lightly.'

Gerald had the grace to look discomfited. 'I did it for Henry,' he said defiantly. 'He wanted me to make money, and there's no room for scruples in business.'

'I take issue with that,' muttered Marcus from his side of the table.

Lavinia finished handing the tea round and sat down. She looked across at Gerald with a steely expression. 'Comparatively lightly,' she repeated. 'How much?'

He looked more uncomfortable than ever. 'Well,' he mumbled after a moment or two, 'I did lose some, but I managed to get most of my money out before the deal finally collapsed. Of course, my money was invested differently; not such a profitable deal as Henry's. I let him have the best offer.'

'Strange then that it turned out worse for him than for you,' said Megan. She wanted to shout but knew that would do no good. Standing up, she began to gather all the paperwork in towards her. 'Something has to be done,' she said to no one in particular. 'But there's no point in talking about it any more. I may be an ignorant little country girl and know nothing of high finance, but I can add up. Folly House will survive, as it's survived before. I shall make certain of that.'

Gerald stood up, 'Of course I can always offer Henry a loan at a very good rate. A loan against the house.'

'No,' Megan and Lavinia both shouted as with one voice, then looked at each other and laughed. It broke the tension, and then Lavinia said, 'I think Megan's idea of sorting it out ourselves is a good one. We'll do that with the help of Angus. You can go, Gerald; you're not needed here any more.'

'And don't think that you'll ever get your hands on Folly House,' said Megan fiercely. 'Because you won't. Not while I'm alive anyway.'

Arthur, who'd been sitting beside Marcus the whole time, wheeled himself over and opened the door. 'Goodbye,' he said politely as Gerald passed.

Gerald's answer was to slam the door on his way out.

No one spoke for a few moments, then Henry said mildly, 'Why would Gerald want Folly House? He has Brinkley Manor.'

'Because he's always wanted it,' said Megan. She didn't add that she feared Gerald, and that lately she'd thought that his desire for the house bordered on fanaticism. Everyone would think she was exaggerating.

'I want to be involved in sorting this out,' said Henry. 'I want to help.'

'What can you do,' snapped Megan, still thinking of Gerald and his invidious ways. Henry was no match for him and never had been. 'How can you help?' The moment the words were spoken she felt ashamed. 'I'm sorry,' she whispered. 'I didn't mean that.'

She tried to catch hold of Henry's hand, but he recoiled from her touch. 'No, you're quite right,' he said. 'I'm no use at all.'

Looking back Megan wondered how they would have survived without Lavinia. They had Henry's paltry pension from the War Office, but no other money coming in on a regular basis. The money from the gardens and farm paid day-to-day bills, but all the customers Megan had acquired at HMS *Mason* had now disappeared.

Lavinia's money was in trust for the maintenance of Folly House, so that was one thing Megan didn't have to worry about.

'That was always Richard's intention,' said Lavinia. 'He always wanted Henry to marry you and raise a large family at Folly House, without the worry of repair bills to an old house.'

'If he were alive today he would be disappointed,' said Megan. 'Somehow I don't think we'll have a large family.'

'There's plenty of time,' said Lavinia, who was blissfully unaware of the fact that Henry and Megan didn't sleep together as man and wife. 'In fact,' she carried on blithely, 'I've been wondering if you are not pregnant already. I've noticed that you've been a bit off colour lately.'

'I'm definitely not pregnant,' Megan told her. 'But I do think I've picked up some stomach bug. I'll visit Dr Crozier if I don't feel better soon.'

'I'll get Bertha to make you up one of her herbal tonics,' said Lavinia.

The visit from Captain Eugene Morgan of HMS *Mason* came on 14 June, the same day as the first of Hitler's new weapons were unleashed on London and the south coast. The weapons came streaming in from their German launch pads at low altitude, wreaking death and destruction wherever they landed.

Captain Morgan arrived in an official car just as the residents of

East End heard the explosions in Southampton. Megan was in the garden and could see puffs of black smoke rising in the sky from Southampton.

The captain walked round from the front of the house and found Megan in the vegetable garden, where she was picking some early broad beans. 'Those are Hitler's new V1 rockets,' he said, nodding in the direction of Southampton. 'They are coming in under the radar, so there's no warning.'

'How awful for the poor people over there,' said Megan. She clutched the broad-bean trug to her chest. His was not a social visit. She knew that.

His gaze was steady and gentle. 'Captain Jim Byrne has been reported as missing in action,' he said simply.

She grasped at the lifeline that was inferred. 'Then that means that there is a chance that he is . . .'

His gaze remained steady, but he didn't smile. 'A chance, but a very small one. As an engineer he went in with the first wave at Omaha. He was building the Mulberry harbour, which he helped design. The casualties were very high on the beach in the first few hours. We've lost over forty thousand men. Not many who landed that day will be coming back.'

I mustn't cry, thought Megan. *Not in front of this man with the kind and weary eyes. Not in front of anyone, because no one must ever know what is in my heart. I mustn't cry. I mustn't.* She swallowed hard, and clasped the trug of beans tightly to her chest like a life raft. 'Thank you for telling me,' she managed to say at last. 'I'm very grateful.'

He reached and briefly touched her hand. 'I'm sorry.' Then he turned to go. 'By the way, officially I've come to tell you that the dower house will be returned to you within the next month. I'm sure Lady Lavinia will be pleased.'

Megan nodded, beyond speech now, and watched as he made his way past the beans and the sweet peas towards the front of the house. Then she turned and watched the black smoke pouring into the sky from the burning buildings in Southampton. It reminded her that she was not alone in her grief. Many more would be weeping tonight.

After supper she took the photo of Jim from the back of her drawer in the office, saddled up Major and rode to their secret place in the forest. Once there she let him roam loose. The old horse looked puzzled to be without his stable mate, but he went to his special spot and grazed on fresh summer grass.

Megan sat down in the hollow and got out the blurred photograph. 'Jim,' she whispered, and then the tears she'd been holding back all day finally came. When at last she climbed back on Major she felt drained. Not a single tear was left. Not one. She felt as if she had wept for the whole world.

CHAPTER TWELVE

The long summer of 1944

Henry was finding life easier as he gradually learned to navigate his way round the house from the gold room, through the hall, which he always recognized when he bumped into the gasmasks hanging on the stand, and into the kitchen, one of his favourite places. He'd loved it there as a child and he still loved sitting listening to Bertha bustling about, peeling, chopping and cooking. He even helped Dottie shell the peas, and tried peeling potatoes, but Bertha took the knife away. 'Too dangerous,' she said.

He was becoming more independent every day, finding his way to the stables and the gun cupboard to clean the shotguns which were kept there. Molly and Pat were happy to let him do that. They liked shooting rabbits which during the summer were plentiful and eating everything in sight if they got the chance. So they did the shooting, and Henry spent happy hours cleaning and oiling the guns, which made him feel useful.

George was not happy. 'I don't like seeing Mr Henry with the guns, not now that he can't see,' he grumbled to Molly. 'He could have an accident.'

Molly dismissed his fears. 'Of course he won't. We never leave the cartridges nearby. They are carefully put away in the box on the top shelf.'

But although Henry was feeling happier he was keenly aware of Megan's melancholy. Of course he knew why. He wondered how many other people knew about her love affair with Jim. In the beginning he'd wondered whether she would ask for a divorce at the end of the war. But now that Jim was missing he hoped that she would stay with him. She belonged at Folly House, always had done; besides now she would have nowhere else to go.

The thought of her loving another man aroused no feelings of jealousy. He felt that he should feel something, but emotionally he was barren. Not totally though, as he felt sorrow for them that their love should have been abruptly severed by the war. The only love there had been in his life since he returned to Folly House had been for Rosie. Yes, with Rosie there had been real affection; now he missed her childish chatter, her unrestrained, loving nature. Perhaps if she had been able to stay he might have learned more about loving. But according to Megan and Lavinia there was no chance of her coming back to Folly House, so like everyone he had to accept that she had disappeared from their lives for ever, and with her his chance of the ice in his heart ever thawing.

But something else troubled Henry. He knew he had to steel his nerves and tell Adam that he did not, and never had, loved him in the way he wanted. He shrank away from it; it seemed strange that Adam had appeared to have forgotten that terrible quarrel they'd had in London. How could he? Adam hadn't lost his memory, but now he behaved as if Henry had never rejected him, continually touching him, talking to him in such loving terms that Henry felt embarrassed and repulsed. In fact Adam's whole demeanour made his scalp crawl. He had to do something to stop it.

He knew now that he'd been a fool not to see what had been staring him in the face all those years before. He should have known Adam was homosexual. Why had he never guessed? The answer was because he didn't want to. He'd been enthralled by the glamorous life Adam lived with his bohemian, theatrical friends. They cast a spell over Henry, bound as he was by science and the often mundane nature of hospital life. The pleasure Adam took in his appearance, his vanity, had been a clue. But there had always been women. Adam slept with many women, but never the same one twice. Now Henry realized it had all been a façade, put up to give an illusion of a normal, red-blooded man. The type of man Adam played so success-fully in theatre and films.

And what about himself? Now Henry was forced to confront the uncomfortable truth of his own character. Why did he have no great passion for anyone? Not even Megan. He'd thought he had loved her, but it was a pallid, restrained affection. Only medicine, his skill at surgery and research really fired his senses. That had been his reason for living. Now that had gone. Destroyed that day on the beach at Dunkirk.

But the most pressing problem now was that he had to grasp the nettle and tell Adam bluntly that there was no hope of any form of physical love between them. He would stop the visits to The Priory now and say that maybe they might build a different friendship in the years to come. He couldn't cut Adam off completely, that would be too cruel. Adam was a dying man although he didn't know it, and Henry knew he couldn't destroy all his hopes. Time would do that.

So Henry steeled himself to tell Adam on the next visit. But when Megan took him, any conversation that day was out of the question. Adam was burning with a fever and hallucinating.

On the way back that day Henry said to Megan, 'You never liked him, did you?'

'I didn't actually dislike him,' Megan said after a moment's silence. Henry could almost hear Megan thinking carefully. Then she said, 'Adam has always been very fond of you, I know that.'

There was something in her tone of voice that made him suspect that she knew more than she was letting on. But surely not. She'd never been in London in their company. She had only ever seen Adam when he been at Folly House, assiduously playing the country gentleman, enjoying himself buttering up Lavinia and the Jones family. Now he thought about it Henry realized that Adam had always more or less ignored Megan.

She said nothing more, so Henry said, 'Yes, I suppose he was.'

'Not was. Still is,' said Megan.

Her reply left Henry feeling certain that she knew more than she was saying.

Since the family quarrel about the money Gerald had stayed away from Folly House. No one bothered to enquire about him, or Violet.

'Good riddance, that's what I says,' Bertha was heard to comment. 'That Gerald never was no good.'

Lavinia had tutted when she overheard but said nothing. How could she, when she agreed with every word? Although she did say that she thought Bertha was becoming a little too familiar.

But Megan pointed out that, for good or ill, they had absorbed the Jones family into their lives; they were involved in the Lockwood family fortunes – or lack of them. Henry had asked them and they'd agreed to take a cut in pay to help out since the loss of his investments. So Megan felt Lavinia couldn't start pulling rank on them now and said so, but quickly changed the subject when Lavinia became annoyed. It was no use, Lavinia was the older generation, and just didn't understand how much things were changing. Instead she asked Lavinia whether they ought to invite Violet to Folly House. Violet was working now. She'd volunteered, apparently to Gerald's fury, to do war work in one of the factories in Southampton.

Gerald had told Henry about it. 'Can't understand the stupid woman,' he'd said. 'How can she work alongside the likes of Mrs Fox on the assembly line? She's in a different class.'

Henry told Megan that he'd pointed out that the war demanded sacrifices from all of them; this made Megan feel guilty as she wasn't sacrificing anything. Unless you counted losing people, she thought miserably. She'd lost Rosie and Jim, and that was a sacrifice.

Apparently Violet was welding aircraft parts. 'She gets up at 4.30 a.m., cycles into Salisbury, and then gets a lorry which takes girls from the surrounding villages into Southampton at 5.30 in the morning.' Lavinia delivered this information in shocked tones to Megan.

'I'd hate to get up so early every morning,' Megan replied. In fact, if Megan were honest she was finding it difficult to get up at all in the morning. Despite religiously taking the tonic Bertha had made for her and drinking mint tea every night, she was feeling more and more unwell, although she tried to ignore it.

But she did telephone Violet and ask her to come over to Folly house on one of her days off. Violet accepted the invitation with an eagerness that surprised Megan.

'It will be so nice to talk to another woman,' she said.

'But you are with women every day of the week,' said Megan.

'Yes, but I can't talk to them,' Violet replied. 'They wouldn't understand.'

It was arranged for Violet to visit the following Saturday, but she arrived unexpectedly on the Friday night, covered in bruises and in an agitated state. That night there had been a fierce summer storm, and Violet had cycled the twenty miles from Brinkley Hall through thunder and lightning, as well as torrential rain without any kind of protection.

Megan and Lavinia were sitting in the gold room, watching the pyrotechnics of the storm over the sea when the door burst open and Bertha came in, practically carrying a sopping wet, exhausted Violet.

'My God!' Lavinia rushed across to her. 'Whatever has happened? Has there been an accident?'

'No accident,' said Bertha grimly. 'Not to my mind anyway.' She looked behind her. 'Dottie, have you got that blanket I told you to get?'

Dottie darted forward with a thick tartan blanket and Bertha wrapped it around a shivering Violet, while Megan pulled forward one of the big armchairs towards the fireplace. 'I know it's summer, Bertha,' she said, 'but I think we need a fire in here. It's suddenly very chilly.'

George came in with some kindling and soon there was a roaring fire in the grate. Lavinia got some warm bath-towels from the airing cupboard and together they rubbed and dried Violet, stripping her of her soaking clothes, and wrapping her in one of Megan's warm winter dressing-gowns.

Henry arrived in the midst of it all. To everyone's astonishment he took charge. He felt Violet's pulse and put his hand on her head. 'Her heart is racing,' he said, 'but she hasn't got a temperature, quite the reverse, she's chilled to the bone. Bertha, please get a large glass of brandy. The sooner she has a sip of that the sooner she'll stop shivering.'

The telephone rang. Violet sat up like a startled rabbit. 'If that's Gerald,' she whispered, 'please don't tell him I'm here.' She reached

LEAVES BEFORE THE STORM

out and grabbed Henry's hand. 'Please don't tell him I'm here,' she repeated.

Henry took the call. 'No, she's not here, Gerald,' his voice was firm and calm. 'Yes, I'll certainly call you if she arrives here. Yes. Yes, it's an awful storm, isn't it. Goodnight.' After the call he turned towards Megan. 'You'd better take her upstairs just in case Gerald comes. I don't think he will, but we'd better not take any chances.'

Bertha passed the brandy to Henry, who placed it carefully in Violet's trembling hands. 'I'll just go and tell Dottie and George that they haven't seen Violet,' she said. Then she nodded towards Violet, who was sipping the brandy, 'Don't you worry about nothing. I'll get George to hide the bicycle and we'll all keep mum for as long as necessary.'

Megan and Lavinia hurried a still trembling Violet upstairs, where she had a hot bath before being tucked up in Rosie's old bed. Megan sat on the side of the bed. 'Do you want to talk now?' she asked.

'I don't know where to start,' whispered Violet.

'Start at the beginning,' said Lavinia, settling herself in the Lloyd Loom chair on the other side of the bed. 'It's usually the best place.'

'Gerald raped me.'

Lavinia gasped. 'How can you say that? He's your husband. A husband can't rape his wife.'

'What else do you call violent sex when you don't want it?' replied Violet.

There was silence. Megan thought back to her wedding night. Suddenly it leapt into her mind, vivid and frightening. Rape? No – she had responded. But would he have stopped if she had said no? Somehow she didn't think so. The memory was humiliating and she shivered.

Then she concentrated on Violet. Lavinia was speaking. Her tone was gentle. 'Start at the beginning, Violet,' she said, 'and tell us how all this came about.'

The unhappy saga of Violet's marriage was revealed in Rosie's cosy, pink, little girl's bedroom, an innocent place at odds with the story. It was a story of violence from the very beginning. The reason for Violet's absences from family gatherings in the early days was because she often couldn't hide the bruises on her face, but when Gerald realized this he hit her where the bruises wouldn't show. She showed them her back, which was scarred from beating with a leather belt. Gerald, it seemed, like to beat Violet into submission and then force her to have sex.

'But why have you only run away from him now?' demanded Megan. 'Why didn't you leave him in the beginning?'

'I didn't think anyone would believe me. He was so handsome and charming to everyone else. Besides I tried to please him. I thought that one day he would love me, not just love my money. But this evening we had a quarrel. About money again. He wanted me to give him control over my private funds, and I said no. That was my mistake. Then, when he began to beat me, I could see that he really hated me. I let him have the sex he wanted and then, when he relaxed his hold on me, I pushed him away and got up and ran. I didn't have time to take one of the cars, and anyway I didn't know whether they had petrol or not; he only puts in one gallon at a time. So I took my bicycle and cycled across the fields so that he couldn't follow me in the car.' She paused for breath and lay her head back on the pillows in exhaustion, then said in a small, tight voice, 'If you make me go back to him I shall kill myself.'

Megan put her arms around her. 'No question of that,' she said firmly. 'You can stay here for the time being.' Violet started up in agitation. 'Don't worry. We'll hide you, Gerald will never know. But we will find you a place to stay that's really safe. I think I know of a place.' The Priory Hospital was running through her mind as a possibility. It was a hospital, the matron was a no-nonsense woman who, Megan sensed, might be sympathetic to Violet's cause. If she would take Violet in until something else was sorted out, it would be ideal. She took Violet's hands in hers. 'Don't worry. Your life with Gerald has finished. You need never see him again, except in court when you get a divorce.'

'Do you think I'll get a divorce? Gerald will say I'm lying.'

'We shall bear witness to your injuries,' said Megan. 'Won't we, Lavinia?'

'Yes, I suppose so.' There was a slight reluctance in Lavinia's voice.

Megan ignored the reluctance. Lavinia was another generation. Divorce never happened in her circles, but in Megan's opinion divorce was the only answer for Violet. However, keeping Gerald away until that happened was another matter altogether. The sooner she spoke to the matron at The Priory the better. It was the only idea she had, and she hoped it would work. But she decided to keep the scheme to herself. If Henry and Lavinia didn't know about it, Gerald couldn't bully them into revealing Violet's whereabouts.

Of course, Gerald did come several days later to Folly House, but by that time Violet had left. The matron, Mrs Curry, was sympathetic and willing to help, and confessed to Megan that she herself had escaped into nursing from a violent marriage in Ireland. Megan, aided by George, smuggled Violet out of the house and took her to The Priory. Only George, Megan and Mrs Curry knew of her whereabouts.

'She can help out on the wards,' said Mrs Curry. 'We don't have many visitors, but when we do she can keep out of the way.'

Megan was in her office, ordering in supplies for the winter wheat. Another month gone, the days followed on relentlessly one after another. Still no word of Jim. Pausing, she laid down her pen. He was so vivid in her mind's eye, his luminous dark eyes, the lock of hair which always fell across his brow, his long sensitive fingers, and the music. She could hear the music. Oh, where was he? What was he doing in this hateful war? Was he still alive? Tears stung her eyes, to be blinked away. Weeping achieved nothing. He was alive. She had to believe that.

Picking up the pen once more she concentrated on her diary, which she used to note delivery dates from the various suppliers. It was then that she noticed the little red tick in the corner of the calendar at the beginning of the month. She always marked the day her period was due with a red tick. She looked again and her heart lurched. Three and a half weeks ago and still no period. Nothing. Suddenly she knew why she had been feeling 'off colour' as Lavinia put it. *I'm pregnant. Pregnant. Pregnant with Jim's child. But Jim has gone and I'm married to Henry.* Yet again she was carrying another man's child, not that of her husband.

Clasping her head in her hands, she slumped across the desk and began to weep. There was no way she could possible get rid of the baby. It was part of Jim, perhaps the only part she'd ever have. But what about Henry? Oh God, what a mess!

There was a tap on the door. 'Go away,' she shouted. 'Go away.' Then, realizing she couldn't behave like that, she jumped up and wrenched the door open, only to stare into the face of a very startled policeman.

Blowing her nose vigorously and muttering, 'A cold I think. In the middle of complicated maths. Sorry I shouted,' she looked at the policeman.

The policeman was too polite to comment and stood hesitantly in the doorway. 'May I come in? Mrs Jones, the cook, said I'd find you here.'

'Yes,' she said, hoping that he wouldn't notice she'd been crying.

'Might be hay fever,' he said helpfully.

'Yes.' Megan composed herself and sat back down at her desk. 'Now what can I do for you, Sergeant. . .?'

'I'm PC Hawkins,' he said, 'and it's not so much as what you can do for me as what you can do for a certain Miss Rosie Barnes.'

Megan's head snapped up. 'What's wrong? Where is Rosie?' She stood up. 'I shall go to London.'

PC Hawkins put up a restraining hand. 'No need, Mrs Lockwood. I have the said Miss Rosie Barnes outside in the police car. She insisted she must come, she said—'

Megan didn't wait to hear any more. Roughly pushing past PC Hawkins she ran from the office, through the hall and outside to where the police car stood on the drive. There was no need for words. She just opened her arms and Rosie tumbled out of the car and fell into them.

'Can I stay?' she cried. 'Say I can stay.'

'Of course you can stay. Of course you can.' Then they both burst into tears while a perplexed PC Hawkins stood by, looking embarrassed and pleased at the same time.

*

Rosie came back to Folly House. She was going to stay for good. Henry even suggested to Megan that they should adopt her, so that she could officially become their daughter. The excitement of Rosie's return even put the worry of her pregnancy to the back of Megan's mind. Her condition didn't show, so she made up her mind to stay as slim as possible until she had decided what to do.

It did cross her mind that she should try and seduce Henry into making love to her, and then she could pass the baby off as his. The more she thought of that possibility the more she thought it was the easiest thing to do. Firmly ignoring her conscience she made up her mind to do it. But every night she found a reason to put it off, and Henry himself never showed any sign of wanting to resume his marital rights.

The event of Rosie Barnes's returning to Folly House was the talk of the village. The V1 rockets, or 'doodlebugs' as everyone called them, had increased in frequency over southern England. Some had even fallen in the grounds of Folly House, in the forest. One had landed smack on Rosie's house in Hackney. It was in the afternoon, when Rosie was at school, but her mother and younger brother were both at home and were killed outright. That day Rosie was collected from school by the social authorities and, as she had no other living relatives, she was put in a temporary children's home in Shoreditch. She had run away. Not once, but three times, and each time she had made her way to the railway station at Marylebone and tried to find a train to Stibbington. Each time she was picked up, and eventually someone thought to ask her why she was trying to get to Stibbington, the trains for which left London from Waterloo, not Marylebone. She told them about Folly House, where she'd been evacuated, and about Mrs Megan Lockwood, who said she could come back at any time. So the police arranged for her to be brought to Folly House and for the said Mrs Lockwood to be asked if she would have her.

Once Megan said yes, the arrangements were made very quickly. There were plenty of orphan children looking for homes, and the authorities were glad to get her off their hands. She went back to the primary school in East End village, and slotted in as if she had never been away.

*

It seemed to Henry that Rosie had a key. A magic key which unlocked his heart. Although he told himself it was a ridiculous notion, something *was* happening to him. He was aware of a warmth which suddenly made life worth living and aware of how sterile his life had been before. But the affection he felt for almost everyone, even Albert Noakes, who used to come up to the stables and do odd carpentry jobs, did not extend to Adam. He still hadn't told Adam that his affection was unwelcome; instead he was gradually easing himself away and hoping that Adam would get the message. But it didn't worry him so much now. He had other things to think of.

He got George to drive him into Southampton to see the solicitors, Paris, Smith & Wendell. This was a family firm who'd acted for the Lockwood family for years. Henry asked them to put in motion the necessary work for adopting Rosie. He didn't mention it to Megan. He wanted it to be a surprise.

But every now and then a niggling, uncomfortable thought reminded him that they could have a child of their own if only he could bring himself to sleep with her. But that was something he couldn't do. He did not love Megan in a physical way. *I should never have married her,* he told himself, but it was too late. He had married her because he needed a chatelaine for Folly House and she had married him because she loved the house. Yes, loved the house, not him. He'd always known that, but had thought they could make a reasonable life together. She had fulfilled her duties as a wife, and would no doubt continue to do so if he made a move, even though she had fallen in love with Jim Byrne. He didn't worry about Jim now. There'd been no word. He must have died along with the thousands of others on the beaches of Normandy.

On Sundays when the family filed off to church to listen to one of Marcus's increasingly rambling sermons, Henry prayed that he'd be able to find a way to live with Megan as a real husband. Not one who lay beside her every night like a block of stone.

CHAPTER THIRTEEN

Autumn 1944

On 8 September 1944 another new and terrible weapon rained down on London. The newspapers said it was a V2 rocket and, unlike the doodlebug there was no warning, no stopping of an engine; instead they fell vertically from a height of fifty miles at faster than the speed of sound and when they exploded the shock waves could be felt for miles.

It cast a pall of gloom over the whole country, including everyone at Folly House. 'Just when we thought things were going our way,' observed Lavinia.

'It *is* going our way,' said Marcus, trying to cheer everyone. 'This is just a little hiccup.'

'Bit more than a hiccup if one lands on you,' muttered Arthur.

But Megan was worrying about her pregnancy. Looking at herself in the mirror she was only too aware of the curve of her stomach and the fullness of her breasts. She chose her clothes carefully, but knew she would have to say something soon.

Sometimes Megan caught her father looking at her and wondered if he had guessed. That was another worry: his health. He was looking very old lately, although he hardly drank now. Not that they had much to drink, the cocktail cabinet was empty these days. Even Arthur grumbled about it sometimes. 'When Jim was around he could usually get his hands on a bottle of bourbon or Jack Daniels,' he said.

'Well, he's not around,' replied Megan sharply. 'So it's no use wishing.'

It was then that she was sure her father knew, for he reached out and clasped her hand as she was passing. 'I pray for him every day,' he said softly, 'and I pray for you too, to give you strength to make the right decision.'

Megan snatched her hand away. 'God isn't listening,' she said harshly, 'if he was he would finish this hateful war.'

Immediately she felt guilty for snapping at her father. The war wasn't his fault, neither was it his fault that she'd fallen in love with Jim, and it was nobody's fault but her own that she was expecting a child.

But mostly there was precious little time to think. Rosie slotted back into their lives as if she had never been away, worked hard at school and did her homework in front of an admiring Dottie when she was at Folly House. Megan was told there was a good chance that she would win a free scholarship to Brockenhurst Grammar School.

Dottie didn't go to school any more as she was too old now, but she often walked with Rosie to the village school, where she stood watching the playground games wistfully. She knew she couldn't go because Bertha had told her so, but she didn't really understand why.

One day she asked Rosie if she missed her mother. She thought she would miss Bertha, even though she never hugged her. Dottie longed for hugs, but Bertha was very sparing with any show of affection.

But Rosie, skipping alongside Dottie, laughed. 'No I don't miss her at all.'

Then she stopped and looked solemnly at Dottie. 'But I pray for her soul every day. Marcus says I must do that, so I do. And I pray for my brother Bertie. I know they're all right now because they are in heaven. Oh look, there's Edie Lee, I must catch her.' Darting ahead she caught up with Edie. They exchanged something from their satchels, then Rosie came galloping back. 'Look,' she said, holding out her hand. 'A blood alley.' She showed the white marble streaked with red. 'She promised to give it to me if I gave her two of my blue ones. Just you wait until I show Henry.'

Dottie was scornful. 'How can you show him? He's blind.'

'He'll be interested all the same,' said Rosie. 'He's interested in everything I do.'

This was true. He *was* interested in everything she did and was spoiling her, according to Lavinia. But Megan didn't mind. He laughed sometimes these days and was following the events of the war on the radio with keen interest. She found herself relaxing in his company, sometimes to the extent that she was tempted to tell him about the baby. He didn't visit Adam much these days, but she didn't ask why.

It became a habit for the family to gather in the gold room in the evening and listen to the news on the radio. The Allies were progressing through Europe, retaking cities and even whole countries at what seemed like breakneck speed.

'Surely the war will be over soon,' said Lavinia.

'Yes, and then perhaps we'll see Jim again before he goes back to the States,' said Arthur. Sitting at the piano he began to play fragments of Debussy, one of Jim's favourite composers.

If he doesn't stop playing that I'll weep, thought Megan. Where was Jim? Was he still alive? But if he was why hadn't he got in touch? Did 'missing' really mean dead?

'Play *The Girl with the Flaxen Hair*,' said Henry. 'I always loved Jim playing that.'

Megan left the room, unable to bear it any longer. She just had to tell someone about the baby. Someone else would have to tell her what to do, because she was incapable of logical thought. All she could think about was the chaos and confusion she would create, the hurt for Henry, the misery for everyone.

In the end it was Violet whom she chose to tell. Violet had settled down at The Priory and was a changed woman. Gerald seemed to have given up looking for her and was spending a lot of time in London with friends in the armaments business. Always thinking about money, he was now lobbying politicians who he thought would be useful after the war. When he was away Violet came and walked along the saltings, which led away from Folly House and into the estuary of the river Stib. Megan joined her when she could, always a little nervous in case Gerald should turn up. But he never did.

They walked on a sunny day at the end of September, and sat on a breakwater, throwing pebbles into the sea. 'I love nursing,' said Violet. 'But I'm not a proper nurse. I wish I was, then I could be nursing in Belgium. They need help there at the moment.'

They were both silent for a moment, thinking of the bad news of the last few days. An audacious airborne operation to capture bridges on the lower Rhine at Arnhem had gone disastrously wrong as, due to bad weather, reinforcements couldn't be flown in to help the British paratroopers already there. Of the original 10,000 men only 2,400 had survived.

It puts my problems into perspective, thought Megan. 'Do you think you could nurse on the front line?' she asked Violet. 'It must be awful.'

'Yes, I know I could. I don't know why I never thought of nursing as a career before. I should have done. But I obeyed my guardians, who said it was my duty to marry and provide Brinkley Hall with heirs.' She laughed, 'Huh!' and threw a flat pebble viciously across the water in a series of skips. 'But do you know what?' She turned back to Megan. 'Once married to Gerald I knew I didn't want his child. There will be no heirs. I don't think I shall ever have a baby.'

Megan could keep the secret no longer. 'I'm having a baby.'

Violet clapped her hands. 'But that's wonderful. Henry must be pleased.'

'Henry doesn't know, because it's not his baby.' Megan tried to keep control, but failed and began to weep. 'It's Jim's baby. You remember him. The American, Jim Byrne. But he's posted missing now, so he'll never know. And I can't bear to get rid of it, and I can't tell Henry because it's so unfair to him and, oh God, everything is such a mess!' Fumbling in the pocket of her jodhpurs Megan searched unsuccessfully for a handkerchief. Silently Violet handed her one. Megan took it and mopped her face.

There was a long silence, then Violet said slowly, 'Couldn't you just keep quiet and let Henry think he's the father. No one would ever know.'

'Henry would know. We haven't slept together since he came back.'

Sitting in the late afternoon sunlight, their feet in the warm waters of the Solent, they talked around the subject for fifteen minutes, but came to no conclusion. Megan didn't see how she could ever come to any answer other than to tell Henry and face the consequences. Violet persuaded her to leave it for the time being. It was hardly a satisfactory conclusion but neither of them could think of anything else. They walked slowly back to the house.

'I'll give you a lift back to The Priory,' said Megan. 'It's dark early this evening, I think there may be a storm.'

The sky, which had been clear all day, was suddenly filling with ominous dark rain clouds, and as they crossed the lawn towards the stable yard where Megan's car was kept there was a rumble of thunder.

Violet stopped. 'Was that a car I heard?' she whispered. 'Do you think Gerald. . . ?'

'Of course not. It was thunder.' But all the same Megan hurried in front of Violet, arriving in the yard just in time to see Gerald's large Bentley drawing to a smooth halt. For a moment she stood stock still; then, realizing Violet hadn't yet appeared she turned around and ran back. Somehow she had to get Violet away.

But it was too late. Gerald followed her and they both reached the corner of the house at the same time. Megan saw the sheer terror on Violet's face as she saw Gerald. Then she turned back and began to run towards the sea and the Folly.

Megan ran too, and so did Gerald, but his long legs overtook her. Violet reached the Folly first, and to Megan's horror began to climb the crumbling stone steps which led to the tower at the furthest end of the Folly. By the time she reached the Folly Violet was out of sight, and Gerald was halfway up the steps.

Megan stumbled up behind him trying to avoid the loose stones and pieces of rock showering down, dislodged by Gerald. On reaching the top she could see Violet cowering on a small stone ledge on the far side of the tower where the wall had crumbled away.

'Violet, come down. It's dangerous,' she called.

Gerald laughed. 'Not as dangerous as me, though.'

Somehow Megan managed to push herself in between Gerald

and Violet. 'Don't think you can come here and bully your wife,' she shouted. 'Leave her alone.'

'She's my wife. My property.' He sneered. 'If I want to bully her, I will.' Grabbing Megan he stepped closer to Violet, who shrank further back against the fragile remains of the ancient wall.

'If you touch me, I'll jump,' she screamed.

Gerald moved and Megan put out her arms to stop him, but again he pushed her roughly aside and moved near to Violet. Megan saw the utter panic in Violet's eyes as she screamed, and at that moment Megan flung herself forward, trying to push Gerald out of the way as Violet stepped sideways. It all happened so fast. Violet's scream, a mêlée of bodies pushing and shoving, then Gerald disappeared over the edge. But he didn't fall all the way. He grasped the top of the wall, and Megan saw that he'd got a toehold as well and was intent on climbing back up. She looked at his fingers holding the rough stone on top of the wall, and started to push at it, trying to dislodge him. At the same time Violet picked up a large piece of flint and still screaming dashed it down on Gerald's fingers. Without a sound he let go and fell the 150 feet down on to the enormous piece of granite at the bottom of the wall. The same granite stone that had killed his ancestor 200 years before.

In one single movement Violet and Megan leaned over and peered down, to see Gerald lying spreadeagled on the stone. His head was twisted so that he was looking straight up at them, his eyes wide open. It began to rain, large, heavy drops, and a brilliant arrow of lightning cracked across the waters of the Solent, followed by a roll of thunder.

At first Violet wanted to confess that she had hit him with the flint because he was going to hit her and that she had wanted him dead.

But Megan calmed her down and persuaded Violet to say that the three of them had climbed the tower to watch the storm that was building up across the Solent.

'We can say the flash of lightning startled Gerald, who was standing on the edge; he jumped, lost his footing and fell. It was a terrible accident.'

'I'm not sure I'm a very good liar,' said Violet, shivering. 'I made him fall.'

'He would have fallen anyway, whether you'd hit him or not,' said Megan firmly. 'I'll tell the story. You just say "yes" every now and then.' Megan took a trembling Violet into the house, found Henry and told him their story. Then he phoned the police.

Two police officers from Southampton arrived. They were feeling harassed and tired, as they'd been on duty in the docks, which were busy ferrying in wounded men from France. Their note-taking was perfunctory, and after looking at the body they gave permission for it to be moved by the undertakers. Bertha hurried Dottie and Rosie out of the way to Silas Moon's farmhouse on the pretext of borrowing more Kilner jars for plum bottling.

Henry sat with Megan and Violet while they answered questions, and held Violet's hand, as she was still trembling and weeping.

'Of course, there will have to be an inquest,' said the sergeant when the two officers finished their questions, 'but it will be an open-and-shut case of accidental death. A terrible family tragedy.'

'When will we be able to arrange the funeral?' asked Henry, who had now taken complete charge.

'Set a date for the day after the coroner's inquest, sir,' said the sergeant. 'We'll send in the report tomorrow, so the inquest should be within a week. As soon as you know that date you can make arrangements.'

A little later Henry walked with the policemen to the front of Folly House. 'A bad business this, sir,' said the sergeant, shaking Henry's hand. 'Give our condolences to the rest of the family.'

Later Violet was dispatched back to The Priory, which was where she wanted to go. She said she would feel more peaceful there and would continue nursing, at least for the time being. Megan hoped that she wouldn't break down and tell the matron the truth about smashing the flint down on Gerald's hands. But by now, she wasn't really certain what *was* the real truth. It was blurred in her mind. Had she pushed Gerald? Or was it Violet? Whatever it was, she was certain that no one mourned the passing of Gerald.

That evening, after a very late supper, she had to go through the whole story again for the benefit of Marcus, Lavinia and Arthur.

'May his soul rest in peace,' said Marcus piously when she had finished.

'One thing is certain, we shall certainly have a little more peace now,' said Lavinia crisply. 'I know it sounds harsh, but I can't bring myself to mourn his passing. He was always a problem rumbling away in the background, even when he was a boy.'

Henry said nothing, but much later that night, when they were together in their bedroom, he said to Megan, 'Now, perhaps you will tell me what really happened up there on the tower.'

Megan made a split-second decision and told him the truth, or at least, most of it. How Gerald had pursued a terrified Violet across the lawn and up into the tower, how she herself had climbed up and tried to put herself between Gerald and Violet. And then somehow, when all three of them were clambering and struggling over the broken stones of the wall, Gerald stepped too far and had suddenly fallen. She left out the part about Gerald clinging to the top of the wall and Violet smashing the stone down on his hands.

'It all happened so quickly,' she said. 'I'm not really sure whether he just overbalanced, or one of us did push him. There was no sound; he just disappeared from the edge and landed on the granite rock below.'

'I see,' said Henry slowly. 'Then the only part which isn't true is the fact that you didn't go up to the tower to admire the view?'

'Yes,' said Megan. 'I lied because I didn't want the truth about Violet and Gerald's violent marriage dragged through the mud by the press.' She looked across to Henry, who was lying on the bed in his pyjamas. He was smiling. 'You're not angry?'

'Not at all, you acted like a true Lockwood. Protect the family name first.' He searched in his bedside locker, found a cigarette and lit it. 'Not that I'm sure that's always a good thing. Sometimes we overrate the wretched family name.'

Megan didn't reply. She climbed into bed and Henry put an arm around her in a friendly embrace. She lay back with her head on his shoulder and wondered whether this was a good time to tell him about the coming baby. Then she dismissed the idea. He'd had enough

LEAVES BEFORE THE STORM

shocks for one day. 'I wonder what Violet will do now,' she said.

'Brinkley Hall would be a hell of a place to live in alone, and now that most of the army have left I understand it's going to be turned temporarily into a civilian hospital,' said Henry. 'London hospitals haven't got the beds, since they've been bombed, and there are plenty of patients to be cared for. Brinkley Hall will make a good hospital; they are even going to start training nurses there.'

Henry sounded almost like the man she had married. Informed and interested. 'How do you know all this?' asked Megan.

'I've been talking on the telephone to an ex-colleague of mine. Senior surgeon at St Thomas's, and he's leaving London to set up a new surgical unit here. He's asked me if I'd like to be involved in the planning meetings.'

'But how. . . ?' The words came out before she could stop them.

'I know, how will I be of use? Well, I'm working hard at getting my Braille up to speed, and he's sending me a parcel of books on hospital administration, all in Braille. The Government has put aside a considerable sum of money, so it should be well-financed for a good many years.'

'But what about Violet? Where will she live when she leaves The Priory? She'll have no home.'

'She can stay here,' said Henry. 'Lavinia will be moving back to Dowager Cottage as soon as we can get it painted.'

'But I haven't made arrangements yet to have it done.'

'I have.' Henry stubbed out his cigarette and gave Megan a squeeze before pulling up the covers on his side of the bed. 'I got Albert Noakes to go round there to have a look. He's quite handy with the paintbrush, so George tells me, so he's going to do it and tidy up the garden as well. He's starting next week.'

'Oh,' said Megan. There seemed to be nothing else to say, as Henry had arranged it all. He was gradually becoming more like his old self and suddenly Megan was not sure she liked it. Would he want to begin organizing the house and gardens and the farm soon? Megan enjoyed her work and had got used to running things her way.

But more than that, if she were honest, was that she'd been thinking that an uninvolved Henry would perhaps accept her pregnancy without making a fuss and would accept the baby into the family. Now she was not so sure.

Sliding down into her side of the bed she pulled up the bedclothes and closed her eyes. But long after Henry was sleeping peacefully she lay awake, worrying about the future.

CHAPTER FOURTEEN

Autumn 1944

Gerald's funeral took place on a misty morning at the end of September. The Indian summer had disappeared and now the air smelled of bonfire smoke, wet autumn leaves, and mushrooms which were sprouting everywhere. Henry, Megan and Violet followed the hearse in one car and Lavinia and Rosie came behind in another. The Jones family piled into their trap as usual, and the Moons and the land girls walked the short distance to the church of St Nicholas.

The Moons were at the lichgate when Megan and Henry arrived. They stood back respectfully, Silas touching his cap before removing it for entry into the church. Mrs Moon and Molly and Pat all looked rather strange, thought Megan, wearing dark hats which had quite obviously been retrieved from the back of a cupboard for the occasion.

'Good thing we got the harvest in,' Silas remarked as Megan passed him. 'I'm thinking this wet weather is settled for a good few days.'

Megan nodded. Like Silas, she'd been thinking along those lines. In fact, the harvest had occupied her thoughts most of the time the last few days; there'd been a rush to get everything in and stored before the weather broke completely. The scudding clouds now threatened more bad weather with a vengeance. It seemed appropriate to be burying Gerald on a dark day that signified the end of things; she wondered how many people were sorry to see him go. As for herself, she was still confused. When they'd been young he'd been exciting and good fun, although there was always an underlying current of darkness which she hadn't understood. Later he'd changed, becoming obsessed with money and power, and then she'd been afraid. There was no doubt; life without Gerald would be simpler.

'The church is almost full,' whispered Violet. 'Maybe he was better liked than we knew?'

Henry gave a wry smile. 'No, it's tradition dating back to the days when the Lockwoods and Brinkley Hall provided most of the work around here. Of course, we don't now, but old habits die hard.'

'My two old gamekeepers are here,' said Violet. 'But that's all the staff I have now. The army has still got responsibility for most of the estate, and the house is being staffed by the new hospital. I shall have a private flat there, but I won't need anyone to help me. There won't be any need for staff again.'

Yes, everything is different and it will never be the same again, thought Megan. Lavinia was wrong when she thought life after the war would pick up where it had left off. Too many people had seen too many changes, the tugging-the-forelock mentality of yesterday had gone for ever. People wanted to do things for themselves, not slave for other people. And as for herself, she just couldn't imagine living the life she had once wanted: a genteel countrywoman with nothing to do but organize a few charity events. She was a farmer now; that was what she liked doing and she'd proved herself good at it. Just as well she had, she thought ruefully, they needed the income. Gerald had made sure of that when he'd embezzled Henry's last remaining money. She idly wondered whether Gerald had left Violet any money, but didn't like to ask and Violet hadn't volunteered any information.

Gerald was laid to rest in the Lockwood family plot, beside his uncle, Sir Richard, and his father William. It started raining as Marcus intoned the last rites and the final sodden clods of earth were dropped on his coffin. Megan slid a glance at Henry, who was standing beside her at the graveside holding Violet's hand as she dropped the last handful of earth on the mortal remains of her husband. She thought of the child she had carried so briefly, that almost certainly had been Gerald's, and then about the child she was now carrying. How long could she put off telling Henry about the coming baby? Perhaps she could delay it until the end of October, but certainly no longer.

The next day a letter arrived for Henry from Mrs Curry, the matron at The Priory. It was not a total surprise to Henry; he'd been expecting someone from the hospital to get in touch, and he asked Megan to read it.

Megan read the letter.

It has been more than a month since you last visited Squadron Leader Myers, and he is getting very agitated and depressed. He has made a miraculous recovery from his last infection, and is now able to walk a short distance on crutches, something I did not expect. He is threatening to walk all the way from The Priory to Folly House, and I fear he may well attempt to do this. Therefore, I am wondering if you could find time to visit him in the near future. I think this will help him further in his recovery.

Yours sincerely,
A M Curry, Matron.

Megan looked at Henry. 'You'd better go,' she said. 'You haven't visited him for ages.'

'I suppose I had. Maybe I should ask Violet to come with me. Perhaps the two of us can cheer him up.'

'It's you he wants to see, not Violet,' said Megan, making Henry wonder yet again just how much she'd guessed or knew about Adam's sexual persuasion.

He visited Adam the very next day; he had managed to persuade Violet to come with him. But Adam was sulky and rude to her. 'If you're a nurse,' he said, 'go away and nurse someone. Henry doesn't need you and neither do I.'

Violet was offended, as Adam had intended her to be, and making a polite excuse she disappeared.

Watching her go Adam lounged back in his bedside chair. 'It's a lovely autumn day,' he said. 'Why don't we go for a walk? I can use one crutch and guide you with my other hand.'

Not really wanting to walk anywhere with Adam clutching hold of him, Henry compromised, and they walked outside and sat on the nearest seat near the cloister wall. When they were seated he took a deep breath; he knew he had to tell Adam now. 'You know I've got my memory back,' he began.

Adam took his hand and Henry tried to draw it away, but Adam clung on tenaciously. 'All of it?' he enquired.

'All of it,' said Henry quietly. Surely Adam would guess something now? But Adam said nothing, just stroked his hand. 'Do you remember that night in London, before I went to France, and you suggested that. . . ?

Adam laughed. 'Oh, you needn't apologize. I only remember the good times we had together. Do you remember when I was playing Hamlet and how the girl playing Ophelia fancied me, and I took her to bed, and then told her that I preferred men. How we teased her after that. They were the good days, weren't they?'

'No,' said Henry slowly. 'They weren't good. I knew then how vicious you could be but at the time I was too infatuated with your world to really notice or object.' He paused, then added, 'But I should have done.'

'Oh, for God's sake! How prissy can you get, Henry?' Adam slumped back on the garden seat and glowered at Henry. Then, in a mercurial change of mood, he smiled. 'But then, I can always forgive you, Henry, because you know I . . .'

'Adam, don't say it,' said Henry quickly.

'Why not? Why can't I say it? I love you, Henry. I want you. I always have, but I've had to make do with poor substitutes, other men and sometimes women. But it's you I want. Surely after all I've suffered you're not going to deny me that?' He reached forward and grasped Henry's thighs with both hands.

'Get off me.' With a cry Henry pushed roughly at his hands and stood up. Stumbling over the edge of the seat he tried to go in the direction of where he thought the cloister archway was, but found himself crashing into the uneven stones of the wall. He heard Adam laughing, and tried to feel his way along the wall to where he hoped the entrance was into the actual cloisters.

'You can't escape, you poor blind sod,' shouted Adam. 'We're meant to be together now. For God's sake, can't you see that?'

The rough branches of a wild brier rose growing along the wall tore at Henry's hands, and lashed across his face. Then his foot caught on the root and he stumbled to his knees. Cursing his blindness, Henry tried to crawl away. He began to weep as Adam's laugh echoed in his ears.

At that moment Violet's voice suddenly interrupted. 'Good gracious. Whatever is happening?'

He felt her soft hands helping him rise to his feet. 'Get me away from here,' he whispered. 'Take me home, please.'

The last thing he heard as Violet led him away was Adam's voice shouting, 'I love you. You sod! I love you.'

A car was organized to take them back to Folly House, as Megan wasn't due to pick up Henry for another hour. Violet mopped the blood from his hands and face, but didn't speak. They made the journey in silence and only when they reached Folly House did Violet speak.

'I think an explanation is needed, don't you?' she said. 'And I think Megan needs to hear it as well.'

'It's not what you think,' said Henry wearily.

'I'm trying not to think anything,' was Violet's uncompromising reply.

When Megan arrived the three of them retired to Megan's office for privacy, and the story came out. How during all the years of their friendship, since childhood, Henry had never suspected that Adam was a homosexual, although he'd always known when they lived in London that his morals were . . . he hesitated for the right word, finally saying, 'suspect'.

'What exactly do you mean by suspect?' demanded Violet sharply.

Megan said nothing. She was thinking of Adam's letter and waiting for Henry's next revelation.

'I suppose I mean loose,' said Henry. 'His crowd, mostly theatre people, took drugs for fun, cocaine and marijuana. Not a lot, just enough for them to lose their inhibitions.'

'You as well?' queried Violet.

'Never,' said Henry firmly. 'I was a doctor; I knew the dangers, so I didn't do drugs, although I joined in the parties sometimes. But most of the time I was working in the hospital, and after I married Megan, I didn't even go to the parties so often. Then I dropped out more or less altogether as Adam joined the Air Force, and then I joined the Army and I didn't see Adam again for months, not until I was sent back to the military mospital at Millbank before I went to France. He came over to London from Biggin Hill, and it was on that last night that he asked me to become his lover.'

'And what did you say?' At last Megan spoke.

'I said no, of course. Surely you don't think that I . . .' his voice tailed off. It was then that Megan told him of the letter which Adam had later destroyed. Henry was horrified. 'And you jumped to the conclusion that . . .'

'What else was I to think?' interrupted Megan fiercely. 'You've not shown me much affection since you returned. You've not been a husband in the true sense of the word. You've not . . .' she stopped, suddenly aware of Violet rising from her seat.

'I'll go now,' Violet said, and put a hand on Megan's shoulder. 'You've helped me in the past,' she said, 'and I'd like to help you both now. So take my advice. Have a good honest talk.'

After she'd left the room there was a long silence, then Henry said, 'Come and sit beside me, Megan.' When there was no response, he added softly, 'Please.'

She knew then that it was time to tell Henry of the coming baby.

Long, long afterwards, in the still of the night, Megan wondered why she had ever been afraid to tell Henry of her pregnancy. The hour they'd spent alone together in her office had taken them forward in their relationship as if they had taken actual physical leaps. She understood what the war had done to the complex man she had married. By robbing him of his sight it had made it impossible for him to lose himself in the world of healing, which had been his whole life. He should never have married her, nor she him. Too late they both knew they had deceived themselves and each other; there'd been no real love, only convenience. But now the wheel had turned full circle and they needed each other as never before. The price had been high, but there was a chance that from the ashes of their dreams they could perhaps forge something worthwhile.

The clock downstairs struck three, the silvery chimes floating up the stairs. One, two, three. That was a number for a family. Three. That was what she and Henry had agreed they would be when Jim's baby was born. Mother, father and baby. His unexpected offer of accepting responsibility for the baby had touched her and she'd burst into tears.

Henry had put his arms around her and held her tight. 'Did you expect me to desert you?' he asked quietly. 'I need you as much as you need me. I promise you we'll make something of this life we've got, and we'll do it together.'

Afterwards they had agreed to tell the family that night at supper. Lavinia and Rosie both flung their arms around Megan. 'A baby,' cried Lavinia. 'Just what I've always wanted.'

Everyone laughed. Later, when they'd retired to the gold room for a celebratory sherry, Arthur said quietly to Megan, 'I'm glad everything has turned out all right.' And she realized that he too had known her secret.

Now, lying beside Henry in the darkness Megan smiled. Suddenly she felt safe, surrounded by love. *I've lost Jim, but part of him will always be here.* The baby was wanted and she knew that he or she would grow up loved and cherished. She slid her hand across her rounded stomach. This baby, she vowed, would be, for better or worse, a Lockwood.

CHAPTER FIFTEEN

Spring 1945

Baby Peter arrived on Saturday 3 March 1945. It was an easy delivery, just as it had been an easy pregnancy.

'Working like a man on the farm has made Megan strong,' Dr Crozier told Henry with a satisfied smile. 'You have a fine strong son. A big lad at eight and a half pounds.'

Lavinia and Rosie burst into the room as soon as they heard the wailing cry, jostling for position to get a glimpse of the baby. 'He's so little,' said Rosie in an awed voice.

'Exquisite,' breathed Lavinia. 'Go on, Henry, hold your new born son.'

Henry reached out a hand and caressed the baby lying against Megan's breast. 'A credit to his father,' he said softly.

'A credit to you,' said Megan quickly and, grasping Henry's hand, raised it to her lips. Would anyone else notice what Henry said? She looked around anxiously, but everyone was entranced by the new arrival.

Dr Crozier laughed, and packed his black bag before slipping his arms into his overcoat; it was still chilly outside, with a strong easterly wind even though there were signs of spring. 'Now,' he said, shooing Lavinia and Rosie from the room, 'let's leave this little family together to have a few moments' peace. Mrs Quinn is going as well, I think.'

The midwife nodded. 'I'll be back later just to make sure you are settled for the night. Make sure you put baby to the breast every now and then so that he can get the hang of it.'

'Looks like everything is going well with the world at last, eh Lavinia?' Dr Crozier's words floated back up the stairs as he shepherded Lavinia and Rosie away. 'The Allies are pushing those damned Nazis back to Berlin, and the Russians have got them on the run in the Balkans. With any luck, young Peter Lockwood will be growing up in a peaceful world.'

Henry sat down on the side of the bed. 'Thank you,' said Megan.

He bent his head and aimed a kiss which landed on her forehead. 'You *are* mine,' he said quietly. 'You and Peter are all I've got. I'll never desert you as long as I live.'

'And I'll never desert you either,' said Megan.

'Not even if Jim Byrne should come back to Folly House?'

The question startled Megan. Jim! She hadn't thought of him so much recently. She hadn't even thought of Jim when she'd first gazed at the face of her new son, because baby Peter had his own quite distinguished personality. He was Peter. No one else.

'No, not even if Jim came back,' she answered. 'This child is yours. You made him yours by accepting him into your life.' But even as she said the words a little flicker of guilt skittered through her mind. It was an easy promise to make because she was convinced now that Jim had been killed in action. It was only a matter of time before he was listed officially as a casualty.

She looked down at Peter and felt an enormous surge of love overwhelm her. Peter's dark-blue eyes ('They are going to be brown,' Dr Crozier had said), looked back at her in a knowing way. *He is a perfect baby*, thought Megan contentedly, and wished that Henry could see him too.

Spring turned into early summer, and as the war in Europe drew nearer and nearer to a close life at Folly House continued on a serene course. Arthur needed to earn some money and applied to the local grammar school for the post of school musical director. He was offered the post, at a lower salary as he wasn't qualified as a teacher, and he took it.

Marcus was pleased, as he was due to retire from the church soon and a vicar's pension was not enough to keep them both. Arthur's salary meant that they could continue to live at Folly House and make a contribution to the running costs.

Megan hardly noticed any of this; she was wrapped in the warm afterglow of Peter's birth, and if occasionally thoughts of another love, a quiet, dark-haired man who played the piano with exquisite tenderness arose, she firmly pushed them away. She was happy, Henry was a devoted father and nothing was going to be allowed to tarnish that. Rosie too adored Peter and helped Henry bath the baby at night.

Megan entered the nursery one evening just as Rosie was lifting Peter up into the air and making him smile. 'Look at the baby,' she cried.

'He's not just the baby. He's your little brother,' said Henry.

Suddenly there was a silence, then Rosie said in a small quiet voice. 'He's not really my brother. I'm just an evacuee. I'm not a Lockwood. I suppose when the war finishes I'll have to go to an orphanage now that my real mother is dead.'

'Certainly not,' said Megan sharply. 'Whatever made you think that? We *are* going to adopt you, aren't we, Henry?'

'But you never said,' whispered Rosie, looking first at Megan and then at Henry. 'Are you really going to adopt me?'

'Of course we are, and we should have done something about it before now. It's just that a lot of other things got in the way. But we shall start making the arrangements tomorrow. I promise.'

'Think of it,' said Henry to Rosie. 'Soon I'll have a son *and* a daughter.'

But neither of them yours, thought Megan, sadly.

Their life together had achieved a measure of closeness, but the final step of making love evaded them. They never talked about it so Megan had no idea what Henry thought. But it was the memory of Jim that got in the way for her; she was unable to imagine herself with any other man.

When Violet, from whom she now had no secrets, enquired about life with Henry she had said, 'We rub along together better than many couples.'

Violet wanted to speak to Henry. 'I feel sorry for him too,' she said.

'No, don't,' said Megan quickly. 'I don't want anything to upset our lives now.'

Violet changed the subject. 'I've decided,' she said, 'that when the war is over and Brinkley Hall reverts back to me, I shall sell it. I don't need a huge house.'

'You might marry again,' said Megan.

Violet shook her head. 'One marriage was enough for me, and anyway no one will ever find enough staff to run a huge place like that. It can never be a home again; in fact it never was a home. It will probably be a hotel or even stay as a hospital. No, Brinkley Hall belongs to another era, when the rich were rich, and the poor were glad of a few crumbs from the rich man's table. But anyway, I'll have to wait until the war is over before I can decide anything.'

That happened on 8 May. Winston Churchill made the radio announcement to tell the whole nation that the war in Europe would officially finish at midnight.

The country went wild. Street parties in all the cities, several days' holidays were declared by most employers, and East End village was no exception. A hasty street party was arranged for the following Tuesday, 15 May, to take place in School Lane, which ran the whole length of the village. Baking began in earnest with what flour, eggs and sugar could be found in store cupboards, and Mr Shepherd, the butcher, began making sausages by the dozen, knowing no one would complain that they were filled with too much bread. Tins of Spam appeared from where they'd been secreted away and last year's blackberry jam was lavishly spread on thick slices of bread.

On Tuesday 15 May the party was in full swing. Megan had baby Peter on her hip, and her arm linked through Henry's. She began to describe the scene to him, ending with, 'I just don't believe all that red, white and blue jelly can be good for the children.'

'They can only be sick once,' said Bertha philosophically. Then she frowned. 'Dottie shouldn't be in there with the children helping herself to jelly. She's much too old.'

George opened his mouth to argue, but Megan interrupted first. 'Oh, let her have some fun. No one minds, and she is a child really. Don't spoil her day.'

Bertha didn't reply, but moved towards the end of the trestle-table, ashamed to be seen too close to her daughter. George snorted. 'She do take on so,' he said and followed his wife.

Megan sighed. 'We're so lucky Peter is normal.'

Henry smiled. 'Give him to me to hold for a moment,' he said. 'He must be heavy for you.'

Carefully Megan passed the precious bundle, and Peter laughed and jigged with glee in Henry's arms. Smiling, Megan watched and then inexplicably she shivered, and remembered the old saying; *a ghost has walked over my grave.* Then she saw Adam. He was standing opposite them, leaning on two crutches and gazing at Henry with mesmerizing intensity.

She shivered again as Adam began to lope painfully along on his crutches towards them. She tried to feel sympathetic for his plight, but felt nothing but fear. He reached them.

'Henry, whose child is this?' he asked.

'My son,' said Henry, and Megan noticed that he instinctively held Peter closer.

Megan moved closer to Henry and the baby. The hatred she saw in Adam's eyes made her blood run cold. But the hatred was not directed at her; his eyes were fastened with a fanatical intensity on baby Peter.

However, much to Megan's relief the tense situation with Adam evaporated almost as soon as it had begun. A male nursing attendant appeared on the other side of School Lane; Megan recognized his uniform of dark green and white and guessed he was looking for Adam. She waved, he came at once and took hold of Adam's arm in a firm but gentle grasp.

'What are you doing out here on your own, old chap?' he said quietly. 'You know you are not well enough.'

'I'm damned sure I am well enough to do as I like.' Adam tried to wrestle out of his grasp, but was not strong enough.

Megan felt a flash of pity, remembering the once proud and handsome man; it was piteous to compare that man to the wreck of humanity now being led away.

'He's gone,' she said to Henry, but he made no reply, merely held Peter more tightly.

The band played on, children began to play hopscotch and ring-a-roses in the school yard, and the adults sat drinking tea and eating scones.

Henry and Megan found a spot beneath the horse-chestnut tree that stood on the edge of the playground. It was heavy with bright green leaves and its iridescent white candle blossoms blazed in the sunshine. Arthur and Violet joined them, and Megan relaxed. Everything was back to normal.

Then suddenly there were cheers from the far end of the lane. Arthur pushed himself forward in his wheelchair. 'Good heavens,' he said. 'Two soldiers have arrived. They must have just been released from the front.'

There were cries of 'God bless them! They've come back alive.' Then another voice cried, 'There's that American.'

Megan's heart stopped. Henry clutched her hand.

She looked closer and saw the two men in uniform, still with their kitbags on their backs. One was a British Tommy and the other in the paler khaki of an American GI. It was not Jim; he always wore a British officer's uniform.

'Is it Jim?' Henry whispered in a low voice.

'No,' said Arthur. 'The American is a GI who went out with our land girl, Molly.'

'And the other is Doreen Foster's boyfriend,' announced Dottie. Molly began to run down the lane, and people cheered and clapped.

Unnoticed amid the general hubbub Megan squeezed Henry's hand. 'Jim won't come back,' she said. 'I'm sure of it, and even if he did it wouldn't change anything.'

Henry remained silent, but Megan could feel him trembling. She looked at Peter, dimpled and smiling, totally unaware of the love mixed with pain that he had brought with him. She knew then that the mixture of joy and guilt would never leave her.

After the victory in Europe life didn't change much. There was still rationing for everything and the struggle to make ends meet continued for everyone, not just those at Folly House. Henry was working now in an office at Brinkley Hall Hospital and enjoyed it; but that in itself was a problem, as he needed to be ferried back and forth in the car, and petrol was still rationed. Eventually it was decided that he would stay over at the hospital four nights a week.

But somehow, Megan and Henry made time to set the wheels in motion for the adoption of Rosie Barnes. She was ecstatic at the thought being officially Rosie Lockwood, and insisted that she should be called that at school. The weeks passed and there was a general election. Winston Churchill, the darling of the war years, and the Conservative party he led were thoroughly trounced, and after what seemed a long wait it was announced that Clement Attlee would be forming the government with the Labour Party.

Marcus was furious with what he saw as the disloyalty of the British population. The Jones family were furious too, as they were fervent Conservative supporters, and they quarrelled with the Moons who were fervent Labour supporters. The two old men refused to work together, and nothing Megan could say would make any difference. Her exasperation was compounded by Silas telling her that 'women know nothing of politicking'. To cap it all George agreed with him. Megan dragged Henry over from Brinkley Hall and demanded that he must speak to them as Master of Folly House. Something she had never done.

Although Megan hadn't planned it she realized afterwards that she had empowered Henry. He sat in the gun room and spoke to the two men, and they accepted his word as the master. Afterwards he sat on alone and felt a warm glow of contentment. He was not useless after all. He was needed at Brinkley Hall and he was needed as well in Folly House. He was still there when Molly made an appearance. She'd come to collect a gun in readiness for an evening's shoot.

'I'll have one last shoot before I leave at the end of the week,' she told Henry.

Henry got the gun down and prepared the shot. 'We'll miss you,' he said.

Molly laughed. 'I'll miss all of you. You know, it's strange but I never thought that I'd settle as a country girl, yet here I am leaving the country to go to a farm in Massachusetts, America. I'm going to marry Luke and live on his father's dairy farm at Sandwich, Cape Cod.'

'At least you already know how to milk a cow,' said Henry. Sandwich, Cape Cod, the name sounded familiar. Then he remembered why. It was where Jim Byrne had come from. Jim, the father of his son, Peter. He felt his heart constrict in apprehension. Supposing Jim was still alive, supposing Molly met him and told him of Megan's baby? He'd be sure to guess. And then supposing he came back to England.

Henry reined in his turbulent thoughts, aware that Molly was still chattering on. 'As I said to Luke, it's strange, isn't it, because Sandwich is where Jim Byrne came from. Luke didn't know of him, and of course he'll never know him now because he was killed, wasn't he?'

'Yes,' said Henry. 'He was killed.' But all the same he couldn't rid himself of the feeling of uneasiness.

Molly took the gun and went off to find Pat, who was joining her for the evening's sport. Henry remained seated in the gun room. Suddenly it didn't seem so warm and a host of unwelcome thoughts buzzed through his mind. Marriage. Molly was going to be married, and she and her GI Luke would sleep together because that's what married people did. So why couldn't he? What was wrong with him? Why didn't he love Megan enough? He *did* love baby Peter and Rosie. He loved them passionately and unconditionally. Was it because they needed him, and Megan didn't? Maybe he should seek medical advice. He was still thinking about it when Violet arrived to tell him dinner was ready.

'You are looking terribly sad,' she said, putting an arm around his shoulders.

'I suppose that's because I am,' said Henry.

Violet hugged him. 'Don't be. The Prime Minister, Mr Attlee is going to announce the end of the war in Japan tonight. At least that's what the radio is saying. At last, the war, all of it, will be finished and we can pick up our lives and put the pieces of the puzzle back together again.'

'Not quite,' replied Henry sombrely. 'I'll never put my particular jigsaw back together again. The pieces won't fit.'

Violet didn't speak for a moment, she just held him close. 'We will make the pieces fit,' she said softly. 'We will, I promise. But the picture will be different.'

On Tuesday August 14 the end of the war in Japan was announced at midnight, and the next day the whole world went mad. Public holidays were announced, bonfires, street parties were held all over again. But at Folly House the celebrations were more muted this time.

Henry's depression affected everyone, and the next evening after the end of the war the family met in the gold room after dinner. The coffee was still the wartime mix of coffee and chicory and Lavinia complained as usual.

'We're at peace now,' she said. 'Surely we can have some decent coffee and perhaps we can all stop digging for victory?'

'We'll still have to dig,' said Arthur, 'because we will still be short of food.'

Lavinia snorted and rang the bell to call Bertha in. 'I don't care if we are still on rations,' she declared, 'but we can still celebrate. The champagne has all gone, but I know, and so does Bertha, that there is one last bottle of *Chateau Neuf du Pape*. Tonight is the time to drink it and toast the future of the Lockwood family, and everyone we know here at Folly House and the village of East End.'

A smiling Bertha retrieved the last precious bottle

'Marcus, will you do the honours, and open the wine and then serve it. When it's had a chance to breathe, of course,' asked Lavinia.

'Delighted.' Marcus levered himself with difficulty from the armchair by the window.

He's getting really old now thought Megan sadly as she watched her father struggling to rise. All their lives seemed to be rushing by too fast. Even Peter and Rosie, playing now on the rug in front of the fireplace, were growing up quickly. Peter's soft blond hair was turning darker now, and his eyes were a deep brown, just like Jim's. He looked nothing like Henry, and Megan hoped everyone would think he took after her. After all, she was a brunette and had brown eyes.

She took the glass of red wine from Marcus and looked across at

Henry. Peter was trying to stand, and was clutching hold of Henry's knee with Rosie's assistance.

'To the family,' said Lavinia, rising and holding up her glass, 'and everyone we love.'

I'm so lucky, thought Megan raising her own glass. *I have a son; I have security, which is much more than many people have.* She moved across the room and sat beside Henry on the settee by the fireplace. 'To us,' she said, touching her glass against his. 'And our family.'

'To the family,' he replied. But he didn't smile.

CHAPTER SIXTEEN

Christmas Eve 1945

A new postman delivered the mail that morning: Silas Moon's son, Benjamin. Megan had felt guilty because she'd not been able to re-employ him when he returned from the army, but Benjamin appeared to enjoy life as a postman.

'Glad to be away from my dad,' he said. 'He wants to talk about the war, and I've had enough of that. I just want to forget.'

That morning Arthur was wheeling himself over the cobbled yard by the stables, waiting for Violet who was coming to take him to church so that he could practise on the organ and collate all the music ready for the Blessing of the Crib service. It was a bitterly cold morning, and Arthur's woollen-clad fingers almost froze to the wheels of his chair.

'Here, let me help,' said Benjamin. He jumped off his bike and took the handles of the wheelchair. 'I've got a letter for Mrs Lockwood. All the way from America.' He put Arthur's chair in position by the stable door, fished a blue airmail letter from his bag and passed it over. 'The young Mrs Lockwood,' he said. 'Not Lady Lavinia.'

Benjamin jumped back on his bicycle leaving Arthur to stare at the blue airmail letter. The postmark was Massachusetts, USA. When Violet drove into the yard Arthur handed her the letter and didn't speak. He waited while she turned it over and, like him, looked at the address on the back.

'I think we'll hold on to this for the time being,' she said slowly, and put the letter in Arthur's music case. 'Do you agree?'

'I'm not sure. Have we right to manipulate other people's lives?'

Violet's mouth tightened into a straight line. 'Sometimes, yes,' she said firmly.

'Well, I'm not sure.' Arthur was equally firm. 'I'll think about it and decide tonight.'

Violet didn't argue, merely helped Arthur into the car. She was annoyed, and he knew why. They both knew Peter was Jim's child and he also knew that Violet was very fond of Henry and wanted him to find some happiness in life. Peter was providing that happiness, he was the light in Henry's dark life, and she didn't want that to be disturbed.

They set off for the church in silence. Violet had difficulty in controlling the car; it constantly threatened to slew sideways on the icy surface. When they reached the end of the lane and joined the main road to the village they both heaved a sigh of relief. The church was in sight. 'Well done, we made it,' said Arthur.

Violet turned her head and smiled. 'About that letter,' she said, but left the sentence unfinished as at that moment a green sports car came round the bend by the church. It was being driven much too fast and the driver lost control. The car slid sideways towards them.

To Marcus standing in the doorway of the church it all seemed to happen in slow motion. The sports car slid with unerring instinct, and screaming tyres, towards the small saloon driven by Violet, and hit it with an almighty impact. The passenger in the sports car somersaulted out and over the saloon, which was crumpling as if a giant's hand had suddenly grasped it.

There was an eerie silence broken only by the sound of hissing steam. Marcus could see the doors to Violet's car were open; Arthur and Violet were lying seemingly lifeless in their seats, trapped by the crumpled bonnet, their belongings scattered in the road. As he reached the car oil started to ooze everywhere, covering everything. Fire! The thought panicked him. He had to get help. He had to get a doctor. He had to get to a phone. If only he were younger. He was out of breath, his legs would hardly function as he half-scrambled, half-slid on the ice towards the nearest house. He fell, slipped into the ditch at the side, then mercifully heard voices. Someone was coming.

'Arthur, Violet,' he gasped, flailing his arms towards the mangled wreckage in the road. 'Help them, please.'

March 1946

Megan could hardly believe it was Peter's first birthday. This time last year had been so different. She'd been happy; Henry loved the baby and had been happy too. He still loved Peter and Rosie, but now, most of the time, he was sunk in depression. Nothing could help him, not even when the final adoption papers came for Rosie.

At Christmas, Arthur and Violet's accident had briefly taken Megan's mind off Henry's growing depression. Frantic with worry, she'd rushed to the hospital; but luckily neither of them had been seriously injured. Arthur had a broken arm and Violet a broken leg. Once they'd recovered consciousness and been bandaged and plastered, they'd been allowed back to Folly House. But Christmas and New Year passed by Folly House unnoticed because Marcus was dead.

He had died that cold Christmas Eve morning in a frozen ditch. No one had noticed at first because they were busy with the accident victims, but when he didn't move, they realized he was dead. The driver of the sports car was pronounced dead at the scene of the accident too. He was a friend of Adam's who'd been down visiting him at the Priory Hospital.

Adam, thought Megan bitterly. Anything to do with him was poison. It was irrational, she knew, but she still thought it. Henry made no comment.

Marcus's death left a huge void in Megan's life. She missed him more than she'd ever thought she would. He'd always been there, an old man getting increasingly set in his ways, annoying sometimes, but there, always there; a continuous thread in her life. Now that thread was broken and Megan suddenly became aware of her own mortality.

It didn't help that Rosie was bereft with grief. 'For the first time I had a real granddad,' she wept. 'Now he's gone.'

Megan couldn't comfort her, but Mrs Fox, who'd returned to Folly House like an avenging angel when she'd heard news of Marcus's death, did. 'Just because you can't see him any more,' she told Rosie sternly, 'doesn't mean that he's not here. He was always preaching about eternal life from that pulpit of his, and now he's got it. Eternal life. You can go and talk to him at his grave in the churchyard. He'll hear you.'

'But he won't reply,' wailed Rosie.

'He will. Although it may not be in the way you expect.'

Rosie started stopping off at the grave on the way home from school. 'Most unhealthy,' muttered Bertha, who didn't approve at all. As far as she was concerned once you were dead, you were dead, no bones about it.

But if it helped Rosie Megan was glad. She had other things to concern her. She wished Mrs Fox could stay for ever at Folly House, but she couldn't afford to pay her, so she went back to Southampton to work in Woolworths. Nowadays she was glad when Henry stayed over at Brinkley Hall; it was a relief from his increasingly depressing aura. She felt guilty about him but didn't know what to do, and anyway she hardly had time to think about it these days. Money was tighter than ever. No matter how hard they all worked it was difficult to pay the wages of the farmhands and the Jones family. Megan did more than her share of work these days, as George was showing signs of his age and had recently become riddled with arthritis. Her hands grew rough and calloused and sometimes she could hardly put one foot in front of the other.

'We'll have to pension off the Jones family,' said Lavinia one evening after supper. 'Get in some younger people.'

'We can't do that.' Megan felt irritable. Lately Lavinia seemed to have no real concept of the world outside Folly House. Now the war was over she thought everything should return to how it had been before the war. The fact that they had hardly any money, and inflation made the cost of everything higher, just didn't register with her.

'It's time for you to take over properly as lady of Folly House,' she said, warming to her theme one evening. 'We could start giving dinner parties for the county set. You've never really mingled with them properly because war was declared so soon after you married Henry.'

'We can't afford it, Lavinia,' said Megan. 'I'm a working woman and have no time for socializing. Besides, although the war has ended food rationing is now stricter than ever, and according to the government is going to get worse. Even bread is rationed now. The country is bankrupt, the taxes are killing us, and we're in for years of austerity.'

But Lavinia didn't want to hear this. 'I've got money,' she insisted. 'There's no need for you to worry.'

She couldn't understand that the inheritance from her husband had dwindled into insignificance due to inflation since the war. She was no longer a wealthy widow. Eventually Megan persuaded her to let Mr Green, the accountant, take over managing her financial affairs, and he confided to Henry and Megan that he thought she was becoming a little muddled in her old age.

For Megan, Lavinia's increasing forgetfulness was one more thing to worry about. If she had not had Peter and Rosie to cherish she sometimes thought she could just walk away from Folly House and everyone in it. Those were the bad days; most of the time she gritted her teeth and got on with it. But even on the good days, there was always the aching, nagging loneliness in her heart. Were there other women like her? Sometimes she felt that perhaps God was punishing her for wanting too much, and trying to grasp it. But other times she felt sorrier for Henry than herself. His memory had completely returned now, and with it came recurring nightmares about Dunkirk. Only once did he confess to her the searing images which filled his sleeping mind. But Megan always knew when it happened. He would awaken, shouting out, covering his face with his hands, sweating profusely and groaning. Afterwards he would lie for hours shivering violently, while Megan lay beside him, unable to help, unable to sleep and constantly worrying about the future.

But sometimes, with Peter in her arms, she knew she was luckier than most. They lived in comfort, unlike many people, crammed together in makeshift accommodation while they waited for their bombed homes to be repaired. And even then, they were not bricks-and-mortar houses, but prefabricated bungalows with tiny rooms, and even tinier gardens. Folly House still had space inside and out. The months went past, Peter reached his second birthday, and Bertha made a birthday cake with black-market flour. No one felt guilty about such small breaches of the law of the land.

Then one evening, when the family had gathered in the gold room after dinner, Violet produced a whole bottle of port, and a pound of mature stilton cheese.

'A whole pound of cheese,' exclaimed Megan in amazement. 'But we're only allowed two ounces a week.'

'Ask me no questions and I'll tell you no lies,' said Violet with a grin, and then produced some water biscuits made from white flour. They looked delicious, with creamy white middles and crispy brown edges.

'The last time I saw something like this it was 1939,' said Lavinia. 'What are we celebrating?'

'Violet and I are going to be married,' said Arthur, beaming from ear to ear.

The room erupted, and Megan hugged Violet. 'I never thought I'd want to marry again, but I hadn't bargained on falling in love with such a lovely man as Arthur,' said Violet. 'We've made lots of plans; Brinkley Hall is going to remain as a hospital, and Arthur and I will have the west wing as private accommodation when we have a family, but before that we shall move to London for a while.'

'Move to London,' echoed Megan. It seemed that more of her world was disappearing. Her father had gone, now she was losing Arthur and Violet as well.

'You'll still see us,' Violet looked seriously at Megan, 'but I know you'll not want to deny Arthur the thing he's always been dreaming of, a place to study at the Royal Academy of Music. He's had an audition and passed and starts next term.'

Megan tried to be glad, as they raised their glasses and toasted the future of the happy pair. But deep in her heart she was jealous. They were about to embark on a normal married life, with the prospect of children. Whereas no matter how much she longed for another child, it would never happen.

Henry didn't say much apart from adding his congratulations, and Megan wondered what he was thinking. It was impossible to guess. She faced the forthcoming wedding with something approaching despair; with Violet in London there would be no one to talk to.

As for Lavinia she immediately began thinking about clothes.

'Let's see,' she mused. 'I've got a whole year of twenty-four coupons. That's enough for a dress and shoes, and maybe a hat if I'm lucky. But not enough for a coat: that's eighteen coupons and I haven't any left over from last year.'

'We're not having a church wedding,' said Violet firmly. 'It will be at the Register Office in Stibbington, so you won't need any fancy clothes.'

Lavinia was disappointed but Megan was relieved. Juggling the clothing coupons to keep up with Rosie and Peter's growing needs was bad enough, without having to think of wedding clothes.

Violet and Arthur were married on a cold, windy April day, more like January than April. Dottie had spent hours in the churchyard picking wild violets so all the guests had violet buttonholes, and the Register Office was decorated with bunches of wild daffodils. Violet wore a restyled lemon suit, so no coupons were needed. Arthur had needed their combined coupons as he'd splashed out on a new suit. Afterwards there was a wedding breakfast at Folly House, overseen by Bertha, who was in her element as usual.

Their new home was a rented house in Cadogan Square, where Arthur had a music room to himself. The couple soon began to enjoy the vibrant post-war London life of theatres, and concerts. Sometimes Arthur thought of the letter from Jim which had been destroyed in the accident, and wondered whether they ought to mention it to Megan. But Violet said, 'No, let sleeping dogs lie,' and that Jim would write again if it was important.

The summer months of the first year of peace passed. Megan employed Dottie officially as a housemaid and started paying her a small wage.

Dottie was ecstatic. 'I'm going to get real money,' she squealed.

'Yes, but it comes to me,' said Bertha. 'You've got no sense.'

Megan had other plans. 'I'll pay half to you, Bertha, to put in the bank, and the other half is for Dottie to spend how she pleases.'

On the Saturday after her first payday Dottie went off to Stibbington market with one pound, ten shillings in her purse. She returned later that afternoon laden with presents. For her mother, a bottle of Devon Violets perfume, for Rosie and Peter a sugar mouse each, and for Megan a bunch of flame red gladioli.

'I knows you like them,' she said in her strong Hampshire accent, blushing shyly as she handed the flowers to Megan.

'Why, I do. You remember that time when I bought the flowers from Miss Cozens.' Dottie nodded and blushed even more.

The flowers were placed in a vase in the fireplace just as they had been all those years before. It brought back memories to Megan. How different it had been then; just as well we can't see into the future, she reflected.

Bertha, of course, thought Dottie had wasted her money, but thanked her grudgingly for the perfume. 'Though Lord knows when I'll get the chance to wear it,' she said.

Megan often thought of Violet and Arthur in London, and would have liked to visit them. But work made that impossible; there was no one she could leave Peter and Rosie with, Lavinia was getting more forgetful by the day, and Dottie, although willing, couldn't be asked to undertake such a responsibility. Bertha, of course, had quite enough to do.

Then Folly House had a piece of good luck. Megan was asked if Folly House would be willing to take two young German prisoners of war for the summer and autumn. The Government was way behind with the repatriation programme and needed places, not prisons, for the Germans to stay. Henry was agreeable, so Hans and Werner came. They were both only twenty, and once Bertha saw that they were two rather frightened young men, she took them to her heart. Pat, the remaining land girl, moved into the box room above the kitchen, and the German boys were billeted in the old stables formerly occupied by the land girls. There were a few rumblings in the village about the 'enemy' being free and living at Folly House, but as the summer wore on the grumbles dissipated, as it was seen that they were good workers and harmless.

From Megan's point of view they were heaven-sent. They gave her the opportunity to have a little free time with the two children. Rosie was growing into a lovely girl, and Peter was proving himself to be quite a handful now that he was walking. He ran everywhere and loved being chased. Megan loved him so much that sometimes she thought her heart would break with the intensity of her love.

As the weeks and months passed Henry tried to drag himself from the depths of depression. But it was difficult. He was afraid to sleep because he knew the terrifying images of dead and dying men would be waiting for him the moment he closed his eyes. He knew he needed to talk to a psychiatrist: someone who could help rid his mind of the demons tormenting him. But he couldn't bring himself to do it.

But strangely enough the arrival of the two Germans helped him a little. Werner, the eldest had been hoping to start training as a doctor before being called into the German army, so Henry found someone he could talk to about things they both understood and were interested in.

They fell into the habit of meeting at weekends in the old stable where the guns were kept. Werner and Hans were both good shots and were helping Pat to learn to shoot now that Molly had left. George had strict instructions from the prison authorities that the Germans should not have access to guns, but he saw no harm in letting them go out with Pat to show her how to shoot pigeons and rabbits.

'The war is over,' he said. 'They are not the enemy any longer.'

Henry agreed, and was glad to resume his duties of cleaning the guns when they came back from a shoot. He gained pleasure from feeling the warm steel barrels and smooth wooden handles, and began to feel less stressed.

Megan noticed this, and when the three men were closeted in the gun room she often took out a tray of tea and cakes to them, accompanied by baby Peter. He adored the attention he received and always wanted to stay.

One hot August afternoon, Henry was in the gun room waiting for Hans and Werner to arrive, ready for the evening's shoot. Megan called in with Rosie and Peter to say goodbye. She was driving the trap into Stibbington where a friend of Henry's, Ken Steadman, had promised to take the three of them out for a sail to the salt marshes in the estuary. Peter kissed Henry goodbye and then climbed into the driving seat of the trap with Megan; she had promised to let him hold the reins.

In the lane Megan passed Hans and Werner on their way to the stables. They waved. 'We're off for a sail,' she called. The two men smiled and stood aside to watch them pass.

The pony and trap trotted down the lane, and as they turned to continue on to Folly House they became aware of a man standing beside them. He had emerged from the copse at the side of the road. 'I've walked through the forest from Stibbington railway station,' he said by way of explanation. He gazed at the disappearing trap. 'Was that Megan Lockwood?'

'Yes,' replied Werner. 'Mrs Lockwood with her son and daughter.'

The stranger took out a cigarette and lit it, then proffered the packet to Werner and Hans. 'The girl is Rosie, I know her,' he said slowly. 'But the boy. Who is he?'

Werner laughed. 'The boy? Why, he is the light of everyone's lives here at Folly House. He is the son of Mr Henry Lockwood and his wife Megan.'

There was silence, while the stranger drew on his cigarette. Werner took a cigarette and handed the packet back. 'Thanks,' he said, lighting his cigarette. There was another long silence and Werner said curiously, 'Do you know the Lockwoods well?'

'Not now,' the stranger replied slowly. 'I knew them once, a long time ago, but . . .' he stopped and put the cigarette packet back in his pocket. He stood looking down the lane to where the trap had now disappeared, and seemed to be thinking. 'I must be going on,' he said. 'I've a long way to go.'

'And where is that?' asked Hans politely.

There was a long pause, then the stranger said, 'I'm not sure.' He turned abruptly and plunged back into the depths of the forest, leaving the two Germans staring after him.

'I wonder who he was,' said Hans. 'Bit strange, don't you think?'

Werner shrugged. He was thinking of other things. 'I wonder if Bertha will give us some cakes this afternoon as Megan is out? Come on.' The two men made their way to the stables, now used as the gun room, where Henry was waiting.

CHAPTER SEVENTEEN

It was a perfect summer's afternoon, and Megan relaxed as Ken Steadman steered the little dinghy out into the saltings on the edge of the estuary. He anchored the boat on a sandy shelf and the children scrambled out and made muddy sandcastles. When the tide turned it was time to go, and reluctantly they climbed back aboard and made their way up the estuary against the flowing tide and into the setting sun.

In the gun room it was as Werner had hoped. Bertha arrived with tea and carrot-cake. The guns were put aside in the old manger by the door ready for later and room was made on the table for the tray. Werner cut the cake and passed it around. 'I don't know how she does it,' said Pat, cake crumbs on her chin. 'Everything she makes is delicious.'

'We're lucky to have her here at Folly House,' said Henry. He sat back listening to the rattling of cups against the saucers, and the banter between the two German boys and Pat. *I enjoy my time with these people* he thought. And although he could not see it he knew the golden sunlight of early evening would now be flooding through the top of the stable door, burnishing the cobbles with a warm glow. When his inner eye could see the good things in life he knew life was worth living. If only it could always be like that.

Then suddenly he heard another sound. Perhaps it was Megan returning early.

Smiling, he turned his head towards the door, and as he did so he heard Werner's sharp intake of breath.

There was a scraping sound as if someone's foot was dragging across the cobbles, then Werner's voice, high and nervous. 'What do you want?' Silence. Then Werner's voice again. Sharp, anxious. 'No! Don't touch the guns, they're loaded.'

'Loaded, are they? How convenient, and how very silly of you to leave them lying around.' It was Adam's voice. Henry knew it in an instant.

'Adam,' he said. 'What are you doing here? How did you get here? Did someone bring you?' He sent up a silent prayer that someone from The Priory had accompanied Adam to Folly House.

'I don't need anyone to help me these days. I know everyone thought I would die, perhaps even wished that I would. But I've regained my strength, although unfortunately not my good looks. I'll never get an acting job again, unless it's to play some poor unfortunate wreck in a horror film.' His voiced was loud, hysterical-sounding, and echoed eerily around the stable. Then he laughed.

Henry shivered; the laugh sounded even more menacing than his words. Then he told himself not to be so silly, the menace was in his head, no one else's.

'You know Henry from before the war?' said Pat, and immediately Henry sensed she was trying to defuse the tense situation. It was not his imagination. She was thinking the same thing.

He wondered where Adam was standing. Was it somewhere near the doorway? And was he pointing a gun at anyone, or was he just holding one? His blindness heightened his senses; he could feel the uneasiness of Werner and Hans as they stood beside him, and he knew they were afraid.

'I'm not interested in talking to farmhands or land girls,' Adam snarled back at Pat. 'I've come to talk to Henry. Come outside with me, Henry.' His voice now had a wheedling sound. 'We need to talk. We've got to get our relationship sorted out one way or another.' The scraping sound of footsteps came again and Henry knew he was nearer. But how near? He wished he knew.

'Henry is not going anywhere with you,' said Pat. Henry felt her hand firmly grip his shoulder. 'He's staying right here with Werner, Hans and me.'

'Mind your own bloody business, woman.'

'It is my business.'

'Get out off my way, damn you,' growled Adam. 'Or I'll shoot the lot of you.'

There was a click and Henry caught his breath. He had cocked the gun. It was ready to fire. 'For God's sake, Adam. You'll hang if you shoot anyone.'

'Do you think the thought of the gallows frightens me, Henry? It will be a blessed relief to leave this world. But I'm not going anywhere unless you come with me.'

That was when Henry realized that Adam was mad. Quite mad. It was not just the words but something in the tone of his voice. Beside him he heard Pat whisper to Hans and Werner. They were going to try and get the gun from Adam. But surely they must realize that he would kill them? He had to stop them. It was his fault, not theirs. He was the cause of Adam's insanity, not they. 'Do nothing,' he said in a low voice. 'Do you hear me? Do nothing.'

'But we must. . .' Hans whispered.

Henry interrupted him. 'Do nothing,' he repeated.

'That's it. Do nothing,' sneered Adam. 'I can hear you. Do nothing. But remember I can wait for ever. Until the sands of time run out,' he shouted theatrically, then dropping his voice to a hiss he added, 'I've waited long enough for you, Henry; a few more hours will make no difference.'

So they waited in silence. Henry knew the sun was sinking in the evening sky because he could feel the dampness of evening creeping in through the stable door. Soon someone would be coming out to see where he was and remind him about supper. He hoped it wouldn't be Dottie: she would panic. If it were George or Bertha maybe he could shout a warning and they could get help. But what would Adam do? Would he start shooting? The more he thought about it the more he knew that it was almost certain that someone was going to end up being shot. Adam would fire, he was certain of it.

It began to get quite cold and Henry shivered. 'What's the matter?' asked Adam with another of his strange laughs. 'Getting nervous?'

Before Henry could reply they all heard the sound of running feet. Small feet. Light feet. A voice called, 'Daddy.' It was Peter. Henry's heart almost stopped. What to do? How could he keep Peter away from the stable? But he couldn't think. He sat there struck dumb, immobile.

Then from beside him Pat suddenly screamed, 'Go away, Peter. Go away. Go back to the house.'

But of course Peter didn't go away. He was too young and innocent to think of danger. He thought it was a game. 'Found you,' he called, laughing as he ran through the doorway.

Then there was a frightened cry, and Adam said, 'Got you. You stay with me until your daddy comes to get you.' He laughed. 'You will come now, won't you, Henry.'

'Daddy,' whimpered Peter. 'Daddy, I'm hurting.'

After that everything happened quickly. Megan arrived. She had on soft linen shoes and no one heard her footsteps. The moment she arrived she screamed, Henry heard the shotgun and felt a hot blast. His brain swirled in terror. 'Peter,' he shouted. There was another shot, and another. He felt someone push him to one side and he lunged forward to where he thought Adam was. He could hear Peter and Megan both screaming, then he felt as if someone had hit him with a heavy fist, right in the middle of his chest. The table was knocked over and fell with a clatter of cups and saucers, and at the same time he felt himself falling down on to the cobbles. He tried to get up, but had no strength in his arms to push himself up, and the cobbles were warm and slippery. He could smell the metallic odour of blood, and tried to shout. But no sound came. 'Peter,' he whispered hoarsely, 'Peter. Is he all right?'

He felt Megan's hands holding him, she was weeping. Weeping as he'd never heard her weep before. 'Peter's all right,' she was saying, over and over again. 'Peter's all right. He's all right.'

Henry relaxed in her arms. There was something he had to say before it was too late. What was it? Everything was blurred in his mind. It was urgent. What was it? 'I'm sorry,' he whispered. 'I didn't know how to love you. I wish, I wish . . .' The words died on his lips as he sighed, a long slow, sigh, then was still.

Megan bent over him sobbing.

It wasn't until George and Bertha came rushing in that Megan was

191

aware of the terrible carnage. Pat was standing by the far wall holding Peter, turning his head away so that he couldn't see the awful sight. Megan realized that she was on her knees cradling Henry's head in her lap, although she had no recollection of how she came to be there. His eyes were closed, and a trail of dark red blood trickled from the side of his mouth. There was a gaping hole in the middle of his chest from which bright red blood was still gushing. Vaguely she thought she ought to stop the bleeding, and looked around for something to staunch the flow.

'I need a bandage,' she whispered.

Werner had the other shotgun in his hand and was standing looking dazed. He came over to Megan, and crouching down beside her put his hand to Henry's throat, feeling for a pulse. 'There's no need for a bandage,' he said softly. 'He's beyond our help now.'

Megan looked around her. She could see Adam lying in a twisted position against the wall by the door, one of the shotguns still clasped in his lifeless fingers. His eyes were wide open, but the side of his head was missing, just a bloody mess where the skull should have been.

Hans was lying near by in a pool of blood, clutching his arm and groaning.

Megan began to weep again. 'Oh my God, oh my God. What shall we do?'

Bertha took charge. 'George,' she said calmly, 'take Pat and baby Peter into the house and get Dottie to start giving them supper. Then telephone the police and tell them there has been a terrible accident. Pat, don't tell Rosie what has happened, and don't let her come anywhere near the stable. Then make sure there's some nice cheerful music on the radio while Dottie's getting the supper, and then, if you could start putting Rosie and Peter to bed . . .

Both George and Pat said 'yes', and hurried off with Peter as fast as their legs would carry them.

'Now,' said Bertha gently to Megan, 'let's get you up.' Firmly she put her strong, plump arms beneath Megan's shoulders and lifted her into a standing position. Megan stood, unable to think or speak, conscious only of Henry and Adam both lying dead before her.

Werner put his gun down in the manger near the door and went across to Hans who was still moaning and clutching his arm. After examining him briefly he said. 'Where shall I take him? I don't want the children to see the blood.'

Bertha thought for a moment. 'Take him to the outhouse at the back of the kitchen. Wait there a moment and I'll bring out hot water and bandages, meanwhile get George to send for Dr Crozier to dress his arm properly.'

Afterwards Megan couldn't remember getting back to the house, but Lavinia told her that Bertha had taken her back through the gold room windows, and then Lavinia had taken over and helped Megan undress and take a hot bath. Dr Crozier came upstairs when he'd finished dressing the wound on Hans's arm, which luckily was a superficial flesh wound. He gave Megan a sleeping draught.

When she awoke next morning the bodies of Henry and Adam had been taken away and, once the police had finished, Silas and a couple of casual labourers from East End farm had come over and thoroughly cleaned out the old stables. Now it was clean and tidy, and when Megan next entered the following evening it was difficult to believe what had happened there the previous night.

Silently she sat on the chair Henry had been sitting on when she'd first rushed in, and tried to think. What had happened then? The police had already asked her, but she couldn't remember. Now, although she was in the stable she still couldn't remember. It was just a confused mess of noise, shrieks and blood. Blood everywhere; she still had the smell of blood in her nostrils.

She shivered at the memory. It was Adam's fault. She had known when she'd first met him long, long ago, before she had even married Henry, that he was dangerous, that he had some kind of malevolent hold over Henry. But Henry had not realized it until too late. What was it Henry had said last night? *I'm sorry. I didn't know how to love you.* His whispered words echoed again around the room and Megan found herself whispering back. 'But I didn't know how to love you either, Henry.'

It was only now that she realized that they had both stumbled through life confused and unhappy, unable to help themselves or each other. *But I am the lucky one,* she thought. *I did find love with Jim, albeit briefly, and I have Peter to remind me.* Yes, I am the lucky one.

Pat had told her that Adam had said to Henry, *I'm not going anywhere without taking you with me.* And it had come true: he had taken Henry. But she was not alone. She was a woman with a son and an adopted daughter, and Peter would inherit Folly House. Her task now was to keep it for him until he reached twenty-one years of age.

Sitting there alone in the deserted stable she straightened her shoulders and raised her chin determinedly. She would turn around the fortunes of Folly House and East End Farm, and she would do it not only for Peter, but for Henry as well. The Lockwood name would be something for Peter to be proud of, no matter that not one drop of Lockwood blood ran through his veins.

Of course the newspapers splashed the news of the double shooting across their front pages for the next few days, and several reporters made their way to Folly House. But after the inquest all went quiet. The coroner's verdict was that Adam's balance of mind was disturbed; he had shot Henry and then turned the gun on himself. Werner had not fired a single shot; he'd told the police that he had every intention of firing but was afraid of hitting baby Peter and Pat, and by the time he was able to get a direct line of fire, Adam had turned the gun on himself.

The Jones and Moon families formed a protective shield around Megan and all at Folly House. She appreciated their loyalty and felt safe, and knew that Rosie and Peter were safe too. Then she sat down and started to make plans for the future.

Food was still in short supply, so there was a ready market for everything they produced. It seemed strange to be so short of food now that the war was over, but Megan knew food was in even shorter supply in war-ravaged Europe. Until the agricultural land in Europe was cleared of mines, bombs and the debris of war nothing much could be grown. Britain exported and Megan concentrated on food that could be grown quickly, packed and sold abroad, even though both Silas and George objected.

'Charity begins at home,' said Silas, when she wanted to plant a whole field of white cabbages.

'I've got a ready market for these,' Megan told him. 'In Germany they use them for sauerkraut. I can't afford to grow stuff just for the home market now.'

As the payment for the exports began to swell her bank balance Megan started to make other plans. Folly House could offer people bed and breakfast for people wanting to take a holiday in the beautiful New Forest. Lavinia was horrified. 'The Lockwoods have never done that sort of thing. And anyway, I was thinking that perhaps I could come back and live here now that Arthur and Marcus have gone. The dower douse is lonely.'

Megan thought about it. True, Lavinia was becoming frailer, but what to do with the dower house. Bertha suggested a solution. 'Why not let people rent the rooms and eat here, or even let the whole little house for holidays? That's what the Truscott family who own Merrymead are doing; they haven't got a bean to their name since young Mr Truscott was killed in the war. My sister works there. This year they let out rooms all summer and my sister Amy says they've done quite well.'

Megan knew the Truscotts slightly, and knew how hard up they were. If Cynthia Truscott, whom Megan had always secretly thought rather useless, could make money from letting rooms, then so could she. So Lavinia moved back to Folly House and had the small bedroom at the back of the house near to Rosie, and the dower house was given a lick of paint inside, ready for the coming spring and summer.

Megan worked hard and enjoyed her spare time with Peter and Rosie. It was only at night sometimes, sitting and looking out into the garden down towards the Folly and the sea that she felt lonely, and wondered whether Jim was still alive. Common sense told her that he must be dead; otherwise he would have got in touch with her. She was sure of it.

CHAPTER EIGHTEEN

Megan missed Henry, but Rosie and Peter were heartbroken. Megan found it difficult to explain why Adam had shot Henry. They didn't understand that Adam had been insane. But Lavinia became a tower of strength, and began taking the children to church every Sunday morning; afterwards they laid flowers on Henry's grave and when they got back to Folly House Bertha would let them into the kitchen, where they had a slice of bread dipped in the gravy from the roast meat to eat before lunch. It was a small ritual they looked forward to and in a strange way it helped to ease their pain.

But there was no such relief for Megan and she coped in the only way she knew how: filling her days with work and plans for the future of Folly House. She decided it would be no ordinary guest house, not like the Truscotts; it would be so fine and beautiful that people would queue up to spend a night at Folly House. This meant the house had to be renovated and the gardens and seashore landscaped. To this end she studied books showing formal gardens of chateaux and palazzi in France and Italy. Her dreams knew no bounds.

In the late autumn of 1946 she set to work intending to do as much landscaping as possible before the winter set in. Apart from a couple of temporary labourers she did all the work herself. Raking and mulching the huge lawns, pruning the tamarisk bushes on the seashore, but her ambition of creating a sheltered bower with sea views of the Solent and the distant Isle of Wight was eventually realized, even if her hands did end up raw and bleeding in the process.

Lavinia watched and worried, and confessed her concerns to Bertha. She often sought her out in the kitchen now that Rosie was at school and baby Peter was playing out in the garden with Dottie, overseen by Megan. She was not trusted to look after Peter on her own now, as she was developing cataracts and her sight was poor. 'It's not right that a lady should be doing all that manual work,' she said to Bertha. 'Megan's hands are now as rough as any workman, and her nails are never really clean.'

Bertha sniffed. She knew only too well what hard work was, unlike Lady Lavinia who had never done anything manual in her life. 'Needs must,' she told Lavinia. 'She can't afford to employ anyone else. Even the men on the farm have to work harder these days. I don't know what we'd do without those two German boys. Thank God they came our way.'

Hans and Werner were still at East End Farm, and both had applied to stay in England and not be repatriated to Germany. Werner was hoping to be accepted into a medical school, provided he could find someone to sponsor him. Megan would have liked to, but couldn't afford it.

But Lavinia worried. 'I only hope all this will work out the way Megan thinks it will. She has no experience of running a real business.'

Bertha stopped slicing potatoes on top of the large Lancashire hotpot she was preparing, and put her hands on her hips. She looked at Lavinia sternly. 'How can you say that?' she demanded. 'Ever since the troubles with Mr Henry's money she's been in charge. He couldn't do it, God bless him, so she took it on. She's been running the business for some years now and it hasn't been easy, and now it's even worse. All this rationing, although why we should have to put up with it now the war has ended I don't know. And now, to cap it all, we have the perpetual threat of electricity cuts.' She went back to her task of slicing potatoes with renewed vigour, and added, 'If we didn't have wood for the kitchen range you'd never get any hot dishes some days.'

Lavinia sat still, thinking of Megan. 'I wonder sometimes whether she keeps herself busy so that she doesn't have time to think.'

Bertha paused again. 'Yes,' she said reflectively, for once being in tune with Lavinia, 'it's a hard life being a widow so young, but there are plenty of them about these days.'

Both women sighed, then Lavinia said. 'So many men didn't come back. Sometimes I wonder what happened to Jim Byrne.' Bertha nodded her head, and Lavinia continued softly, 'He was like one of the family, we all loved him. But I suppose he is dead, like so many others.'

Bertha nodded again. She had her own ideas about Jim Byrne and often thought she could see a likeness in baby Peter. But she kept these thoughts to herself, not even mentioning them to George. Live and let live had always been her motto, and if Megan had taken a brief chance at happiness who could blame her?

Megan struggled on, falling into bed at night exhausted. No time for make-up or to have her hair done, she just scrubbed her face and twisted her long dark hair up in an untidy bun, which, although she did not know it because she rarely looked in the mirror, was very attractive. Sometimes she worked in the garden until the first stars of evening appeared, only then would she stop, but often wished she didn't have to. For then, when alone in the garden as dusk began to fall, and lights from the houses on the Isle of Wight twinkled across the waters of the Solent, she thought of Jim and Henry. They had become intertwined in her mind. Henry was the young man she'd thought she'd loved in the years before the war, when it seemed that nothing could possibly go wrong, and Jim was the passion of her life in later years.

Jim! She ached for him. The mere thought brought hot tears to her eyes. Alone in the garden she gazed at the sky; was he somewhere on the other side of the world looking at the same moon? If he was alive did he remember her? Or had he forgotten the English girl he'd met during the war?

For the sake of the children she kept cheerful, always making time for them before bedtime. Occasionally she sat down and read the newspapers, but not often, the news was so depressing. The wars in Europe and Japan might have finished but there seemed to be fighting everywhere else. China, Palestine, Indonesia, Vietnam, and even the Russians, once British allies, were now the enemy. Sometimes she wondered why anyone had bothered to fight the war, because it seemed that one set of problems had been replaced by another, and there was no limit to man's inhumanity to man.

In Britain new draconian rationing laws were being implemented, and many private industries were being nationalized by the Labour Government, setting neighbour against neighbour as everyone seemed to think differently when it came to politics.

But most of this passed by Folly House; life continued much as it had always done. She struggled on through the cold, dark days of a bitter December and by the time Christmas 1946 arrived Megan had virtually finished the garden. New bushes were planted, winding pathways created and by the foreshore a secluded bower had been created. Megan could see it in her mind's eye, a mass of fragrant yellow and pink blossoms in the summer.

At Christmas Rosie got the part of the Virgin Mary in the school nativity play and was very cross about it.

'But darling,' said Megan when Rosie was stamping about being bad-tempered. 'The Virgin Mary is the most important part, except for Jesus.'

'No it's not. I just sit there wrapped in a blue curtain holding a doll. They only gave me the part because I've got a club foot and limp.'

'Rubbish,' said Lavinia. 'They gave you the part because you are the prettiest girl in the class.'

Only Dottie cheered her when she told her she was the star of the play.

Megan allowed Peter and Rosie to do all the decorations in the house, and Dottie helped, willingly taking directions from Rosie, clambering up and down the stepladder festooning the rooms with paper chains, and sticking holly and ivy behind the paintings and mirrors.

'All those berries will dry and fall off on to the floor,' was Bertha's caustic comment watching Dottie giggling on the top of the step-ladder, 'and Dottie's nothing but a big baby.'

'That's exactly what she is,' said Megan gently. 'She can't help it, and it's lovely that she can get pleasure from such small things.'

'That's what George always says.' Unconvinced, Bertha stomped back to the kitchen, watched by Megan, who wished that somehow Bertha could accept Dottie and enjoy her the way she was.

Arthur and Violet arrived on Christmas Eve in time to go to

church for the blessing of the crib. Arthur was badly missed at the organ, which was now played by Miss Jennings, an elderly lady who'd recently moved to the village. She was very willing and enthusiastic, but singularly lacking in technique. Her enthusiasm regularly caused her to slip off the seat whilst pushing hard at the organ pedals.

But as Lavinia remarked with a heavy sigh, after one such episode, 'beggars can't be choosers.'

The two children from Folly House, along with other village children, took their gifts to be blessed by the Christ Child. Watching their shining faces lit by the candlelight around the crib, Megan felt a momentary shaft of joy. But most of the time it brought back bitter-sweet memories of previous Christmases, when Marcus was alive, and when Jim had played the organ. Those Christmases seemed a lifetime away.

The new vicar of East End, Alistair MacKinnon, was a young ex-army officer who had recently been discharged from active service. He was invited to Folly House for Christmas lunch by Lavinia. He was unmarried and Megan could see the gleam in Lavinia's eye. There was no way Meagn was going to let her start matchmaking and told her so the moment they were alone.

'Lavinia, I shall never remarry. So you can forget any ideas you might have about Alistair.'

'But he's such a nice young man,' protested Lavinia.

'I had enough religion to last a lifetime when I was a vicar's daughter. I don't want any more.'

Lavinia retired defeated, but the idea disturbed Megan more than she'd thought possible. It had nothing to with the vicar or religion, but everything to do with loneliness. Twenty-six years old, with many years stretching ahead; the thought was daunting. Peter and Rosie were company now, but they would grow up and go their own ways and then she would be alone again. She thought again of Jim and felt sad and guilty at the same time. The guilt was because she knew she would never be able to tell Peter who his true father was.

Glad when Christmas was over, she threw her energies into reorganizing the house ready for the summer visitors she hoped to attract. Gardening books were replaced with books lavishly illustrated with pictures of grand rooms in stately homes the length and breadth of England. The classical schemes gave her ideas. The gold room was repainted in a cool green with the moulded coving and ceiling roses picked out in white and gold leaf. A woman from the village helped Megan recover all the chairs and sofas with a delicately muted gold material, and new curtains were made for the tall windows from the same material. The overall effect was to make the room seem larger and give it an air of tranquillity and grandeur.

Lavinia and Bertha were the first to see the final result. 'Well, I never did,' said Bertha solemnly. 'If anyone had told me that a change of colour could change a room like this I would never have believed them.'

'It's absolutely beautiful,' said Lavinia breathlessly.

'It cost more than I thought,' Megan admitted, 'and that means that I won't be able to do the same with the rose dining room for this year. But in the meantime I'll get the guest bedrooms done in a simple English country style. That won't cost too much.'

'It would be lovely, though, if the rose room could be decorated in the same manner,' said Lavinia. 'I think you should go ahead and do it.'

'I told you. I haven't got the money.'

'But I have.'

Megan was about to interrupt and remind Lavinia that Mr Green was managing her financial affairs, and that she was not as well off as she thought she was, when Lavinia said serenely. 'I shall pay for the rest of the repairs and decorations to Folly House. It's the least I can do.'

'But . . .' began Megan.

'Don't tell me I haven't any money because I know that, but I do have diamonds, and diamonds can be sold.'

Without waiting for a reply from Megan she rushed from the room and returned five minutes later with two boxes. In one, lying on black velvet, was a pair of exquisite diamond and emerald drop earrings, and in the other a large pendant set with matching diamonds and emeralds.

Both Megan and Bertha gasped. 'I can sell these,' said Lavinia triumphantly. 'I haven't worn either the earrings or the pendant since Richard died, and I never really liked them. Too flashy for me.'

No time was wasted. The jewellery was sold at auction in London in the beginning of January 1947, and once the money was deposited in the bank Megan lost no time in designing and ordering the materials for the renovation of the rose room and the rest of the house.

'I'll be able to employ men to do the actual work, thanks to you,' Megan told Lavinia, showing her the plans she had sketched out in readiness. 'Albert Noakes has got together a team of men and they are reporting for duty next Monday, the twenty-seventh of January.'

But on Thursday 23 January the inhabitants of the New Forest woke up to a deathly hush. At first Megan couldn't think what it was. The light in the bedroom was unnaturally bright for a winter's morning and the silence was uncanny. But she knew as soon as Rosie burst into her room shrieking with excitement. 'There's snow everywhere, tons and tons of it.'

Throwing back the bedroom curtains Megan saw an unfamiliar sight. The snow was deep, up to the downstairs windowsills; a smooth blanket of white stretching down to the shore. Rosie and Peter had to be persuaded to have breakfast before going out, and during breakfast they listened to the wireless. It was reported that snow had fallen heavily during the night over south and south-west England. Many villages were cut off because of the depth of the snow.

Folly House was no exception and was well and truly cut off, even from East End Farm. Hans and Werner cleared a narrow path from Folly House to the farm at East End so that they could collect some fresh milk.

'Thank goodness we put all the cows inside at the first cold snap. At least we'll be able to feed and milk them, although goodness knows what we'll do with the milk; the lorries will never get through today to pick it up.'

'We'll cope like we've done before,' said Bertha firmly. 'Ivy Moon and I will try to use as much as possible, and the rest will be tipped down the drain once the new calves have had an extra treat.'

'What do you mean?' demanded Rosie. 'An extra treat.'

'Well, they'll get to drink their mother's milk instead of

watered-down stuff.'

'Oh.' Rosie digested this bit of information and went back to the rose room to tell Peter.

Because of the weather the renovation of Folly House was put on hold. There was no school, as there was no coal to heat the big pot-bellied stoves that warmed the schoolrooms. The roads were impassable even after they'd managed to clear footpaths to the village, and the temperature regularly dropped to minus four degrees Farenheit night after night. Snow spread all over the country and because there was virtually no transport, as everywhere was affected by the snow and sub-zero temperatures, there was a coal shortage and electricity was cut off most days from 9.00 a.m. in the morning to 12 noon, and then again from 2.00 p.m. until 4.00 p.m.

At least Folly House was able to provide hot meals, as Bertha used the big wood-fired stove in the kitchen, but even then Megan had to ration their wood as the wood-pile in the field was frozen into a solid block which, despite the best efforts of Hans and Werner, could not be broken. The wood store at the back of the old stables was still accessible and Megan knew it would have to last until a thaw began. Like everyone else Folly House ran out of coal, so the house was cold and extra layers of clothing were needed.

Day after day the bitter cold persisted and the frozen snow remained, making normal life impossible. One morning Benjamin Moon arrived with an armful of post; amongst it was a letter from Arthur. Megan sent Benjamin on his way with half a dozen eggs and a small loaf which Bertha had baked the day before. Eggs and bread were still on ration and he was grateful for the extra food. 'I heard on the radio yesterday that a farm in Essex was digging parsnips with a pneumatic drill,' he said. He shook his head. 'Don't know what the world is coming to. It's nearly the end of February and there's no sign of a thaw.'

After Benjamin had gone Megan sat down in her office with Arthur's letter, pulling an old woollen shawl around her and keeping her mittens on, but even so her hands were still permanently blue. Arthur's letters were always full of news about his studies, and the concerts he'd been to and now was even being asked to play at. It was news of another world, and sometimes Megan wished she could escape from Folly House, just for a little while, and join him.

Slitting open the envelope she began to read.

I was booked to play at St Martin's in the Fields for an evening concert, and I had to play by candlelight as there was a power cut. Luckily I knew the pieces well, some Chopin and Schubert, and didn't need to read the music. How I wished you could have been there, Megan. The church looked magnificent when it was totally lit by candles and had a wonderful feeling of mystery and beauty.

Violet and I often think of you down in the New Forest and hope you are not suffering from the cold too much. But I know you, and I expect you've organized everything very well and that you have plenty to eat and drink.

By the way, we tried the new whale meat the government has imported to help with the meat ration. We had Moby Dick, that's what they call whale meat and chips, in a restaurant. It's supposed to be like steak, but Violet and I thought it tasted very fishy and didn't like it. We shall stick with vegetables if there's no meat, but even those are difficult to come by in London at the moment as everything is frozen.

By the way, we did eat out at the Savoy Hotel the other evening, a special treat. Who do you think we saw? It was Jim Byrne. At least I think it was Jim Byrne. He looked extremely smart and the woman he was with was very glamorous. But he was right over the other side of the room and I didn't get to speak to him or even get closer as there was another sudden power cut. By the time the hotel staff had lit all the candles Jim and his companion had vanished, so I'm not sure if it was him or not.

Megan let the letter fall into her lap. It was impossible to read more, she was blinded by tears. Jim in London! Why no letter? Why no phone call, or visit to Folly House? The answer was, of course, he had forgotten her.

CHAPTER NINETEEN

Winter 1947

Arthur regretted having mentioned the sighting of Jim, not least because Violet was furious with him. 'Surely you must know how much it would upset her. To think that Jim is in England and hasn't bothered to get in touch. It must be devastating.'

'Of course, we're not really sure it was Jim,' said Arthur defensively. 'I did say we were not sure.'

'You shouldn't have said anything,' replied Violet grimly. 'When we see Megan again for heaven's sake do be careful what you say.'

'God knows when that will be,' said Arthur, feeling guilty as well as gloomy. 'Unless it stops snowing we'll be marooned here in London for ever.'

Down in Hampshire life became increasingly difficult after another heavy snowfall blocked all the roads on 27 February. More snow and a dramatic fall in temperature, just when everyone was thinking that a thaw must be just around the corner, caused Megan to lose patience. Idleness was not good for her peace of mind and she decided that at least she could strip the paintwork in the bedrooms. She reasoned that if an ill-educated workman could master the art of stripping paint then so could she.

George had two old blowtorches in the garden shed and filled them paraffin for her. 'This is dangerous work,' he said disapprovingly. 'Things can be set on fire.'

'Have you used them?' asked Megan, 'And did you set anything on fire?'

'No, of course not,' said George.

'Well, there you are then,' said Megan, taking the two blow torches from him.

'But I'm a man,' said George.

This remark was greeted with an angry snort from Megan and that was the end of the argument.

But it was slower and harder work than she'd anticipated and by the end of the first week in March she'd only managed to strip halfway round one bedroom. George sent one of the farm labourers, Alf Beeson, to Megan with an offer of help. 'I've done all me own cottage, stripped the lot,' Alf said. 'Dab hand with a blowtorch I am.'

Megan was only too glad to accept the help, and together they scraped away at the blistering paint. Although it was often ten degrees below freezing outside and blowing a gale as well as snowing, they both sweltered in the heat from the blowtorches.

Lavinia always came up to remind Megan of lunch and both she and Alf left their work and went downstairs, Alf to the Jones's kitchen and Megan to join Lavinia by the rose room fireplace, where a meagre little wood fire was glowing, waiting for Bertha to get the children and bring in the lunch. 'You look exhausted,' said Lavinia one morning. When Megan didn't reply, she continued, 'For nearly two hundred and fifty years the Lockwood family has lived in this house while it has grown around them to what it is today. And now the only people living here are not Lockwoods. You and I are Lockwoods by marriage, not by inheritance, and yet you are half-killing yourself to save the house and the estate.'

'I've always loved Folly House, and I'm saving it for Peter. He's a Lockwood.'

Lavinia poured them both a small glass of wine from the decanter on the table. 'Yes, there's Peter, a Lockwood in name,' she said softly. 'Henry's joy, the boy he gave his life for. He was a loving father in every way save one.'

Megan felt a cold hard knot grow inside her. 'You know,' she whispered.

'Yes, I know. I've always known, even before Henry told me. I knew because you and Jim had that special glow when you were together, the glow that only true lovers have.'

'What are you going to do?'

Lavinia turned in surprise. 'Do?' she echoed. 'Nothing, of course. Why should I? You gave Henry more joy in the last years of his life than he expected by sharing Peter with him. I'll always be grateful for that. Besides I know the price you paid. Lost love is always hard, and doesn't get easier as the years pass by.'

A single tear trickled slowly down Megan's cheek. 'Peter is all I have now,' she whispered.

'Nonsense.' Lavinia suddenly sounded like the Lavinia of old, firm and slightly abrasive. 'You have me while I'm still alive, and you have everyone else here and in the village. They will always be here for you and your son. That's the advantage of living in a small place, you are never completely alone. Not the way you can be in a big city. That was my life before I married Richard and came to the country. Although I was never lucky enough to have children I shared in the upbringing of Henry and Gerald, and the little vicar's daughter, who always wanted to live in Folly House.'

Megan wiped her eyes and smiled. 'Was it always so obvious?'

'Perhaps only to me. I too would have hated living in that big, ugly vicarage. That's the one good thing the Luftwaffe did, dropping a bomb on it.'

Megan laughed. 'Maybe the war wasn't all bad after all.'

'Nothing is ever all bad. We've been picked up and tossed around, but now it's time for those of us still here to settle down. New life will blossom, you mark my words, and Folly House will always be here, just as it has been for the last two hundred and fifty years.'

Her positive mood was infectious and after she'd gone Megan, when she resumed paint stripping, worked beside Alf with renewed vigour.

It was even colder that night and Werner got up to fetch his greatcoat and put it over his bed as an extra blanket, so it was he who saw the vivid finger of orange lick up the chimney-breast at the far end of Folly House. He rubbed his eyes and looked again. But there was nothing, just darkness, and the black slumbering hump of the house against the vivid whiteness of the snow. He turned to go to bed, but hesitated and turned back, sensed something and waited. This time yellow and orange, no mistake, it was a spit of flame caressing the ancient brickwork of the chimney like a malevolent hand. This time it didn't disappear but lingered before leaving, and after it left he could see a string of sparkling red embers, throbbing with life as they started spreading away from the chimney and along the roof. The thatch of Folly House was on fire. As he watched he realized that all the tiny threads of flame were creeping along the roof, faster and faster. Then he heard it, a roaring sound. The cold easterly which had been blowing for days straight from Siberia was gathering strength and acting on the fire like a great pair of bellows.

Throwing his greatcoat over his pyjamas and struggling into his yard boots he called out to Hans. 'Hans, Hans, the house is on fire. Come on. Come on.'

Hans stumbled outside with Werner. There was no mistaking it now. The roof was on fire. They got the fire buckets and ran to the cattle trough. But it was frozen solid.

Werner swore. 'We'll have to get water from the house.'

'No,' shouted Hans. 'We must get everyone out first.'

Megan awoke to the sound of the wind. She'd fallen asleep that night more exhausted than usual, and now woke reluctantly. For a moment she lay listening to the sound of the bitter easterly wind which always howled along the rooftop, and thought with longing for the soft southerly breeze of summer, which brought with it warm misty rain, not snow and ice. Snuggling down in bed she pulled the blankets up, then pushed them down again. What was it she could hear? Surely not the sea lapping near the house. But it was the wind, and it had a roar to it she'd never heard before. Then she heard the voices of Werner and Hans, they were shouting. Suddenly she was aware of heat, and the acrid smell of burning wood. Folly House was on fire.

She jumped out of bed, threw on her jodhpurs and sweater and thrust her feet into a pair of boots. She opened the door and raced down the corridor in the darkness to where Peter and Rosie slept.

She tried to switch on the lights but there was no power. In the darkness she stumbled towards Rosie's bed. 'Rosie,' she screamed, 'get up, put on a coat and shoes and follow me.' The next moment she picked Peter out of his bed, wrapped him, still half-asleep, in a blanket, made sure Rosie was by her side, then the three of them staggered downstairs into the hallway.

Hans was there with a torch. 'Come,' he said urgently, his panic making his German accent almost unintelligible. He grabbed Megan's arm and tried to drag her through the doorway to the gravel drive outside.

Megan thrust Peter into his arms and shouted to Rosie. 'Stay with Hans, I must get Lavinia.' Without waiting to see if they did as she said, she turned and rushed back up the stairs to Lavinia's bedroom.

Lavinia wasn't awake properly when Megan dragged her from her bed. She threw a thick blanket around a dazed Lavinia and led her downstairs. It was difficult in the pitch black with choking smoke now eddying around them. Lavinia was racked with coughing, but Megan pushed and pulled until at last they were able to get outside into the bitterly cold, fresh air. Only then did Megan realize that Lavinia had no shoes on. But Lavinia didn't complain. She was shocked into silence as they stood in the icy snow, watching Folly House being engulfed by fire.

Werner was there with Bertha and Dottie, all clothed in dressing gowns. 'The phone is not working and there's no power,' he told Megan. 'But George has gone to the village on his bicycle.'

'Why didn't he take the car? cried Megan, 'it would have been quicker.'

'It wouldn't start. Everything is frozen. We must take water from the kitchen tap while we can, the trough is frozen solid.'

Bertha took charge of Lavinia and the children and took them into Hans and Werner's rooms in the old stable. People from the village came and helped form a chain, passing buckets of water to and fro, but it was too little to quench the fire. When the fire engine arrived Megan heaved a sigh of relief. But her relief was short-lived.

The outside fire hydrant was frozen solid and by the time the firemen managed to thaw it out for use with their hoses Folly House was reduced to ashes. The only part left standing was the original old nurse's cottage in which the Jones family lived, and even that was uninhabitable now as it was soaked with water, blackened by soot and full of grey ash. As dawn began to break they stood together in the bitter cold and looked upon a scene of utter desolation. The once beautiful house was now a mountain of smouldering ash with blackened timbers pointing like accusing fingers to the sky.

Lavinia and Bertha both wept. Rosie clung to Megan. 'What shall we do? Where shall we live?' As she began to weep so did Peter. Megan was silent, holding Peter and Rosie close. Their small soft bodies were a kind of comfort, but she had no answer for Rosie. Everything was lost, even Peter's beloved teddy. And the photo of Jim, that too had evaporated into smoke. When she thought of that she began to weep as well.

Her soul was filled with a gut-wrenching despair; she felt she could hardly breathe. It was the end of everything, the past, the present and the dreams for the future. Now there was nothing.

Peter began to cry again. 'He's cold,' said Rosie, her teeth chattering.

Megan suddenly realized that both her children were blue with cold. She had to do something. 'We will all have to use the dower house today.' She looked at Bertha, who was moving towards her. 'I supposed it's still locked, and we won't have a key now; it's somewhere in . . .' She looked at the ashes and couldn't bring herself to say Folly House.

'George has picked the lock,' said Bertha. 'We'll get a fire going in the sitting room for you and one in the kitchen, then we'll be all right.'

We'll never be all right thought Megan with a heavy heart. *Nothing will ever be the same again.* But she said, 'Thank you Bertha, I don't know what we'd do without you.' Gathering the children to her she walked down the drive through the hard frozen snow towards the dower house.

Werner followed, carrying a shivering Lavinia.

May 1951

Lavinia, Megan and the children had moved into the West Wing of Brinkley Hall after the fire. It had been redecorated and furnished for Violet and Arthur's use, but as they were staying on in London it was an ideal solution as a temporary measure. That had been four years ago and there was still no sign of Folly House being rebuilt; the insurance was complicated, and really not adequate to build the beautiful country house Megan wanted. Violet offered to help, but Megan refused to borrow money. She said she would save money from the proceeds of the gardens and farm and then build another Folly House, but the truth was her heart wasn't really in it.

The stables and outhouses had all survived the fire, as had the Jones's part of the house which, once cleaned up and redecorated, was fit to live in again. George and Bertha still lived there; Bertha was more or less semi-retired and George stayed on, working on the gardens of the estate. Dottie had got a job washing glasses in the East End Arms, which she loved. Megan had decided to merge East End Farm and the Folly House gardens and fields into the East End Estate, making Hans the manager. Silas Moon had retired and George was retiring soon, both taking advantage of the new, improved old-age pension the government had instituted. Werner, sponsored by Violet and Arthur, had gone off to medical school in London, and after Pat had married Hans, Megan gave them the tenancy of the dower house as part of their salary.

Megan had to admit that living in Brinkley Hall was the last word in luxury. They had a maid and a part-time cook on a daily basis which worked well, although Megan missed the companionship of the Jones family. But most of all she missed the sound of the sea, and the lovely gardens of Folly House which sloped down to the shore. But in the years since the fire she'd learned to be patient and tried not to look back too often, nor look too far into the future either. As Lavinia wisely said, 'Live for the moment, my dear. Once a moment has come, it becomes history all too quickly.'

Now today in May 1951 she sat beside an over-excited six-year-old as the train clattered across the countryside of the Home Counties into Surrey and to their final destination, Waterloo Station, London.

It was difficult to believe that Peter was six years old, or that Rosie, who was staying with Violet and Arthur, was eighteen and would be starting medical school in the autumn of the year. The years had flown by, and most of the time Megan was happy. She still worked hard on the farm, but had more spare time now for Peter and Rosie as she'd passed some of her duties on to Pat and Hans.

Peter chattered on, and Megan listened with half an ear. Her thoughts skittered over the past, and the future. Life was getting easier, she had to admit that: she had a beautiful and talented daughter in Rosie, and an adorable son who showed every sign of inheriting his father's and Arthur's musical ability. This was something Megan was determined to nurture. They were coming to London to hear Arthur play in London's new Royal Festival Hall.

Peter was keen to go to the concert but even more keen to see the sights of London. He ticked them off on his fingers, 'I want to go on the underground, go to London Zoo and see the bears, go to the Tower of London and see the Beefeaters and see the torture instruments in the Bloody Tower – oh, and see the King and Queen.'

Megan laughed. 'We're only going to be there for five days, darling. But we'll squash as much in as we possibly can. Rosie and Violet will be our guides.'

They were met at Waterloo by Violet and Rosie and, much to Peter's joy, caught a double-decker bus to Knightsbridge. He would have stayed upstairs on the bus for ever if allowed to, but eventually got off and went to the house in Cadogan Square where Violet and Arthur lived. When he was eventually asleep Megan sat with Violet, waiting for Arthur to return from the Festival Hall; Rosie had gone there to meet him and help him with his wheelchair. 'I can't believe how grown-up she is,' said Megan, and felt a pang of sorrow. She was no more a child, no more dependent on her.

'She'll always come back to Hampshire and you,' said Violet, guessing Megan's thoughts. She changed the subject. 'Arthur and I love it here,' she said. 'This part of London somehow miraculously escaped most of the bombs, and when I look out at the garden in the square it's almost like being in the country.'

Megan gazed out. Yes, it was beautiful, the garden in the square was awash with early roses, surrounded by tulips and wallflowers, and the pavements were covered in pink blossom blown like confetti from the flowering cherry trees. 'Yes, it's lovely. But no sea,' she said.

Violet laughed and watched Megan. She's still very beautiful, she thought even though she's thirty-two now. But with no make-up, and her air coiled up in a chignon she manages to look both elegant and very young at the same time. She should be living in London where she would meet people, rather than being buried in the country and never meeting any eligible men. Violet put her thoughts into words. 'Why don't you move to London once Rosie starts university? Hans can run East End Estate, there's no need to bury yourself in the New Forest.'

Megan shook her head. 'I can't leave Lavinia. She's increasingly frail now. In fact I've asked Mrs Fox to stay with her while I'm away now, just to make certain she's OK.'

'Perhaps she could stay permanently,' suggested Violet. 'I understand she only rents rooms in Southampton.'

Megan shrugged: a tired gesture, Violet noticed. 'No, I've got to stay and sort out the finances for the Folly House rebuild, although at times I despair of it ever happening.'

Violet changed the subject. 'We'll have dinner as soon as Rosie and Arthur get back from the rehearsal. Then we can have a relaxing evening.' She didn't mention that she was worried that the visiting American pianist, a James Byrne, might be their Jim Byrne. Violet thought he must be, as apparently he had only started as a soloist at the end of the war. She'd not wanted Megan to come at all, but it was difficult as she'd already been invited to Arthur's first prestigious concert. She hadn't mentioned it because Arthur was insisting that they should find out if it was 'their' Jim, as he called him, and whether he was married. Although there was nothing they could do about any of it. They couldn't prevent Megan from going to the concert and once she had seen him, and if it was Jim, what then? Not for the first time Violet wished that they hadn't interfered, but had told Megan about the lost letter. It was too late now, life had moved on. What will be, will be, Violet thought in resignation. Tomorrow they would all know whether James Byrne was the Jim Byrne of the war years.

It was dark the next night when Megan arrived at Waterloo Station. It was 3 May and London was in festival mood. Crowds everywhere, people wearing Union Jack hats and waving flags. But Megan might as well have been all alone, so immersed was she in her own private world of misery.

Earlier it had been so different. Along with the rest of the family she'd set off in high spirits. Violet was a little nervous but Arthur had assured her that he thought James Byrne was a different man, not the Jim they knew. He hadn't managed to actually meet him, but had seen his photo and he looked different, also his wife was an opera singer and apparently they had been together for years.

Megan, along with Peter and Rosie watched the King at the opening of the concert at the Festival Hall. Afterwards Arthur had got them tickets to attend the reception for all the artistes along with the King and Queen. Peter had been in raptures to see a real King and Queen, although bitterly disappointed that neither of them was wearing a crown. But all this passed Megan by. She could hardly think straight. All she could think of was Jim.

From the moment she had seen him walk on to the stage and take his place at the piano she'd been incapable of rational thought. It was difficult to keep the tears from her eyes as she watched him play. Everything was so painfully familiar, his broad shoulders, his shapely hands on the piano keys, and the familiar lock of hair which fell across his forehead as he concentrated. She could hardly breathe as they waited to be introduced at the reception. He was standing with a group of other musicians and singers. Stepping forward she saw the recognition light up in his eyes as she smiled at him. At last, after all this time, they were together.

But before either of them could speak Arthur spun himself forward in his wheelchair and manoeuvred himself between them. 'You remember Jim, don't you Megan? he said.

Megan stared at him. Why was his voice so strange? Remember

Jim? Of course she did. Everyone did. What was he talking about?

Jim spoke next. 'Megan,' he said and, stepping forward, clasped her hand. There was a long silence while they stared at each other, and then he said slowly, 'Of course I remember you.' He looked down and Megan was suddenly aware of her rough farm girl's hands and tried to draw them away, but he held on.

The tall blonde woman at his side laughed gently. 'You must introduce us, darling. Don't keep her all to yourself.'

'You look just the same,' he said, staring at Megan.

Again Megan tried to draw her hand away, conscious of the crowd around them, and especially of the blonde woman. 'I am the same,' she said. 'Nothing has changed, except that I have a son.' She nodded towards Peter at her side.

'Henry must be very pleased and proud. Please give him my regards.' He dropped Megan's hand and held out his hand to Peter, who took it and executed a stiff little bow.

Megan thought: surely everyone around them must have heard her sharp intake of breath as she realized that Jim couldn't know that Henry was dead. For a moment she hesitated, wondering what to say. But Peter filled the silence, his voice clear as a bell. 'My daddy is dead. A nasty man shot him and then he was shot as well.'

'Don't let's talk about that, darling.' Megan pulled Peter firmly to her side. 'Let's talk about the concert, about more cheerful things.'

The blonde woman stepped forward. 'I second that,' she said. 'There's far too much talk of war here in Britain.' She turned to Jim. 'Tell them about us, darling. About our concert tour here in the UK. Introduce me.'

'This is my wife, Greta Lavelle,' said Jim. Megan remembered her from the concert. She was a lyric soprano. 'It was Greta who persuaded me to give up engineering and go back to music.' His wife slipped her arm through his and smiled at Megan.

Megan forced herself to smile back, and suddenly realized why Violet and Arthur were looking so worried. They had been as unprepared for this meeting as she had. Clasping Greta's hand, she managed to say in a steady voice. 'It was lovely to hear Jim play once more. I must say that I never expected to see him in England again.'

'Oh, Jim and I often pay flying visits here, but we both really prefer New York, don't we, darling?'

They look right together, thought Megan sadly. They belong to this glamorous world of music, and I belong on the farm and in the forest. For a brief moment she wondered if Jim remembered the sunlit rides through the forest in the weeks before the D-day landings. Now he looked so elegant in his evening suit. He was not the man she had ridden out with.

Jim didn't say anything but went on looking at her until Megan felt she had to say something and get away. 'Well, this is just a flying visit backstage to see Arthur,' she said hurriedly, 'and I have to go now as I promised to take my son to see the royal procession as it makes its way back to Buckingham Palace. It's been lovely seeing you. Good luck with the tour. But we really must dash now.'

Everything was a blur from then on. She vaguely remembered dragging Peter away, but how she got through the rest of the afternoon and evening she didn't know. Of course Peter noticed nothing; he was much too interested in the King and Queen. But back in the house in Cadogan Square Megan knew she had to get away from the proximity of Jim and his wife. 'I can't stay. I can't stay,' she said, weeping as she packed her case. 'Will you take Peter for a few days? I'll say that I've had to go back for business reasons.'

Violet agreed, and Peter hardly listened to Megan's excuses, he was totally centred on the promised sightseeing trips in London, including a ride on the big dipper at Battersea Park Festival Gardens. That evening a reluctant Violet put Megan in a taxi for Waterloo station.

By the time Megan eventually arrived at Salisbury and found a taxi it was one o' clock in the morning and she was exhausted from the effort of trying not to weep in front of people.

'Nurse going back on duty, are you?' asked the taxi driver as he dropped her off at the hospital entrance.

Megan let him think that and didn't ask to be taken to the west wing, her private entrance. After he'd driven away she picked up her suitcase and began trudging round the building. Now, when no one could see, she let the tears stream down her face, oblivious to the busy world of the hospital inside the building.

When she arrived she tried to let herself in through the big wooden door which fronted their apartment, but the door wouldn't budge. Then she realized that Mrs Fox, who was caring for Lavinia, was not expecting anyone, and had barred and bolted the door for the night. It was the last straw. Exhausted she slumped down on the suitcase, leant her head against the doorframe and closed her eyes.

'Whatever are you doing here at this time of the morning? I thought it was a burglar.' It was Mrs Fox, a formidable figure in her red-check dressing-gown, and with rollers in her hair. She was gripping a large cast-iron frying pan.

'I couldn't get in.'

'I know that. Well, come in now.' Mrs Fox's brisk matter-of-fact tone was strangely comforting. She made no mention of the fact that Megan had obviously been weeping, but ushered her into the kitchen. 'I'll make a cup of tea,' she said.

Megan searched unsuccessfully for a handkerchief, sniffed, then said, 'It's what the English always do when there's a problem. Make a cup of tea.'

'Nothing wrong with that.' Mrs Fox passed her a clean handkerchief. 'It's the doing of it that helps. The Lord helps those who help themselves. I've always believed in keeping busy; no time to think then.'

Megan rested her head on her arms on the kitchen table and wondered what it was that Mrs Fox was trying to forget. Was it the alcoholic husband she'd once had, or the constant lack of money? Whatever it was she never complained, just got on with life.

'I do try to keep busy,' she said tearfully.

A heavy hand grasped her shoulder and gave it a squeeze. 'I know, ducks. Forgive me for speaking plain, but I've seen you struggling through your marriage, trying to manage the farm with no money to speak of, and bringing up two children with no father in sight. We all admire you, you know.'

Megan raised a tear-stained face in astonishment. 'Admire me! Who admires me?'

'Why everyone in the village and all around . . .' Mrs Fox petered off, then said, 'I've spoken out of turn. I'm sorry, Miss Megan.'

'I don't think people would admire me if they knew the truth of everything.' Megan wiped her eyes and picked up the cup of strong tea placed before her.

'The truth. Aah, now there's a thing,' said Mrs Fox slowly. She leaned across the table and gazed at Megan. 'The truth, my dear, is your business and no one else's. And it's for you to decide who you tell, when you tell, and if you ever tell. The only thing to remember is that our Lord knows the truth and loves you for it or despite it.'

Megan drained the tea from her cup and smiled. Suddenly nothing seemed as bad as it had half an hour ago. 'You should take up preaching, Mrs Fox,' she said. 'You'd make a lot of converts.' She stood up and dragged her case to the kitchen door. 'I think I'm ready for bed.'

Mrs Fox held the door open for her. 'Goodnight, dear. I'll leave you in the morning. Come down when you're ready.'

When she was ready for bed Megan drew back the curtains. A full moon was high in the sky, and everything was black and silver in the formal gardens of Brinkley Hall. The topiary trees cut in the shape of cockerels stood guard, black sentries before a silver path, and the gnarled branches of the ancient wisteria, which was now covered with early blossom, tapped against the pane of the sash window. It was a mild night, so Megan unclipped the catch on the top of the sash, and pushed the bottom window up. The smell of damp earth and the delicate eau de cologne fragrance of the wisteria floated into the room. Megan sniffed appreciatively.

But it was not the salty tang of the sea: the smell of Folly House, which she'd always loved. There was an edge to that, a wildness, which was lacking in the formality of the gardens at Brinkley.

Leaving the window open she climbed into bed, and at last let herself think about Jim. Why had he not come back? The answer was, of course, that theirs was a wartime romance. Chance had thrown them together, and then separated them again. Maybe if they had not discovered Henry at that concert things might have worked out differently. But it was just a maybe, not a certainty.

The moon continued its journey across the heavens and Megan lay in bed and watched it. She felt strangely peaceful now. She remembered the saying: *it is better to have loved and lost than never to have loved at all.* It was true. The golden memories she had would always be there, to be kept in her pocket, golden pebbles, to be looked at whenever she needed to.

But now the path before her was uncluttered with useless hopes and dreams. She would grasp reality, accept Violet's offer of money, and begin work on the reconstruction of Folly House. A new house would be built with a new name, because there would be a mélange of families belonging there in the future. One day the true story of the Lockwoods would be revealed, because she would write it all down.

She turned over in bed and pulled the bedspread up to her chin. She'd tell Violet and Arthur in the morning of her decision to start work on the new house. They would be pleased.

CHAPTER TWENTY

Summer 1991

Of course the name of the house was never changed. But the house was rebuilt. It was much larger and completely different, but it remained Folly House, because as Arthur said, 'Whatever kind of house is here it will always be Folly House because we still have the Folly standing guard down on the shore.' So it remained Folly House, home of the Lockwood family.

Megan walked unhurriedly across the lawn in the warm dusk of a summer's evening. Her progress was slow because she stopped every now and then to enjoy the view. Across the expanse of sea the lights on the Isle of Wight gradually appeared, tiny stars in the night. She was seventy-two now and as slim and upright as she had been in her youth. Years of working outside in all weathers had given her strength. Although in these last years at Folly House hard manual labour had not been necessary, she still did a fair share because she enjoyed it. But mostly her work had been involved in the administration of the Folly House Music Academy. In the forty years which had elapsed since the house had been rebuilt many things had happened and changed, and yet for Megan some things were still the same. She was still alone, and sometimes tender memories of her time with Jim would flood her mind; those memories were as real and clear as if it had been yesterday. But it no longer seemed important that he had not loved her enough to seek her out. There was Peter. That was enough.

Other times she thought of Henry. Arthur was right: she should never have married him, but if she had not then she wouldn't be here now, neither would Peter or Rosie, and maybe not even Folly House.

Life, she reflected, was like a jigsaw, except the humans involved had no say in how the pieces fitted together. That was left to the hand of fate.

When she reached the shore she sat on the granite stone. It had been chiselled now into a rough seat and no longer reminded her of Gerald's death. That too was history. Now, it was a seat with a panoramic view of the Solent, nothing more nor less. Megan shifted on the stone until she was comfortable, then relaxed listening to the sound of a music rehearsal starting back in the house. A flute was playing a haunting refrain, the notes drifting down into the garden then floating out across the sea into the dusk.

It was the beginning of the summer season for the Folly House Music Festival, and this year a new opera was to be performed. Megan smiled proudly. The opera had been written and was being directed by Peter Lockwood. Quite how Folly House had morphed from a farm into a music school she still found difficult to believe. Originally set up to help Arthur, who had found touring as a soloist more and more difficult as his arthritis made him increasingly disabled, it had small beginnings.

But it had grown from a small music establishment specializing in piano into an internationally acclaimed music school for singers and instrumentalists, as well as having a famous summer festival.

Peter had fulfilled his early promise as a musician and was now a well-known composer and conductor. He was married to Klara, a lieder singer, and had two children, Siena and Gabriella. The two girls had grown into lovely young women and were now at university, although they came back to Folly House as often as they could. Megan loved it when the house was full and Rosie teased her, saying she just wanted to be the centre of attention, playing the dominating matriarch. But Megan didn't feel like a matriarch, that sounded far too old. She didn't feel old. Where had all the years gone? She was still young in her head.

Footsteps sounded behind her and she turned to see Rosie coming across the lawn carrying a tray. 'I've brought us both a glass of lovely cold white wine,' she said as she got near. 'Some chardonnay, I know you like that.'

Megan moved up and made room for her on the stone seat. That was another bonus. Sometimes she couldn't believe she deserved all the happiness she had from having Rosie as a daughter. Who could have wished for a more loving child and grown-up daughter. They couldn't be closer, not even if she had actually given birth to her. Although always musically talented, Rosie had decided to become a doctor, eventually coming back to work at Stibbington Hospital, where she had met and married another doctor, an amiable man named John Edwards. They were happy; the only sadness in their lives was the lack of children. When Lavinia died they moved into part of Folly House and Megan was never alone. Rosie was fifty-eight now and had decided to retire from medicine and take up the reins of running the Folly House Music Academy and Festival, so that the three founders, Violet, Arthur and Megan could take life a little more easily.

Megan nodded back towards the house. 'It's a little late for the orchestra to start rehearsing, isn't it?'

'Yes.' Rosie passed her a glass of wine. 'Peter's got some visiting bigwig in there whom he met in New York when he was on tour last year. This man wants to hear the opening overture of the new opera. Maybe with a bit of luck Peter will get an invite to take the opera to the States.'

They sat in silence, listening to the music. A chilly gust of wind blew in from the Solent rippling the smoothness of the sea so that the shingle surged and sighed.

'I'll go and get a wrap for you,' said Rosie, and went back towards the house.

It was beginning to get quite dark and Megan shivered. *A ghost walking over my grave*, she thought. Suddenly they were all there, the ghosts of the past pressing in on her, demanding her attention. The Jones family; how she missed Bertha's cooking, and Dottie's ever-anxious-to-please face. And Lavinia, tall and elegant; even when age had robbed her of the knowledge of who she really was she had retained her elegance. They were all there, Hans and Pat, who had eventually returned to Germany, to a farm in Bavaria amongst the lakes and mountains. Silas Moon, his greasy cap always on his head and a hand-rolled cigarette stuck in the corner of his mouth. Mrs

Fox, Albert Noakes and all the others. Now, all long gone, although in Megan's imagination still treading the familiar paths.

But new people were jostling to take their places. Different children rode on their bikes along the lanes to the foreshore, shouting and laughing, without a care in the world. They never noticed the shadowy figures of past inhabitants, not did they see the soldiers lining the shores, ghosts of the men who long ago launched their crafts and set out to sea to fight a battle from which there was no return. The only reminders of those days were the enormous cast-iron bollards, half-sunk into the sand and shingle. But Megan could still hear the sounds and see the sights of those days; the air throbbed with them.

The music stopped. Glancing over her shoulder she saw that the lights in the house had all been switched on. Now there was laughter and the clink of glasses. The house was vibrant, alive with fresh life and suddenly Megan felt alone. She turned back and gazed out to sea. A sea fog was beginning to form, soon it would come rolling in. The weather was always changeable at this time of year along the coast, one moment warm and balmy, the next, when the sea mist crept in, cold and clammy. The cold made Megan's joints ache. *Perhaps I've lived too long.* The thought was depressing. She wasn't ready to go yet, she wanted to live on and find out what else life had in store for her.

'I've brought your wrap.'

A man's voice startled her. Megan turned. A tall erect figure with broad shoulders was silhouetted against the lights of the house. Her heart thudded. It couldn't be. But it was. It was him. He had come back after all. But it was too late. Far too late. Surely he knew it was too late? All the same though, she couldn't suppress the little flicker of joy in her heart.

But as she peered at him through the deepening dusk she realized with disappointment that it was an old man. It wasn't anyone she knew, just an old man walking with slightly faltering steps over the rough turf at the foot of the Folly. When he reached her he leaned forward and gently placed the wrap around her shoulders.

'Thank you,' said Megan. He sat down beside her without

speaking and Megan looked at him. She felt uneasy. There was something about him that filled her with disquiet. Then he turned his head towards her and smiled.

Her heart thudded. How could she have been so blind? It was his smile. It was the smile that had warmed her heart the first time she'd seen it in St Nicholas's church so many years before. It was Jim. The old man was Jim. For a moment she felt confused, then realized why. The Jim of her dreams had remained forever young. But of course he had aged just as she had. It was easy to forget that when she was young inside.

'I'm sorry I'm late,' he said.

'Why didn't you come back before, when. . .' she stopped. There was something ridiculous about asking a question fifty years too late.

'I took a different route.'

She nodded slowly. 'I suppose we both did.'

He reached out and took her hand. 'There's a lot to say. I'm sorry . . .'

Megan put a hand to his lips, stilling the words. 'We can talk later. That is . . .' now she hesitated. 'If you are staying for a while?' Would he stop? She waited.

'I'd like to. If you will have me.'

'Nothing has changed. You will always be welcome here at Folly House.'

'Are you two coming in? It's getting cold out there. You'll catch your deaths, both of you.' Rosie came hurrying across the lawn towards them.

It seemed natural to slip her arm through his as they walked back towards the house. They didn't speak. Being together was enough. The warmth and light of the house reached out and drew them in to the heart of the family.

As they entered Megan looked back over her shoulder and for a fleeting moment thought she could see the past fifty years, a silvery shimmer behind them like the wake of a ship that passes in the night. Then with a whisper it disappeared, borne by the wind into the enfolding sea that lapped the ancient walls of the Folly.